HIDDEN ANGEL

KEEPERS OF THE LIGHT 1

TAMAR SLOAN

V.P. ALLASANDER

KEEPER
CHRONICLES

Cover by Laercio Messias
https://laerciomessias.com.br

I

GABBY

"That is so freaking pretentious," Gabby says under her breath as she takes in the sight before her.

She's standing in front of a set of open, ornate gates that require her to move her head up and down, left and right just to take in their gigantor size. Ahead, a curved gravel driveway powers through emerald-green lawn, large trees dotted around, spreading lush shade and dignified serenity. Somewhere beyond is an even more daunting building.

Gabby hoists her bag a little higher, stopping herself from throwing her arms out wide as if she could hug the whole scene. "And I freaking love it!"

She ducks her head, conscious that she said that louder than she intended. Students are wandering the lawn, carrying books and hunched over their cell phones. Fellow students.

No two words could be more exciting and intimidating.

It's super important that she makes a good impression on her first day.

Honk! Honk!

Gabby spins around, her heart surging up throat. A red

sports car is right behind her. She was so enthralled with the grand entrance that she didn't even hear it approach.

Hooonk!

The drawn out sound pummels her ear drums. A guy is behind the wheel of the sleek, obviously expensive car, waving his hand at her impatiently.

Her own hands land on her hips. No doubt a rich kid who didn't need a scholarship to come here, expecting her to jump out of his way with little more than a flick of his wrist.

Well, he hasn't met Gabrielle Heartley.

Honk! Honk! Honk!

The guy slams his hand onto the steering wheel in frustration and instantly winces. She swears she sees him mouth an apology.

Gabby knows she should move. Technically, she's the one blocking his way. But something has her digging her heels into the gravel driveway. Maybe it's the fact that he's treating his car more courteously than her.

Maybe it's the strange sense of protectiveness that rushes through her. That compels her not to let him past.

She cocks her head. "Rude, much?"

The car door opens, lifting up rather than out. A large body unfolds from its depths and her eyes widen as the guy straightens. Her mind flatlines for long seconds, followed by one word plowing through.

Holy-shit-he's-hot.

Wine-colored hair—the deep clarets rich people would say has velvety, earthy tones—frames strong, wide features. His gaze meets hers, chocolatey and deep, and very pissed off.

"What part of 'get out of my way' wasn't clear?" he demands as he strides toward her.

Up closer, he's even more arresting.

"I think the part that was missing was the 'please'," she snaps back.

The guy's eyes narrow. "I'm late for work. Use the sidewalk like everyone else."

He waves his arm to a smaller gate beside the large ones, a footpath leading up to it. Two girls who were just about to pass through it pause, eyes lighting up in hope. But the guy looks away, unaware of the disappointment that has their shoulders dropping an inch.

Seems Gabby's not the only one who's noticed how hot he is.

But as he turns back, she stiffens. Her eyes widen a little. Every muscle tightens as the need to guard the school behind her explodes.

Beneath the guy's handsome features, something moves. Something dark. Something that has his earthy eyes glittering red.

"Get back!" she shouts.

The guy blinks, shocked at the verbal assault, but quickly recovers. "Look, I don't know what your problem is, but I'm just trying to get past."

"Not. Happening," she bites out, every muscle ready to fight.

The guy's eyes roam from her head to her feet and back up again. He's obviously sizing her up. His gaze flickers to the right.

Is he considering picking her up and moving her? The nerve!

Gabby's hands clench by her side. If he lays one of those strong looking hands on her...

"Is there a problem?" comes a voice from behind her.

She spins around, her whole body flushing when she sees a short man with a balding head and the features of a bulldog approaching them.

Crap. Shit. Crap-shit-crap.

He looks exactly like a professor of this school would.

The guy straightens. "I was just trying to get through, sir. But she won't move out of the way."

"Is this true, young lady?" the professor asks with a frown.

Gabby clasps her hands together. "Ah, yes...I was just—"

"What's your name? I assume you're a student here?"

She nods. "Gabrielle Heartley. I'm just starting today." She smiles weakly. "But Gabby is fine."

"Gabrielle," the man says slowly. "It's your first day, and already you're creating trouble. You haven't even stepped foot inside. If you think this is acceptable behavior at Mercy Academy, then I suggest you reconsider entering these gates and walking back the way you came."

The flush deepens as Gabby presses her hands harder together. "I'm sorry, sir. It was a misunderstanding." She flashes a glance at the guy, who's now standing with his arms crossed. "A misunderstanding that lacked a few manners. But it won't happen again."

"I hope not, Gabrielle. Behavior like that won't be accepted at this academy."

Shame and anger keep the red staining her cheeks alive. "Of course. Once again, I apologize."

The professor, possibly the dean of this whole place, nods sharply before spinning on his heel and walking away. "Don't dally. The welcome speeches are about to start," he says over his shoulder, the sun glistening off his agitated head.

Gabby turns back to the guy. Wanting to punch him. Never wanting anything to do with him again. But he's already back in his car. The engine revs as he pumps the gas and Gabby steps out of the way, just like she should've in the first place.

She wanted this first day to go smoothly. To make a good impression. To look...normal.

He winds his window down as he slowly drives past. His lips twitch. "Don't dally, remember? You don't want to be late."

"Assbutt," she mutters under breath.

She walks to the footpath and passes through the smaller gate. The one she didn't see because she was too busy building a future in her mind. A beautiful, wonderful, ordinary future.

Entering the grounds, Gabby sees a group of students beneath one of the nearby trees. One or two quickly look away, as a few others snigger and whisper.

Freaking great.

She suppresses the desire to stomp over to them and ask if anyone has a problem. That's not what nice, normal girls do.

Just like nice, normal girls don't stop guys from entering an academy just because they thought they saw—

Gabby shakes her head. Her back tingles, two hot lines scorching down, parallel to her spine. She can't afford to lose control.

A few more whispers follow her as she makes her way along the drive. The guy and his shiny sports car are nowhere to be seen. Gabby straightens her spine and lifts her chin. Today is her first day at Mercy Academy. It's supposed to be the beginning of something great. Her dream come true.

She just needs to put the whole unfortunate incident behind her.

The academy appears as she rounds a bend, rising up and dominating the view. Several stories high, the monstrous brick building stands proudly, rows of windows gazing down as students flock to enter. Four large columns are the foundation of an imposing entrance, the balcony above shading two ornate wooden doors built for giants.

The excitement returns, tingling along Gabby's nerves.

So damned pretentious.

So freaking cool.

A bell rings somewhere within, loud and jangling. Realizing she's the last one still outside, Gabby rushes up the steps. Dammit, she's dallying! She slips through the massive wooden doors just as they shut.

Inside, she finds herself in a wide foyer, photos lining the wall that she doesn't have time to look at. The open space is empty, and as much as she hates that hot-guy was right, she can't afford to be late.

She rushes through, almost at a run as she reaches the door on the other end. She pushes it open, pulling up quickly when she sees rows of people. Working to get her breathing under control, Gabby slips through and closes the doors. As she shuffles to the back of the crowd, she realizes she's in a great hall of some sort. The roof soars high above, a glass dome filling the vast room with natural light. Two curved staircases lead to the second floor.

In between stands a man on a dais. He steps up to the lectern with a mic, and the room hushes.

Except for two muffled giggles beside Gabby.

She glances over and stiffens. Two girls have their hands over their mouths, stifling their laughter. It's the girls who were on the footpath when Gabby was having her, er, discussion with the guy. The ones who looked like they wanted to jump his bones.

Gabby snaps her gaze back to the professor who's about to make a speech. They're not laughing about her, she tells herself. If she can forget the momentary brain glitch, then so can everyone else.

The professor scans the room, and she realizes with a sinking heart it was the same professor who spoke to her outside. His gaze moves over the crowd, one so much bigger than Gabby had anticipated.

"Welcome, students, to the Mercy Academy of Arts." His eyes continue to rove, never settling.

Until they reach Gabby. He stops, his gaze inscrutable as he keeps talking.

"My name is Albert Roberts, dean of the most prestigious, esteemed, and sought after arts academy in the country."

His eyes move on, skimming over the crowd of tomorrow's talent.

Crap. Shit. Crap-shit-crap.

She's already made an impression.

And it wasn't a nice, normal one.

The dean keeps talking, and Gabby tries to pay attention, she really does. There are snippets of words like excellence and expectations, but the soliloquy that she's sure he's repeated with every new batch of students can't compete with the emotions dancing through her.

She's at Mercy Academy. A freshman. As in, one of the students enrolled here. Gabby surreptitiously pinches herself, then winces at the sting. She's definitely not dreaming.

Excitement is like sunshine through her veins. Awe has her feeling like she's filled with helium. She wants to sing and dance and do a triple pike...even though she's never taken gymnastics.

She's finally found the place she belongs.

"And so, without further ado," Dean Roberts intones, "I once again welcome you to Mercy Academy. May your truth shine."

The students all clap politely and Gabby quickly joins in. The speech is over? She looks around, panic tickling at the base of her skull. What the hell did she just miss?

A quick glance at the podium shows the dean is already gone, although it's not like she's going to point out she missed most of his speech...while standing in the same room...after he chastised her. The students disperse, a low hum of chatter filling the room but Gabby stays where she is, knowing she's supposed to be somewhere next, but having no idea where that is.

Great. She's really failing at blending in. At belonging.

Quickly falling in behind the throng of students heading out a door on the far right, Gabby makes her way down another hall, relieved to find a line leading to a desk. A guy sits behind it, scowling as he passes something to a student. He doesn't look happy to be working in customer service. Somehow, she doubts he's there by choice.

The line moves slowly but steadily, and Gabby uses the time to look around and get her bearings. Like the other corridor she was in, the walls are pale with artwork dotted across them, strategic lighting angled above. The students ahead of her are as diverse as she expected and the excitement starts to effervesce again.

These people are the future of philosophy, arts, journalism and theater. And each and every one of them are her peers. She has to stop herself from pinching her arm again.

She reaches the front of the line and her happiness dims a little. The guy's wearing all black and he's obviously decided to match his mood to his attire. "Name," he snaps, not looking up from the paperwork in front of him. Actually, it's not paperwork, but a newspaper.

"Gabby, ah, Gabrielle Heartley."

He drags his focus away from whatever he's reading and skims a sheet beside it, flicking to the next page. "Yep. There you are."

The headline grabs Gabby's attention and she internally winces. Ritualistic murder of couple in Golden Heights. The photo of two smiling middle-aged people is beneath it. It seems like an odd thing to be reading while volunteering to give out ID cards, but she doesn't say anything. Maybe the guy's a news buff. Or he's playing the role of a detective in an upcoming play. Or, he hasn't realized reading macabre stuff will put a person in a bad mood.

He flips through a stack of ID cards, pulling hers up. The photo she sent with her acceptance, the one deliberated over for hours, is already printed on the front. He stares at it for a long second, then frowns up at her.

Gabby holds out her hand to take it, but he doesn't move. She smiles politely as the seconds stretch out awkwardly. He's looking at her like he's expecting something.

She clears throat. "Ah, thanks."

Surely he didn't also see her moment at the gates. He looks as if he recognizes her or something.

Blinking rapidly, he passes it to her, his frown deepening as he looks away. "This will get you into your dorm room. Room 615. You'll also need it to borrow books from the library and to photocopy."

"Thanks," she says brightly. She's not going to let one person's bad mood ruin hers.

He grunts, passing her a folder with papers inside. "There's a map inside. The residences are in the west wing."

Gabby moves on, holding her ID card like it's a key to Santa's workshop. She's about to see the room she'll be living in for the remainder of the school year. The skip in her step almost turns into a trip. Please, let her roomies be people from the awesome side of the tracks.

She follows the map easily, finding herself in another corridor, this one lined with doors. Several students mill around, entering or leaving, each smiling at Gabby as they pass. She makes sure to dazzle them with her own smile. A little part of her wants to hug each one of them.

She finds the door of room 615 open and she stops in the entrance, rapping on the door jamb. "Hey, roomies," she chirps.

But her smile drops faster than her hand. The two girls who turn to face her are the duo who saw her have the brain glitch with the guy in the car. The same two who were giggling when she joined the assembly.

They glance at each other. One is tall and slender with long brown hair, skin pale enough to be a vampire's, and large round glasses. The other is shorter and curvier, her black hair in ornate cornrows, and wearing the most amazing makeup Gabby's ever seen. Her eyeshadow morphs from red to orange to yellow, like a glorious sunrise bursting over each of her dark eyes.

"OMG, you have to teach me how to do that," Gabby breathes.

The girl grins, her cherry lips widening to expose perfect white teeth. "Only if you tell me if that guy contributes as much to global warming as I think he does."

Gabby laughs, pushing away the disquiet the guy in the red car triggered. "He was jalapeno level hot."

The brown haired girl sighs. "I loved his car more. A Jaguar. Probably an F-type."

Her friend shakes her head. "We need to get your glasses tested, Maya." She turns back to Gabby. "I'm Kalisha, by the way."

"Gabby, nice to meet you Kalisha. Maya." She grins. "Roomies."

Kalisha smiles back, waving her arm dramatically in the compact room. Each wall has a bunk bed against it, an arched window between. Three small desks are the only other significant furniture. "Welcome," she says brightly, like a hostess on a game show. "And, as your prize for being the last to get here, you win the top bunk!"

Gabby makes a show of squealing and clapping her hands. In truth, a top bunk is a small price to pay for spacing out during the welcome speech.

They all break into laughter. Gabby walks the rest of the way in, feeling like her first day is finally what she imagined it to be. Like, actually fun.

Maya sits on one of the bottom bunks, crossing her long legs. "The guy who gave us our ID cards said our luggage would be delivered shortly," Maya says.

"Oh, I didn't get more than a handful of words out of him," says Gabby.

Maya scrunches her nose, making her glasses move up. "He was kinda rude."

Kalisha sighs. "Actually, I know him. He lives in my neighborhood in Golden Heights."

"Golden Heights?" Gabby frowns. That was the location of the ritualistic murders.

Kalisha nods. "Yeah. The couple murdered were his parents."

Maya gasps as Gabby frowns. "Oh, I didn't know. Poor guy." No wonder he was focused on the newspaper. And so surly...

Kalisha nods again. "The worst thing is, every seven days there's been two new murders." She grimaces. "Two other couples have been killed since then."

"Can we change the subject please?" Maya tucks her knees up to her chest. "This stuff freaks me out."

"Sure thing, honey," Kalisha coos. "Why don't we all get to know each other a little better?"

Maya brightens. "Or we could draw up the bathroom roster? It'll mean everyone knows when their shower time is." She glances at Gabby, suddenly looking unsure.

Gabby's heart softens at the vulnerability that flashes

across the girl's face. It reminds her that everyone else is probably trying to figure out where they fit in, just like she is.

"I love a good roster," she says warmly even though it's the farthest thing from the truth. Words like structure and routine weren't programmed into her genetic code. But Maya's smile returns in a rush, totally making the lie worth it.

"And I'm going to need a good forty minutes," adds Kalisha. She gracefully flicks her hand across her face. "You can't rush art."

"Yay," chirps Maya. She reaches over and pulls a pen and pad from the nearby desk, the Mercy Academy crest stamped on both. "Now, who's an early riser like me?"

Kalisha and Gabby groan simultaneously, triggering another round of giggles. As Gabby grabs one of the chairs at the desks and sits down, she pushes away another wave of uneasiness. She's fitting in. She's making friends. She's on her way to normalville.

She's not going to wonder what the hell is going on. Why seven days is significant.

Or whether that means more murders are coming.

2

COLT

Colt flips through the newspaper he found in his room when he first arrived along with the wine basket. Seems Mercy Academy likes to welcome their teachers with the same subtle opulence the rest of the academy is shrouded in. Beyond his room, the chatter of students fills the afternoon air.

Leaning against the bedhead, he lifts a knee as he flips to the third page then the fourth. He was hoping to find something to take his mind off the unsettling altercation with the beautiful girl at the gates, but the distraction didn't have to be as extreme as every page covering recent murders in Mercy City.

He frowns. Several of them. The first was a man in an apartment. The second was a couple in an up-market suburb. In the next, another couple in a park. A serial killer is on the loose. And a sick one at that.

"Humans," Colt mutters.

They call demons monsters, conveniently ignoring what their own kind is capable of. Humans rejoiced in being granted free will, ignoring the responsibility that comes with it.

He's about to throw the paper away when he stills, every

sense on high alert. Slowly, he lowers the newspaper, the hair on the back of his neck rising.

Across the room, a small flame dances at the edge of the linen curtains, quickly becoming bright flames gobbling up the material. Within a blink, they're devouring the intricate designs and spitting out charred blackness. The fire travels upward, not stopping until it reaches the steel holder, and then vanishes all of a sudden.

As if it was never there.

The window unlocks and the panes are flung open. The force explodes the glass and it shatters, shards crashing to the ground like deadly raindrops.

Colt jumps off the bed, curious yet wary. Surely, they haven't found him already. Steadying his breathing, he moves forward, careful not to cut himself on the glass. A breeze caresses his face as he reaches the window, glancing up and bracing himself. But nothing is up there, waiting, hovering. Ready to attack.

He slowly tilts his head toward the ground below. Two stories down, he sees him. A man is looking up and grinning, but it's not the cold, malicious smile that has every muscle in Colt's body coiling. It's the crimson glow that throbs in the man's eye sockets. No, not a man's. This person is not a who. But an it.

A demon.

As if the being was waiting to be silently named, the demon unfurls his midnight wings, the afternoon light catching the crimson red at their tips. He opens his mouth, revealing teeth shaped like fangs, sharp and pointed. The wings contract and the man shoots upward, racing to attack Colt. He leaps back, no longer caring about the glass as he prepares himself to fight.

He doesn't care who they sent, they won't be taking him back with them.

Except the demon doesn't come. There's no messenger of death flying through the window, those sharp teeth glistening with the saliva that anticipate his end. Colt keeps his breathing steady, counting out the seconds.

One.

Two.

Three.

And still nothing.

Cautiously, he walks with silent steps and primed muscles toward the window again, his palm extended and ready. The fires of Hell burn deep within it. Very little can survive such a blast.

Suddenly, goosebumps race along his skin. The air around him becomes icy, and pale vapor wafts out of his mouth as he exhales. The plummeting temperature only confirms what he already knew.

Colt takes another step closer to the window, ready to strike. Before he can take a second look, a blast of energy sends him sailing backward. He slams into the hardwood headboard of his bed and pain explodes like a grenade through his brain. An unwilling groan tumbles from his mouth as he tries to right himself. He's too vulnerable. The demon is going to pounce on him any second.

His vision blurs and the room swims, everything becoming shades of shadow and pain. His body feels cold and heavy, like it's now carved from stone. He wills his healing to work faster.

If it doesn't, there will be nothing left to heal.

Several blinks and his vision clears, the pain in his head shrinking to the point on his head that hit the timber. Colt is already on his feet before the healing process is finished. Ready to fight.

He frowns. The room he's standing in looks the same as when he lay down to read the paper. The window is closed, the curtains open but most definitely there. Nothing is burned. Nothing is destroyed. The floor is clean except for the newspaper he was reading, the pages strewn after he threw it aside.

Rubbing his head even though it no longer hurts, Colt tries to figure out what just happened. Did he doze off and was dreaming? Hallucinating? Or is someone messing with him...

Bending down, he picks up the sheets of newspaper, his mind still whirling. For some reason, he assumed he'd be safe at Mercy Academy. Heck, he even had a nap. Maybe his subconscious was trying to warn him of becoming complacent and that's why he just saw everything he did.

He straightens and a piece of paper slips out of the newspaper and floats toward the ground. His gut clenched, he picks it up. The message scribbled on the note is short, but even before he's read it, his pulse jackknifes. The writing is illegible to humans. Only his kind would be able to read it.

They know you're here.

Colt's fist curls, crumpling the paper in his palm. He stares at it, a little surprised his anger hasn't incinerated it and a curl of smoke isn't coming up from his hand. He came here to escape. To disappear. The academy had felt like one of the safest places he's found so far. But it seems he was wrong.

But before Colt can move, there's a knock on his door.

Brows furrowed, he opens it, ready to tell whoever's on the other side he's busy. But the words evaporate when he sees who's there.

It's her.

The girl who had refused to move out of the way as she stood in the middle of the road. The one who was full of fire and attitude and a sultry sexiness he wished he hadn't noticed. She said her name was Gabrielle, Gabby, but he refuses to acknowledge that. She's just another youthful human at the academy.

"Yes?" he asks.

But the girl just stands there, her blue eyes strangely unfocused.

"Can I help you?" he says a little more forcefully.

She doesn't answer, remaining still and silent.

Frustrated, Colt bends his knees a little, bringing his face closer to hers. His gaze connects with pure, electric blue and he stills, too. In fact, he loses the ability to move.

No, that's not true. He wants to move more than he ever has before. He wants to jump. Leap. And fall into the oceans of possibility he just discovered in this girl's eyes. As the seconds draw out, his eyes scream for him to blink. His lungs start to burn.

But, inexplicably, confusingly, he's found somewhere he wants to stay.

Her lush lips part, and he's not sure if it's on an exhale or an inhale, but even that small motion is enough to snap him out of whatever spell was just woven. He straightens, pulling down a ferocious frown. He waits for her to explain why she just knocked on his door. Surely enough time has passed for this to be getting awkward.

But still, she says nothing.

Colt crosses his arms. He's not sure what's more unsettling —the mouthy girl who stood in front of his car, or this silent, mysterious creature who trapped him with just a look. His arms tighten. He should just close the door in her face. It would be the most effective way to show he's not in the mood for playing games.

"What do you want?" he asks, this time raising his voice.

The sharp tone snaps the girl out of her trance. She blinks. Then blinks again. Her eyes focus on him and then widen. "Oh... uh...nothing...," she squeaks. She looks around, speaking under her breath. "Holy shit, how the heck did I even get here?"

Colt frowns as his sensitive hearing picks up every word.

That's going to be her excuse—some sort of temporary amnesia?

"Can I help you? he repeats.

"I'm...ah...looking for a friend..." her voice trails away, her face twisting as if even she knows how lame that sounds.

"Your friend isn't here," he growls.

The girl looks around again. "My goodness, you're right." She pulls up a blinding smile that's as artificial as the fluorescent lighting above her. "Silly me."

She's lying. And behaving even more strangely than earlier today. Colt gently, suspiciously, probes her mind, looking for answers. There's something about this girl that has his instincts on high alert.

Except he slams into a wall. An impenetrable wall. He recoils as he realizes this girl holds enormous power. Few people can prevent him from exploring their mind.

Who is she?

And more importantly, what is she?

"I suggest searching for your friend," he grinds out the last word, "in the girls' dormitories, not in the section for teaching and administrative personnel. And definitely not in the men's section."

At that, her eyes widen as she realizes where she is. But instead of looking chastised, she smiles sweetly. "Surly and rude as always, but right, as annoying as that is."

Without waiting for a response, she spins on her heel, her thick curls flicking over her shoulder, and sashays away. Colt watches her for longer than he should. For longer than he wants.

He tears his gaze away and shuts his door with a sharp thud. Not getting involved with anyone or anything is his golden rule. It's how he's stayed alive despite the wanted sign branded on his back. This girl isn't going to change that. He refuses to think of her again.

Quickly changing into a blue collared shirt and dark slacks with a gray tie, Colt decides it's time to learn about this new job he's signed up for. He's waited long enough for the initial excitement of arrival day to have waned. Now that it's late afternoon, the staffroom should be empty.

Making his way through the labyrinth that is Mercy Academy, Colt climbs the circular staircase that will take him to the third floor. He memorized the floorplan of this overgrown building before he arrived. He's well aware of all the entrances and exits. Interestingly, the entirety of the property is surrounded by a six-foot hedge, the only way in is through the large entrance gates. The ones where he first saw the girl.

Colt frowns, annoyed that she's already crept into his thoughts so quickly. He'd decided he wouldn't think about her again. What the mudda is wrong with him? His frown morphs to a scowl. Now she has him cursing in Bahamian.

The ornate door to the staffroom is open and Colt enters, his stride smooth and confident. He may only be here to teach martial arts, but he's still a member of the staff, so he's going to act it. He's found that the more assured he looks, the less likely people are to ask questions. And questions are one thing he prefers to avoid.

Just as he expected, it's empty. The large open space is divided into cubicles. He already knows his is in the back corner, a space befitting a newly recruited teacher. He's taken two steps when he senses he's not alone. The faint scent of human tickles his nostrils. He's about to spin on his heel and come back another time when a head pops above one of the dividers on his right. A young man wearing thick-framed black glasses registers Colt and a beaming smile spreads across his face. "Ah, another dedicated soul here, in the staffroom before classes have started, late in the day."

Colt nods, letting the man believe that if he wants. "Hello, I'm the new—"

"Martial arts instructor," says the man, stepping around his desk and extending his hand. "Colt Grayson. Welcome." He pumps Colt's hand enthusiastically as he studies his face just a little too intensely. "My, my, and just as young as they said."

Colt suppresses a frown, not liking that others knew he was arriving. And have been talking about it.

"Oh, I mean, you look young for your age," stammers the man, misreading the silence. "In fact, you look great for your age." He stops, a flush creeping up his cheeks as his eyes slide away, quickly releasing Colt's hand when he realizes he's still shaking it.

Colt unwinds, deciding this young man is harmless. "Thank you." He glances around the staffroom. "I was just getting myself familiarized with the academy."

"It's a maze, if you ask me. I've been here two years and I still get lost. You're best sticking to the main areas. Just getting from the lecture halls to our dorm rooms is enough of a challenge for some. And they think a one day Orientation is enough for the students," he scoffs. "Youth of today are so used to having everything spoon fed to them. Expect to be asked for directions every few minutes for the next few weeks, maybe months. And after you explain where to go, you'll be finding yourself escorting them there, practically holding their hands." The man sighs. "At least you're teaching martial arts, I suppose, which I don't expect has much of a theoretical component. Marking those first essays is an instant headache. The first few sentences resemble what you've covered in lectures...the rest is an opinion formed after watching the latest Netflix series."

Colt blinks through the barrage. He doesn't even know the man's name.

"Oh, goodness me, I sound like a fopdoodle. I haven't introduced myself. I'm Sam Knowles, history teacher, I mean, professor." He rolls his eyes. "The academy does like their titles."

"Nice to meet you, Professor Knowles," says Colt. "And I don't think you're a foolish man." Awkward and over-talker, but not stupid.

"Sam, please," he says, eyebrows raised. "You know medieval English?"

Colt chuckles. "I dabble in languages." Mostly because he's lived through most of them.

Not wanting to continue this line of conversation, he moves to the window, staring outside into the evening gloom. His eyes rove over the grounds, as restless as his mind. Tomorrow is Orientation. Then classes start following the weekend. His new persona as a respectable teacher of martial arts was also supposed to begin.

Except for what he saw in his room.

Unless it was all in his mind. His imagination getting out of hand after centuries of being on the run. Nothing but manifestations of his worries now that he's found somewhere he wouldn't mind staying.

He's about to turn away when something catches his eye. A man is standing beneath one of the large sprawling trees. His arms are crossed as he stares back at Colt with sharp intensity.

"What is it?" asks Sam, coming to stand beside him. "Foolish freshman already testing the curfew rules? They'll find out quickly how strictly those rules are enforced."

"No, no students," says Colt. "Just that man under the tree."

Sam leans closer to the window. "What man?"

Colt stills when he realizes Sam can't see what he does. Either Sam has poor eyesight, or...

"Excuse me, I'm going to rest up for Orientation."

Without waiting for a response, Colt strides out of the staffroom, intending on returning to his dorm room, even as he wonders if that's safe.

Surely they haven't found him already.

3
GABBY

Is this what people feel like when they do drugs?

Or has she had a knock to the head she didn't know about?

Maybe she was accidentally dropped as a baby and this is some sort of delayed reaction...

Gabby rubs her temple as she reaches her dorm room. She just rocked up at Mr. Rude and Surly's room, and she has no idea how she got there. Or why.

She steps in, closing the door behind her. The last thing she remembers is climbing to her top bunk, agreeing with Maya and Kalisha that they suddenly felt exhausted. She must've fallen asleep. She glances at her two roommates, who are still snoozing.

But it seems she woke up and went for a wander. And she has no recollection of getting up and leaving, of navigating the corridors until she ended up in the professor's wing. In fact, her next memory is being snapped out of whatever weird-ass trance she was in by Mr. Rude and Surly himself, being rude and surly.

Her cheeks heat at the thought of the second time she's

made a fool of herself in front of him. She couldn't answer his questions as to why she was there. She still can't.

She's acting about as far from normal as a girl can.

Her stomach rumbles as she walks over to Kalisha, reminding her that if they're not quick, they'll miss dinner. Maybe the stress of today, along with low blood sugar can explain her brain glitch...

"Kalisha," she says, her voice low. "Wake up. It's past dinner time."

She doesn't respond.

"Hey," Gabby tries again, this time nudging the girl's shoulder gently. "Come on, sleepy head."

Kalisha draws in a half-snort and her breathing once again falls into a regular, snuffly rhythm.

Frowning, Gabby moves over to Maya. "Wakey, wakey, roomie." Maya's brow twitches, giving Gabby hope. "Come on, Maya. Surely you've put eating on the schedule."

Her nose twitches as if she's being bothered by a bug. She rolls over with a groan and falls back into the deep sleep she doesn't want to be roused from.

Gabby straightens, her hands hoisting onto her hips. "Was there something in the water?"

Her stomach rumbles again, almost as loud as Kalisha's soft snores. Gabby was too excited-nervous to eat most of the day, and her stomach is now objecting to being ignored for so long.

Deciding there's no way she can wait until breakfast, especially considering how strict the academy seems to be about their curfew, she heads to the door. "I'll see if I can bring you back something," she calls to her sleeping roommates.

Not entirely sure where she's going, Gabby follows the few students milling around. She's relieved when she finds herself inside a dining hall. The place is part high-school cafeteria with its rows of tables and a serving station at the back; part architectural greatness with its exposed beams slicing through the ceiling and dangling lights that look like giant glowing orbs. Gabby instantly loves it like every other place she's seen at the academy.

Joining the back of the line, she scans the room, hoping to spot a familiar face from this morning. When she doesn't, she checks again. There's no one she recognizes.

Maybe all the freshmen ate earlier? Gabby shifts uncomfortably. Has she broken some unspoken rule that newbies don't get here late?

She takes a step forward to ask the two girls in front of her only to pause. The need to immediately draw back is almost overwhelming. Gabby notes their straightened hair, cute tops and tight jeans. Nothing out of the ordinary. And yet, alarm is tingling up and down her spine, making her shoulder blades heat.

Gabby surreptitiously takes a step back, frowning. This has happened to her before—the sensation is always too powerful to ignore. She's just never been sure what it means.

Are these girls bullies?

Do they wear some perfume that she has an allergy to?

Or are they something else...

Pushing away the thought, Gabby focuses her attention back on the crowd in the dining hall. Surely, there's someone here she can recognize. But no one has any semblance of familiarity. In fact, they all have the casual, comfortable expressions of students who have been here before. They all look like seniors.

Is this why Kalisha and Maya stayed asleep? Because freshmen don't eat in the dining hall on the first night?

Gabby spins around, ready to hightail it back to her dorm room, when she bumps into someone. She pulls back, apologizing, taking in the short, plump, pimple faced girl.

The girl smiles, pushing her glasses up. "No biggie. I wasn't paying attention, either."

One of the girls on Gabby's other side sniggers. "Look at her. She's pouncing on the first freshman she finds, hoping to make a friend."

The girls giggle, turning their backs and dismissing them.

Gabby stiffens. Seems the girls are definitely bullies.

But the girl rolls her eyes and shrugs. "Ignore Dianna. She always has something to prove. My name's Klae, by the way."

Gabby debates what to do, then acknowledges she doesn't want to make any more waves today, so she relaxes and smiles. "Hi, I'm Gabby. First day."

"I'm a third year student here, drama major," says Klae. "Best academy there is, you know, for theater and stuff. Have you given any thought to what you will be majoring in?"

Gabby shakes her head. "I haven't."

Which is true. From what she had read in the prospectus, the academy offered drama and theater, singing, creative writing, culture and philosophy, the study of theocracy, and political science among many other subjects. All of them looked interesting to an eighteen year old girl who has yet to know what she wants to do with her life.

"You should totally choose drama," Klae gushes. She smiles broadly, her cheeks a little pink. "I can tell you'll be amazing at it."

Gabby's not sure how this girl has already come to that conclusion, so she nods politely. "Sure, I'll think about it."

Klae bounces a little. "Tomorrow's orientation, and if you choose drama, you totally have to audition for the lead role in the play I want to direct." She clasps her hands to her chest. "It's untitled, but it's going to be the most spectacular love story."

"Ah, sure," she responds, trying to be polite but noncommittal. Klae barely knows her and she's already trying to recruit her for a play. The girl's lovely, but weird. And Gabby was hoping to steer clear of weird.

The line moves forward and Gabby turns back, seeing that the blackboard with the menu is now visible. Avocado salad, fried fish filets, pork chops, and spaghetti with red chicken sauce. Dessert is a choice of chocolate lava cake or raspberry cheesecake. Wow, another reason to love Mercy Academy.

Klae speaks over her shoulder. "This is why I love the day you freshies arrive. The special menu is always amazing."

Gabby nods, realizing that makes sense. Although she got a scholarship, she saw the annual tuition of the academy. Even though it almost made her faint, all those numbers after the dollar sign wouldn't cover regular meals like this.

Her turn at the counter arrives and she thanks the server as she's passed her tray. She walks a few feet away, scanning for an empty table, quickly seeing that there isn't one. She tries again to find a familiar face, hoping she can ask to sit and try to make some new friends, but the room gives her nothing.

Looks like she's best going back to her dorm room and sharing what she has with Kalisha and Maya.

Klae appears beside her. "I have my own table," she says proudly. "You can join me if you like."

Gabby hesitates. It's clear Klae is a social outcast. Will associating with her on her first day annihilate her social life even before she's done orientation? But as she glances down at the short, dark-haired girl, their gazes connect. And she sees the layers Klae's bubbly exuberance covers.

Vulnerability. A familiarity with rejection. Knowledge she doesn't quite fit in.

And Gabby can't be another one to add to that. She smiles brightly. "Sure, lead the way."

Klae's smile is so big, her braces practically glint. "You're going to love Mercy Academy," she gushes as she weaves through the table. "It really brings out the best in people. It's an opportunity to show off your talents, sometimes ones you didn't even know you had!"

Gabby nods even though she's not sure the second part applies to her. She doesn't have any hidden talents.

They reach the far end of the dining hall and Klae stops beside the one and only table in the place that's empty. It's a little shorter than the others and pushed against the wall. It's clear it's empty because no one wants to sit here. They'd be labeled a loner and a weirdo.

Klae slips into her seat. "Grab a seat," she says warmly, either clueless to the social self-sabotage, or she stopped caring long ago.

Sighing as she wonders if this first day could get any worse, Gabby sits across from her. But just as she's planted her butt, the lights flicker. The hum of conversation stutters and stops.

Klae looks up. "Huh, must be electricity problems."

Suddenly, a strident alarm bell rings. Several students gasp, one or two scream.

Gabby tenses, conscious that it feels like the air has thickened. A fire would be the perfect cherry on her first day cake. Except the air cools, as if the temperature is plummeting. Across from her, Klae shivers. Gabby glances over her shoulder and stills.

Across the room, a dark figure is standing in the doorway, its eyes scanning the hall as if it's looking for someone. Eyes that are a crimson red.

Dread, as icy as the air, clamps around her throat. The figure continues to scan, its hellish eyes eventually falling on Gabby. The moment it does, it turns and runs.

She turns back to her plate.

Obviously someone's playing a stupid prank and she has no intention of reacting to it.

* * *

Gabby opens her eyes, blinking rapidly. Cold air caresses her skin and she draws in a sharp breath. She's no longer in the dining hall.

She's in a corridor of some sort, the lights turned low. How the flock did she get here?

She creeps forward, keeping her footsteps light. The corridor turns right and she peers around it, gasping and reeling back.

Mr. Rude and Surly stops in his tracks. "What are you doing here?" he asks, that scowl of his back as he hikes his hands on his hips, the shadows seeming to cling to him like water, slipping down his body as if they don't want to let him go.

Looking at his biceps, that broad chest, a little part of Gabby can't blame them. She mentally shakes herself. She's obviously exhausted and mildly delirious.

"I thought I told you to stay away from this area," he snaps.

Gabby's mouth works like a fish. One that just got caught somewhere it's not supposed to be...for the second time.

Of all the people she could've run into...

"I...ah..." Freaking great. She's got nothing. "I was going—" She quickly stops herself. She has no idea where she was going. Or how she got here.

"Going where?" Those piercing chocolate eyes trap her.

For some strange reason, the truth hovers on the tip of Gabby's tongue. As if part of her feels she can trust this guy. Sheesh. Is she really that much of a sucker for a handsome face? Even if it's a strikingly, deliciously handsome face. Her gaze roams over him, noting the shirt, tie, and dark slacks. One with a striking, delicious body...

Horrified, she steps back. "Anyway. I won't keep you." She

turns, flushing. She's not running into an acquaintance at the grocery store! "I'll go back to my room."

"I'll escort you," he says resolutely.

Gabby stops in her tracks. "I don't need escorting," she says indignantly. Being escorted back to her room is going to mean others asking questions.

Mr. Rude and Surly arches an eyebrow. "You expect me to believe you'll just go back to your dorm?"

"That's what I said, isn't it?"

"No wandering around areas that are off limits on your first day? Then giving flimsy excuses when you're caught?"

She chews her lip, the fight inside her gone as quickly as it came. "Believe it or not, that's pretty out of character for me."

He blinks, as if he wasn't expecting that response. "Then hurry up and get moving," he says gruffly. "In case you missed it, the academy has a curfew."

For some reason, she's smiling before she realizes it. "It's been mentioned once or twice."

He blinks again but Gabby quickly turns away, not wanting to find out how long this leniency will last. No doubt Mr. Rude and Surly will be back if she hangs around.

She quickly makes her way through the halls and corridors, finding herself back at her room. Inside, she leans against the door, noting that her roommates are both still asleep. Just like she should've been.

Gabby climbs up to her bunk bed and sits, her back against the wall. The day hadn't gone as well as she'd hoped. There was too much weird threaded through it. She expressly planned on not being weird. And there was a witness to her weirdness. Twice. A hot, brooding one. She rubs at her temples, trying to unjumble everything that's happened.

And failing.

Her cell phone rings, making her jolt. Glancing at the

screen, she smiles. Just the person she would want to talk to at a time like this. "Hey, Ari."

"Why are you talking so quietly?" her younger cousin asks.

"My roomies are asleep."

"Already? I thought you would've been talking well into the night."

Yeah, well, today hasn't really lived up to expectations. "It's been a big day," says Gabby. "Everyone's tired."

"Tell. Me. Everything."

Gabby smiles. Arielle is more like a sister than a cousin. Her mom found herself a single parent two years after Gabby's mom did. The two sisters stayed in their family home, raising their daughters together. Gabby and Arielle shared baths as toddlers, shared clothes as children, shared makeup as teens.

"The photos didn't lie. It's big and pretentious," she says, connecting with the excitement of being here all over again. "With a long list of dos and don'ts. They even have a curfew."

"Uh oh," Ari teases. "Rules. You're not so good with them."

Gabby giggles. "I'm going to conform, remember?"

"Wow. You're going to undo eighteen years of...being you?"

Although Arielle's still teasing, the words sober Gabby. She wanted to be a success at Mercy Academy. Someone her family would be proud of. Especially her mom.

But she hadn't been particularly successful at doing that today.

Not one strange memory lapse, but two. It's as if something's wrong with her...

"Gabs, is everything okay?" Arielle asks when Gabby doesn't answer.

"Sure," she quickly reassures. "I just...miss you all."

Homesickness washes through Gabby, tugging at her heart. She took for granted the sense of belonging she feels with the people she loves. Right now, that practically seems impossible at Mercy Academy.

"We miss you, too," Ari says warmly. "Your mom is freaking out about these murders. We had to take the stairs at the mall, even though we went to just about every floor."

"The stairs?" Gabby's mother isn't exactly a gym junkie. She's usually looking hot and flustered after cleaning the oven. Although admittedly, with the amount of burned material on there, it can be quite the job. Even if she does it weekly.

"Yeah. The latest victims were found in a lift. The couple got in on the ninth floor, and when it opened on the ground floor and people went to enter, they got a rude shock. Lots of blood, and the victims' blood was made into some weird shape around them. Like a symbol of some sort."

Gabby frowns. "That's awful."

"Almost ritualistic," says Ari, her voice hushed.

Gabby shifts, her spine straightening. Her mother is a worry wart, but these murders are definitely unsettling everyone. Maybe Mercy Academy isn't where she's supposed to be...

"Maybe I should come home for the weekend. After Orientation tomorrow."

"What? No! It's your first weekend at college. You can't come home already!" There's a pause. "Are you sure everything's okay?"

Gabby's hand tightens around her cell. "It's just harder than I thought, that's all."

It's far easier to believe she's just a regular girl like everyone else when she's at home. A mom who loves to worry and burn food, an aunt who's been a second mother to her, and a cousin-sister who knows everything about her.

"Since when did hard stop you?" Ari asks fondly. "Remember when you were determined to do the impossible and finish a shampoo bottle at the same time as a conditioner bottle?"

Gabby smiles in spite of herself. "My hair turned to frizz, I was shampooing it so much."

"But you did it. Even if you looked like you'd been electrocuted."

Gabby giggles. "I did."

"You're meant to be there, remember?"

Gabby draws in a breath. That's exactly what she told Ari, that she's meant to be here. It's why she got the scholarship.

"Thanks, Ari."

She knows her cousin would be missing her. That she didn't want Gabby to go. But here she is, giving her a pep talk. That's what family's all about—putting those you love first.

"You got this, Gabs. And it won't hurt your mom to take a few more sets of stairs every now and again."

They say their goodbyes and I love yous and hang up. Gabby nestles down into her bed even though she still has to get changed and brush her teeth.

Screw Mr. Rude and Surly. Everyone has a bad day every once in a while. She'll prove to him and everyone else what she's capable of.

Tomorrow is Orientation. It'll be a new start.

Tomorrow she'll be normal.

4

COLT

Colt strides past the large banner saying Orientation Day across the entrance to the academy, his hands shoved in his pockets. He tightens his jaw as his sensitive hearing notes how many bodies are in the foyer beyond, filling the place with excited chatter. Crowds are a double-edged sword. Easier for him to blend in, but full of hidden threats. And he needs to know what he's dealing with before he's comfortable being amongst them.

Taking a sharp right, he strides around the side of the monstrous building that will take him to the side entrance. He hadn't slept well, his night full of strange dreams and half-remembered scenes. There was murder and blood. Red-eyed demons. And the beautiful blonde girl, running, her blue eyes pleading for him to help her.

He'd got out of bed long before the sun was up and gone for a punishing run. But even those several miles, his feet pounding the grassy perimeter that stretches around the vast grounds of the academy hadn't rid him of the uneasiness crawling under his skin.

Maybe coming here was a mistake. It's not looking like the

safe haven he was hoping it would be. And admittedly, he accepted the offer to be a martial arts instructor here in haste.

Except the other option is to leave.

And Colt's running out of places to hide in this shrinking world.

He sighs. Mostly, he's tired of constantly moving. Of uprooting whether he likes it or not, forced to find somewhere else to disappear. He's even become attached to this body. In fact, he's kept it longer than any of the others. It just seems to...fit.

Pushing open the door, he steps into the narrow corridor, welcoming the quiet, cool air. That's what he needs to be right now—quiet. Cool. Calm. In fact, he's not normally this easily rattled.

He pauses as he realizes it's because he's become attached. To this vessel. To the life he could live here at the academy, if even for a little while. Shaking his head, he makes his ways up the spiral staircase at the end of the corridor, his fingers lightly running over the wrought iron bannister.

He knows better than that.

Buddha said it himself. Attachment causes suffering.

If he has to leave, he'll do so, and never look back. Free of regrets. Free of the shackles of connection or emotion or responsibility. It's how it's always been, and always will.

Colt reaches the second floor and steps to the railing that overlooks the floor below. The students mill around, varying shades of nervousness or excitement coloring their faces. The throng slows as it forms a bottleneck, everyone lining up to enter the assembly hall for instructions. Colt studies each face carefully.

If there are demons here, then he needs to know about it. If they are, then his bag is already packed.

But it's one person who captures his attention. And doesn't let go.

The girl is standing with two other females, whom Colt quickly discounts. The dark-skinned one is obviously determined to stand out with the colorful paints across her face, and demons don't try to attract attention. While the pale one, with her tightly clutched books and hunched shoulders, looks like she's trying to take up as little room as possible, and demons would never cower.

But the girl...she's looking around with intense curiosity, like she's trying to absorb everything around her.

He remembers her standing between the gates of the Academy, her hands on her hips. Not in the least scared of him. Although most humans don't know the supernatural exists, they have an instinct when it comes to an angry demon. And he was most definitely angry. She was obstinate and rude. And totally unafraid of him. Just like she was when she turned up at his door later the same day, and then again in the corridor. Practically unapologetic, even though she was in the wrong.

There's a fierce determination about her. A strength that belies the sweet beauty of her features. Maybe that's why he's so fascinated. Too many contrasts. Questions. Contradictions.

She smoothes her hands over the short skirt that leaves her slim legs bare, as if to exemplify his very thoughts. She's nervous, but obviously isn't afraid of being seen. Colt's hands tighten around the railing as he finds himself drawing in a deep breath, trying to catch a trace of lily and rose.

Her shoulders stiffen and her brow crinkles as she glances around.

Surely not...

The girl's eyes, the ones he already knows are the color of a clear summer sky, begin to climb up. As if they're unerringly seeking him out. Colt steps back hurriedly, instinctively seeking the shadows before she can see him.

"Skata," he mutters under his breath, spinning on his heel and continuing to the wide, marble-tiled corridor. The Greek curse word is a favorite of his, and this is all definitely feeling like shit.

He needs to stop thinking about this girl, no matter how beautiful or fascinating she is.

He's here to teach martial arts. Lie low. And move on when the time is right.

Glancing at his watch, Colt registers he only has a couple of minutes. Picking up his pace, he makes his way to the first door on the left when he sees a flicker of something out of the corner of his eye. His senses tingle and muscles tense.

As if whatever just caught his attention isn't human.

A quick glance confirms the door is closed, so he quickly walks past, determination hardening his features. If there are demons here, he needs to know who they are. And who sent them.

Colt rounds the corner, the sensation growing and making the hairs on his arms stand on end. But the body he finds in the hallway is far from what he expected.

An old man walks toward him, his back curved over the walking stick he's using. Tap. Tap. Tap. Colt frowns as he registers the man's clothes. Dark blue shirt, gray trousers, and a silver name tag pinned above his breast pocket.

Nicholas Bishop. Head of Security.

And the same man who was staring up at Colt when he was in the staffroom.

The man stops short a few steps away, his raspy breathing filling the foyer. "Lost, young man?"

For some reason, Colt doesn't relax. Although this man looks old enough to have been a server at the Last Supper, and very unlikely to be the threat he thought he was, there's something off about him. Something that's nudging at the edges of his memory, but refusing to come into the light of consciousness.

Colt smiles politely. "I thought I saw something."

"Ah," says Mr. Bishop, his pale blue eyes twinkling with intelligence. "And you thought you'd investigate?"

If all the security guards are of similar caliber to Nicholas, then maybe it's necessary. "Old habit, I suppose." He unwinds his shoulders, trying to relax. "I thought maybe a student was lost."

"Like the girl?"

Colt stills. The old man had been watching when she arrived at his room? Or when she turned up in the corridor? "Ah, yes. She was quite confused. But I directed her back to her dorm."

"You were more patient than I expected. It surprised me."

Colt keeps his face neutral even though he's frowning internally. The man's speaking as if he knows him. "I'm not sure what you mean, Mr. Bishop?"

"Just that you're different." He smiles, those eyes once again belaying the wrinkles of his skin. "Ignore the ramblings of an old man," he says with a wave of his hand. "I'd best be going. Orientation is a busy day for everyone."

He tap, tap, taps past Colt, his breath quietly wheezing again, and disappears around a corner.

Shaking his head, Colt returns to the door he'd been planning to knock on three minutes ago. Now, he's late. He dislikes being late.

He raps on the ornate timber and it opens almost immediately. A man—the same man who spoke to Colt and the girl at the gates—stands on the other side. He's short and squat, resembling a toad. He pulls up a tight smile. "Mr. Grayson. Only a little late."

Colt smiles back, cataloging the barb. The email that arrived in his inbox this morning had been short and straightforward.

Meet me at 8:50am. My office.

Regards.

Colt wonders if it was a test, checking whether he's monitoring his email early on his first day. He planned on turning up early to prove he's as professional as his resume claims he is...

He nods differentially. "Your academy is quite the maze, Mr. Roberts."

The dean of Mercy Academy chuckles. "It can be Hell to get around, can't it?" He steps back, indicating for Colt to enter before returning to his desk.

Colt enters the large, rectangular room, noting the plush maroon carpet beneath his shoes, the academy emblem in the center. The walls are lined with shelves of dark timber, while above a modest chandelier twinkles, most likely from the Victorian era.

He's taken two steps when a chill trickles down his spine, once more putting Colt on high alert. He angles his head as he registers a low hum, almost rolling his eyes when he notes the air-conditioning vent above him. First thinking the old security guard was a threat, and now this.

He's getting skittish.

And he doesn't like being skittish.

The dean slips around his mammoth mahogany desk and takes a seat in the large leather chair. Two more are on the other side of the desk, also leather, but slightly smaller. Colt takes one, crossing his legs and clasping his hands. Is this meeting more than just a test of his conscientiousness?

Mr. Roberts picks up a pair of black-rimmed glasses and slips them on, perusing the paperwork in front of him, and Colt notes it's his resume. The dean glances up, puffing up his chest. Once Colt had done a little research, he wasn't surprised to find that a Roberts family member held the position, despite the short stature. The Roberts are an old, rich family in this area. They have a finger in every pie Mercy City has to offer. "How have you settled in, Mr. Grayson?"

"Very well, thank you. My room is as impressive as the rest of your academy, Sir."

Mr. Roberts' eyes narrow, almost disappearing into the flesh of his face. "Excellent."

There's a knock at the door and a matronly woman's face appears. "Three minutes, Sir."

"Thank you, Martha. I'll be there shortly." She closes the door and the dean returns his attention to Colt. "I like to run on time."

Colt bristles. He was one minute late to this dean's test. He doesn't appreciate the condescending tone from a man who is hundreds of years younger than him. Hasn't seen what Colt has. Doesn't know what he does.

Colt loosens his tight hands. To the dean, he's simply a young man with excellent qualifications. They could've hired someone with more experience, but he's here because he was cheaper, his wins in the martial arts tournaments and impressive references—admittedly all forged—were enough to get him over the threshold.

And Colt needs a safe haven right now. Until he learns Mercy Academy isn't, he's going to have to defer to the dean, no matter how much it chafes.

He pushes to his feet. "I won't hold you, then." He smiles, still refusing to apologize despite his best intentions. "I hope Orientation goes well."

"I've looked at your schedule, Mr. Grayson. I know you're

already handling martial arts for us, with classes every day but Friday."

Colt remains where he is, realizing he's here more than just to check up on his punctuality. "Yes, that's correct."

"And all your classes are in the afternoon, some in the evening."

Colt waits, wondering where this is going.

"Which leaves you free the rest of the day." The dean picks up Colt's resume, perusing it as if he wasn't doing that a moment ago. "And it seems you're proficient in music. Is this true?"

"Yes, it is."

Music is the one thing Colt's found that transcends time itself. Its beauty simply evolves with each era, discovering and rediscovering itself in each decade and century.

"I can play a few instruments, guitar and piano mostly."

And every iteration of them through history and culture. The kithara, the lyre, the lute, even the Spanish vihuela that predated the guitar. And the pure tone of the dulcimer, the strident harpsichord, then the depth of the modern piano. He's loved them all.

"Wonderful," beams the dean. "Your familiarity with the instruments makes you a great candidate for assisting with our music class."

Colt doesn't respond, unsure what to say. He doesn't really want to teach music.

But Mr. Roberts has already chalked up a strike against him for being one minute late.

Skata.

"Music classes are in the early morning," the dean continues. "In the gazebo outside the gardens, in fact. A glorious morning of music and sunshine. What do you say, Mr. Grayson?"

"Can I ask why the sudden need for a music tutor, Mr. Roberts?"

The dean sighs, his aged face falling. "Our long term tutor has recently passed away. Terrible, tragic way to go." He frowns. "May his soul rest in peace."

Colt wonders if this has anything to do with the murders he read about in the paper. "I'm sorry to hear that."

"Thank you." The dean leans forward. "So, you'll take the role?"

"Of course," Colt responds, even though his jaw is tight. He can't afford a second black mark against his name.

"Excellent," beams the dean. "I'll let the faculty members know."

"Thank you, Mr. Roberts. I appreciate the opportunity to be of service," says Colt, proud that he didn't choke on the saccharine words.

"I'm glad to hear that, Mr. Grayson." The dean raps the stack of paper on his desk. "We took a risk hiring someone so...young."

Colt smiles, for the first time, the motion almost genuine. If only Mr. Roberts knew exactly how old he is...

The door opens and Martha appears again, keeping the door open this time and standing stiffly beside it.

With an incline of his head, Colt exits and quickly makes his way down the corridor. He finally allows himself a frown when he reaches the landing he saw the girl from less than half an hour ago. The foyer below is now empty, all the students in the assembly hall waiting to begin orientation. He's glad for the quiet as he digests what just happened in that short meeting.

He's now helping with a morning music class.

And he's been reminded his place here at Mercy Academy is tenuous.

5

GABBY

Gabby smoothes her skirt, wishing she'd packed some longer ones as she hurries to the Assembly Hall, then rolls her eyes. She didn't pack any because she doesn't own any.

Kalisha shoes her hands away. "You look hawt, girlfriend. And that maroon skirt is even in the academy colors."

Gabby grins, pleased that someone noticed. She spent hours shopping online trying to find just the right shade. Then again, of course Kalisha noticed. "It matches your eyeshadow beautifully," Gabby points out.

Kalisha grins right back, fluttering her thick black lashes, the ones that came straight out of a packet. Her makeup is art, as always, the deep burgundy of the academy gracing her eyelids in a metallic stroke of color, offset by midnight eyeliner in a perfect, bold wing. Contrasting with Kalisha's dark skin, the effect is striking.

Maya flicks the brochure in her hand. "Hurry up you two, I allocated four minutes for us to make it to the Assembly Hall."

Gabby and Kalisha grin at each other as they salute. They join the throng of students making their way there. Gabby smiles even wider when she discovers she's a few minutes early.

Maya glances at her watch. "Next time I'll allocate five minutes," she mutters to herself.

Gabby scans the students around her, wondering who might be in her classes, when a prickling sensation dances over her skin. She glances up, feeling as if she's being watched, but the landing above is empty. She shakes her head. She needs to get a grip.

The crowd moves forward and they take their place toward the back, close to where they stood yesterday. Gabby marvels that it's been less than twenty-four hours. So much has happened. Her smile dims and she quickly pushes the thought away. She woke up feeling refreshed and excited all over again.

Today is a fresh start. She's going to personify future-success-story-of-Mercy-Academy, no matter what it takes.

There's movement on the small stage and the same man who spoke yesterday steps up to the lectern. "Welcome class, to your day of orientation," he says sternly. "Today, you become one of us."

The words thrill through her. This is why she's here—to belong.

Dean Roberts scans the room and Gabby surreptitiously slips behind Kalisha and Maya. Maybe Kalisha's bold makeup will take the attention away from her. His gaze sweeps past the three of them and Gabby lets out a breath. It's best if the dean forgets she exists.

"And as one of the hallowed members of Mercy Academy comes responsibilities," Roberts booms, his mustache twitching. "We have a culture of discipline and order. We do not tolerate tardiness, poor behavior, and rule breaking."

"Whoa," whispers Kalisha. "Did we sign up for military school or something?"

"Rules must be respected," he continues. "Including the curfew." His hawk-like gaze glares at the room with intensity, leaning over the lectern. "No one is to move beyond their rooms after ten o'clock. Sharp."

Yes, it sounds strict. Maybe even a little draconian.

But Gabby's excitement doesn't wane. The brochures had talked of expectations, even expulsion for those who didn't do the right thing. She actually likes the idea of it. She's looking forward to some order and structure. Neither of them are a strong suit of hers.

Roberts takes the room's silence as assent. He straightens. "Respect Mercy Academy and Mercy Academy will equip you with some of the most sought after qualifications in the arts, culture and philosophy faculties. Your career will be an illustrious one in your field of choice." His mustache twitches again. "And the academy's reputation will be secure."

"Which is what this is really about," mutters Kalisha and Gabby elbows her.

"Now," says Roberts. "We have volunteers, seniors of Mercy Academy, to take you on campus tours in groups of twenty. Monday, your classes start."

There's a polite round of applause as the dean steps down and walks away. Gabby suspects he's not really a relationship-focused kind of teacher. It's possible he doesn't know how to smile. The knowledge makes her feel a little better. His annoyance with her yesterday wasn't personal. He's probably already forgotten she exists.

A young man with bright red curls and more freckles than skin approaches them. "Do you have your group of twenty?"

Maya nods firmly. "Yes. These people here." She indicates to a group of what Gabby guesses is exactly twenty people. She hadn't even noticed Maya corralling them.

"Excellent," the guy beams. "My name's Donald Lovecraft,

and I'll be your tour guide for the morning." He taps his finger on his clipboard. "Let's get started."

Maya claps, seemingly unaware that she's the only one and Donald beams even wider. He brandishes his clipboard wide. "We'll start with the classrooms."

The next hour is spent winding their way through the corridors of the first and second floor. Donald explains that each area is dedicated to a subject—philosophy, religion, humanities, anthropology, journalism, mass communication, public relations. All heavy sounding topics that have Gabby a little bored and a lot overwhelmed. Maya, on the other hand, seems closer to orgasm with each word.

Donald continues, pointing out that remembering their classrooms is much easier once they memorize the subject areas. Gabby nods, quickly noting the silver plaques with names and numbers. She's always had a good memory. An almost photographic one. Recollecting details, even the time and date someone said something, has always come easy to her.

Donald's face turns serious. "Because you don't want to be late."

Kalisha crosses her arms while Maya scribbles notes in her book. She's already onto the fifth page of scrawls.

Donald leads them to another of the spiral staircases, the ones who can fit four people abreast, as he heads for the third story. He looks over his shoulder. "Those taking a theater major are in for a treat."

They step into a theater that looks like it occupies half the third story. A huge stage stretches to the left, while rows of maroon covered seats march throughout most of the space. The walls are dark and padded, a large chandelier hanging from the roof. Gabby presses her hands to her stomach to quell the fluttering. The place is empty and it's already full of atmosphere.

"At the end of each semester, there's a play students can

take part in," says Donald. "Actually, several of them. Director and producer roles are generally undertaken by seniors, but we encourage you to try out for roles. Next, the library."

Maya squeals. "Ooh, the library!"

Gabby smiles, excited, too. Books were the first worlds she ever belonged in.

Donald leads them up another broad, curving staircase and they step onto the fourth floor. Maya gasps. Kalisha blinks. Everyone else looks around in wonder.

Gabby smiles so hard it hurts. The library of Mercy Academy appears to extend over the entire floor, emerald carpet stretching out like thick Irish moss. Shelves, mahogany and gleaming, are everywhere, holding countless books. And the ceiling above curves higher than should be possible.

"How?" Gabby asks in a whisper.

Donald grins. "It's an optical illusion, painted on by the creator of Mercy Academy."

Maya walks away as if in a trance. "I...I've just got to..."

Kalisha rolls her eyes. "I'm going to follow just in case she doesn't want to leave."

The others in their group disperse, running fingers over warm looking wood, craning their necks to study the ceiling, or drawing in deep breaths, as if they're hoping to suck in the mountains of information stored here.

Gabby stands where she is, letting the feeling of awe soak into her pores. Everything that happened yesterday and last night fades away. The theater. The library. Just the whole freaking place.

Mercy Academy is where she's supposed to be.

"It's pretty amazing, isn't it?"

She turns to find Donald is beside her. "It's beautiful."

He turns to look at the love child of architecture and literature. "There's not a library larger or more beautiful," he murmurs, almost to himself. "Apart from Veritas, that is."

"Veritas?" Gabby asks, her curiosity piqued. There's somewhere even more magnificent than here? "I haven't heard of it."

Donald blinks. "Oh, ah, somewhere I haven't been since I was a kid." He turns to smile at her, a little too brightly in her opinion. "Anyway, let's keep moving." He taps his clipboard. "We have a schedule to stick to."

He claps his hands, far more softly and almost reverently, as if he doesn't want to break the spell of silence in the library, then spins and walks back out. Gabby watches him, wondering what that was all about.

"Come on, Maya," grunts Kalisha, dragging her by the straps of her backpack. "It'll still be here later."

"So many books, not enough time," Maya says mournfully.

"Have you heard of a library called Veritas?" Gabby asks her as she falls into step beside them.

"The Truth Library?" Maya asks thoughtfully. "Veritas means truth in Latin. No, never heard of it."

"Huh." Gabby watches as Donald makes his way down the stairs, their group following. But then she shakes her head. She doesn't want to know.

Donald leads them outside, talking over his shoulder. "The lawns and gardens around the academy are a wonderful place to study on days of nice weather. They're open to all students." He turns to look at them more fully. "Except after curfew. You shouldn't be outside your dormitories, let alone beyond the walls of the academy."

Kalisha huffs under her breath. "In case we'd forgotten in the twenty minutes since he last mentioned it."

They're showered in sunlight as they make their way down the gravel drive to a large statue surrounded by circular gardens.

"And here he is," Donald says proudly. "Sir Jeremy Mercy Davenport."

"Ohmigod," Maya breathes. "The genius himself."

Donald beams. "Yes, the architect of Mercy Academy."

Gabby looks at the statue more closely, impressed at how life-like it looks. Sir Davenport was a serious looking man, his shoulder-length hair, pencil mustache, and aquiline nose all exquisitely carved. He's staring at Mercy Academy, his features pensive as one hand grips a lapel. Possibly looking a little proud.

He should be, Gabby thinks to herself. The academy really is something special.

"Sir Davenport was born in 1626," Donald says. "He moved here when it was little more than a village following Salem Witch Trials of 1692, determined that education was the way forward. He completed the academy six years later. He died at the age of eighty-nine, after designing many of the buildings in Mercy City."

For the first time, Maya isn't writing anything down, simply nodding as Donald speaks. No doubt because she already knew all this.

"Mercy Academy has withstood the tests of time, and was even unaffected by the American War of Independence. It has become known as a place of great learning for all."

Maya sighs, clutching her notebook to her chest, possibly crushing on the almost-five-hundred year old dude. Although Gabby can't blame her. He was a visionary. She reaches out, brushing her hand over his stone fingers, drawing them back quickly when her own tingle. Someone glances at her strangely so she looks away, knowing static electricity isn't going to be a plausible excuse.

Donald glances at his watch. "And that brings us to lunch

and the end of your tour. I'll be joining you in the cafeteria if you have any further questions."

Gabby joins in the murmured thank yous, falling in behind as everyone makes their way back to the building. She rubs her fingertips against her palm, thinking maybe she just imagined it.

She's just stepped off the lawn and onto the gravel drive when she glances over her shoulder.

And instantly wishes she hadn't.

Tucking her head between her shoulders, she hurries to catch up to Kalisha and Maya, wishing she could unsee what was just seen.

Why didn't she keep her hands to herself, just like everyone else? Why did she have to turn around?

And see the statue frown.

6

COLT

Colt flexes his shoulders as he walks in circles around the gym. He glances up at the large clock hanging high on the wall, noting it's almost five o'clock. The first class will be starting shortly and he's surprised to find he's a little nervous.

Until now, he's taught individuals. Adults. Those willing to pay premium prices to have one on one instruction from a young man known as a prodigy in the industry. It's one way Colt's youthful looks have been advantageous. A guy who looks like he's in mid-twenties thanks to a little glamor magic, and yet is unbeatable in the arena, quickly earned him respect and high-paying clientele.

That is, until a demon attacked him, telling him that Belphegor wanted a word before he dispatched her.

Colt had packed his scant belongings and left that day. The offer from Mercy Academy arrived that night.

Thanking Fate, he'd left before morning.

The sounds of students talking and laughing reaches him as a group of twenty or so enter the gym. They're already dressed in various shades of active wear and are carrying water bottles.

Good. They read the instructions he emailed to come prepared.

They congregate before him, looking at him curiously. Colt meets each of their gazes, unsmiling, but not frowning either. He's here to teach them valuable skills, they're here to learn. That will be the nature of their relationship.

He does a quick head count, finding twenty students now in the group. "We seem to have some people missing." His schedule says there should be thirty-six.

"Those in Social History are probably late," says a young woman in the front of the group, smiling. "It's not unusual for Professor Stokes' class to go overtime."

Colt nods curtly. Sam certainly seemed to enjoy talking. "I see. Well, we'll get started anyway."

His classes are focused and intense. And unlike the dean seems to think, punctual. He doesn't know how to do anything differently.

He scans the group again, getting a sense of their levels of fitness. Seems there's the full spectrum of those who have partaken of too much fast food and those who love to workout, and are proud of it judging by the tank tops and tight shorts.

"Who here has studied martial arts?" he asks. Understanding ability level is next.

His only response is silence and the odd shuffling of feet.

He frowns. "No one?"

He'd been hoping he wouldn't be starting with a bunch of novices.

The students glance at each other, as if hoping someone can answer yes, but no one raises their hand. Not one student has thought it would be worthwhile to invest time and resources into learning how to protect themselves.

It's a testament to the safe world they assume they live in. One flash of his wings and they'd find out otherwise...

He suppresses a sigh. "We'll start with the basics then—"

His sense of hearing hones in on the sounds of approaching footsteps. What must be the remainder of the class shuffle through the door, one or two muttering they can't believe they've already been given an assignment on the first day. A girl or two glance at him, then the class, before their gazes dart back to him.

"Oh, he's young," one whispers.

"And hot!" says her friend.

Colt's about to turn away, wishing his hearing isn't so acute when a third girl speaks.

"Who is?"

He stills, recognizing the voice.

Her.

Her gaze dances around the room before finding him. Her lashes flicker before she looks away. "He's not that hot," she mutters.

For some reason, her words have him stiffening. He's been told this body is very pleasing many a time. In fact, a strategic smile and a warm word has created many opportunities for him.

And yet, this girl doesn't seem to agree with the consensus.

He contains another frown. Not that it should matter.

The group approaches as he affirms to himself that it doesn't. What this girl thinks of him is inconsequential. "Thank you for joining us," he says, his gaze sweeping past every student but her. "My name is Colt Grayson and I'll be your instructor for this class. You may call me Colt." Although he's almost regretting the decision to not use his surname. It would've been a reminder of his role and responsibilities with the girl. "I was just asking if anyone had any prior experience with martial arts."

The same silence from before is his response. His mind

reviews the basic moves they can start with, when someone moves.

And she steps forward.

She arches an eyebrow. "I've been training at a local dojo in Mercy City since I was eight."

"What form?"

"A mixed bag," she says with a shrug. "Not exclusive to one."

Sounds like some backyard self-defense course. "I'd like to test you, if that's okay."

She takes another step forward. "Sure." She tilts her head. "I'm Gabrielle by the way. Gabby."

He nods. He knows her name from their first meeting at the gates of the academy. Doesn't mean he intends on using it. He indicates to the mats behind him. "Shall we?

Her eyebrow twitches again as she sashays past. She's not wearing a mini-skirt today, although her shorts aren't much longer. The smooth length of her legs is...distracting.

She reaches the center of the mats and slips into a fighting stance. Colt surveys her as he takes his own. Legs braced but loose. Hands forming strong fists, one held in front of her face, the other in front of her chest. It's a stable, solid stance.

Facing her, he flicks his fingers, indicating for her to come at him.

She doesn't move a muscle.

Interesting. She's getting a sense of him just as much as he is of her. Very well. Let's see if she's all confidence and show.

Colt executes a short, sharp punch to her chest, already intending on reigning it in several inches from her nose. But he never gets there. Swiftly, almost as if it's second nature, the girl flicks out a block, knocking his arm away with enough strength to make their contact sting, her hands returning to their protective positions.

Not only is she faster than he expected, she's stronger.

Also interesting.

This time, Colt moves a little quicker. He throws out a kick aimed straight for her head. She ducks, dropping to the ground and executing a swift sweep, trying to knock him over. Colt leaps, landing to a chorus of "oohs" from the students.

Finding his center of balance again, he refocuses. He watches as Gabby returns to her defensive stance, muscles coiled and ready once more. She's far more capable than he expected. Possibly a professional.

Deciding it's time to find out, he attacks with a series of strikes. A punch to the head, one to the abdomen. A spinning elbow followed by a sharp uppercut. She blocks and parries each and every one of them. Becoming more aggressive in his attack, Colt moves faster, strikes a little harder.

The outcome is the same each time.

Not one punch or kick makes contact with the girl.

What's more, each time their bodies collide, there's an undeniable spark of electricity that jolts over his skin.

He's not sure which one he finds more irritating.

Determined, Colt's gaze locks with hers, finding the same resolve in her summer eyes. They practically flash with blue fire. A responding fire flares within him. A fire he's never felt before.

One he doesn't want to.

Tightening his jaw, he goes on the offensive again, this time barely holding back. His techniques become more advanced, the volleys of strikes and kicks more relentless. His aggression is met with an equally determined defense. He doesn't make contact with his intended target once.

What's more, the moment there's an opening, she becomes the attacker. With lightning fast movement, she spins and flicks out a kick. It connects straight with his chest, shoving him backward.

Colt quickly regains his balance, but not his equilibrium.

Who is this girl? He can't remember the last time someone landed a kick on him. Not even seasoned fighters.

Gabby straightens and drops her hands, a smile hovering over her lush lips. "Must've been a lucky shot."

The murmurs around them snap Colt out of the strange cocoon of awareness he'd found himself in. He bows to the girl, realizing he'd started using her name, even if it's within the confines of his mind. "Indeed." He turns to the rest of the class. "We'll begin with a warm up. I'd like five laps of the gym, and each time you pass this point, ten sit-ups and five push ups, please."

There are few groans but the students do as they've been asked. Gabby—the girl, he corrects himself—flicks her ponytail and jogs past him, that half-smile still there, a flare of triumph in her eyes. Lily and rose tickle his senses, but he tells himself the increase in his pulse is due to the short fight.

And the unmistakable uneasiness scratching away at his nerves.

Ever since Belphegor began sending demons out after him, he's been on high alert. Maybe his paranormal senses here at the academy haven't been wrong.

Maybe Gabby's the threat he needs to be cautious of.

Maybe she's more than human.

* * *

Colt enters his room and drops his bag beside his bed, mind still whirling even though the class is long finished.

The idea that Gabrielle is a supernatural of some kind has taken root. She'd trained like all the other students, the only sign of her remarkable fighting skills apparent in her easy grace and the way she executed each move with familiarity. In fact, she'd barely made eye contact with him the remainder of the session.

But she landed a kick on him. That makes her exceptional.

And it's undeniable Belphegor wants Colt.

If the girl is a spy for that bastard, Colt needs to be careful. The moment she catches him unawares, he'll find himself back in the bowels of the underworld, kneeling before the one who sends ripples of fear coursing down his spine.

And yet, he can't sense demon on her. Nor can he smell the sulfurous, ashy-laden scent of Hell. He may not have smelled it for hundreds of years, but it's one he'll never forget. Although demons can hide their aura from other supernatural beings, there is always a trace, no matter how small. And Colt's trained himself to detect it. His life depends on it. If the girl really is a demon, then she's learned to mask it well.

Unless...

Colt dismisses the idea before it can take hold. No angel has entered the mortal plane in eons. On the other hand, demons poured into the world seventeen years ago when a Tear opened up in the Middle East. It's since then that he's been hunted by the forces of Hell.

Which means, if Gabby is a demon, she's a powerful one. One capable of almost anything. One more powerful than him.

Colt's just closed the door when his curtains flutter. The memory of the strange vision from a few days ago has him tensing. As he watches, scribbled words appear on the glass.

Run. They know what you are. They have found you.

The words, written in a language far more ancient than human memory, have Colt's breath disintegrating. Who wrote this? And why?

He glances around the room, expecting someone to materialize. Is someone trying to help him? Or does someone want him to leave the academy?

His hands form tight fists. Unless there's a trap outside. And the demons hunting him are lurking, waiting to pounce as soon as he steps outside of the gates?

Too many questions. And none of them with an answer.

Frowning, he connects with the trace of magic as the ominous words fade. And is met with a wall. That means the demon is strong, probably old. Maybe older than he is.

The older ones are fond of hunting. With a whole lot more practice.

That thought has him rushing to the wardrobe where he pulls out his duffle bag. He'll take his chances outside of the walls of the academy. He's not staying.

Most of his clothes are still packed, like they always are. He likes to be prepared. Grabbing the few possessions littered around the room, he zips up the bag and slings it over his shoulder.

It's twilight as Colt descends the stairs, every muscle wound tight. He'll find somewhere else. He has to.

He's just reached the front foyer when there's a soft tapping noise behind him. Colt spins around, already intending on using his duffel bag as a weapon, only to quickly stop himself.

Mr. Bishop walks toward him, his back curved over the walking stick he's using. Tap. Tap. Tap. Colt frowns, unhappy with the delay.

The head of security stops short a few steps away, his raspy breathing filling the foyer. "Leaving already?" he asks, one bushy brow raised.

Colt nods, thinking fast. "Yes. I know it's early and sudden, but I got a call from my mother. Seems like my father's hospitalized and I need to be there for him right now."

The wrinkles in the man's face fold in concern. "Of course, family's important, young man."

Relief powers Colt's smile as he turns to leave, only for the man to speak again.

"But the gates won't open until dawn tomorrow."

Colt has to unclench his jaw as he turns back. "Not even for an emergency?"

"You'd need the dean's permission for that," the man replies. "You know how strict they are about that."

"Yes, I've noticed," Colt remarks. The place is practically a prison for students and professors alike once lights are out. "Luckily, I have the dean's permission."

He slips his spare hand behind his back, hoping the old man's hearing won't pick up what he mutters under his breath. A piece of paper appears in his hand and he holds it out to. Mr. Bishop takes it, reading each word carefully, alternating between holding it close to his face and extending his arm as he tries to focus.

Colt chafes as he waits. He's tempted to just turn around and walk out. It's not like the guy could catch him.

The man hands the paper back to him and says, "Looks good."

Colt nods. "Have a good night, Mr. Bishop."

"You too, Mr. Grayson."

Mr. Bishop turns and tap, tap, taps his way toward the offices. Shrugging, Colt walks toward the parking lot and gets into his car. Tomorrow, Mercy Academy will be nothing but a memory, just like the countless other places he's lived.

He reaches the parking lot and climbs into his car, turning the ignition and gently pumping the gas. The Jaguar purrs with enthusiasm. There are few things that he's let himself get attached to during his time on Earth, but beautiful cars have been the exception. As human technology evolved, so have their vehicles. It means the Jaguar he now has is a sleek, sexy, state of the art machine.

Colt rubs the dash affectionately. "We'll find somewhere. It'll be fine."

He pulls out of the staff parking lot, and makes his way to the gates, the slip of paper he showed to Mr. Bishop once again appearing in his hand. He'll show the guards and they'll open the gates, even though it's something that rarely happens after curfew.

And he'll be on the road again.

As Colt makes his way down the gravel drive, his eyebrows twitch when he sees the gates are open, the two security guards standing to the side, chatting over half-smoked cigarettes. It seems getting away will be even easier than he expected.

He accelerates a little, wanting this over and done with. If he's leaving Mercy Academy, then he'll do it quickly. Without looking back.

The security guards look up, surprised that someone is approaching them at this time of the night. Colt's just about to wind his window down when something grips him by the throat. His hand flies up, ready to rip the invisible threat away.

But he doesn't get a chance.

He's yanked backward with enough force to snap his seat. For him to plough through the plush interior. To tear straight through the metal frame of the car as if it were paper.

As he sails through the air, he watches as his car continues forward. The moment it reaches the gates, it bursts into flames. Then explodes as if it were a giant grenade.

Colt doesn't have time to understand what's going on. He crashes to the ground, the impact wrenching a groan out of him. His body tumbles and crumples, bouncing like a rag doll. Cracks echo through his mind as bones break, pain explodes with each collision of gravel driveway.

When he finally stops, he stares at the starry sky above him, blinking slowly, even that motion hurting. Flames flicker somewhere in the periphery. Beyond his harsh, gasping breaths, there's silence.

Closing his eyes, Colt knows he has to wait. His skin feels shredded. His body mangled. There's no doubt in his mind that if he were human, he'd be dead right now.

He's focused so hard, willing it with such determination, that he feels the moment the healing starts. His body twitches as bones realign and mesh back together, tendons and muscles reconnecting and bringing his skeleton back into alignment. He sighs as skin unites and binds, healing as if it was never torn apart. The pain abates, breath by breath. Slowly, he drags himself onto all fours. Then upright.

Beyond the gates, his car is a fireball. It would be magnificent if it wasn't such a tragic loss.

The security guards haven't moved from where they were beside their booth. They're both motionless, mouths wide and eyes wider. Colt can't blame them. Even he's not sure what just happened, and he's seen pretty much everything.

Carefully, his senses alert for another invisible attack, he walks toward the closest gate. He places his hand on the wrought iron, drawing in a sharp breath as his palm burns. There's definitely some power buzzing through it.

Definitely something designed to keep him inside the walls of the academy.

Though not demonic.

He frowns, unable to place it.

A few feet away, one of the security guards twitches. "Wh— what...just happened?"

The other blinks, the cigarette dropping from his lifeless fingers. "The car just...it just..."

Colt rubs his forehead, stifling a sigh. He needs to take care of this. Humans can't know of the supernatural. They simply can't handle it. It scares them, and scared humans are dangerous humans. Usually violent and aggressive humans. He's seen it too many times.

Colt steps into their line of sight and the two men freeze all over again. He watches the terror climb in their eyes and their muscles lock as they realize there's no chance of escape.

Not from the winged being now steadily approaching them. He expands his wings so their splendor is all they'll be able to see. Black as night, the tip of each feather dipped in red, they shield the rest of the world from what's about to happen.

The tips of Colt's fingers glow with crimson fire as he raises his hands. The men take a few stuttering steps back, but it's too little. Too late. He places his palms on the side of their heads, focusing his energy.

The glow brightens.

The men scream, their heads tipping back as their cries are thrown to the sky.

But Colt has no choice.

He just hopes he can do it quickly.

7

GABBY

Kalisha flops onto her bed, groaning. "Ohmigod, I am so tired!"

Maya giggles as she climbs onto her own. "Although you're not the one who took on the instructor."

Gabby rolls her eyes. "I thought we'd decided that conversation was over and done with."

"That's what you suggested over dinner," says Kalish, pointing a fire-engine red nail at her. "We've still got days of ribbing to milk from this."

Sighing, Gabby climbs onto her bunk. "I told you, it's no big deal."

She'd had a lovely, normal day until martial arts class. Social History had been her favorite, even if they already had an assignment. She soaked up every word the professor said as those around her furiously took notes. But Gabby didn't need to. She was fascinated. Focused. She found herself totally immersed in how the world has changed through the ages, and why.

"Kicking the hot instructor in the chest is definitely a big deal," says Kalisha with a grin.

Gabby flops back onto her pillow. She hadn't meant to. She'd just wanted to show him—Colt—that she wasn't a complete air head. That she was actually capable at something.

But he was good. Very good. And she got a little...competitive.

"How old do you think he is?" Maya asks dreamily.

"Twenty-five, maybe a young twenty-seven," Kalisha guesses.

Maya shakes her head. "I mean, he's an instructor at the academy, and even if he's twenty-five, that's too old. I was just, ah, wondering."

Gabby leans over her bunk, pushing her curls out of her face as she looks at Kalisha below in surprise. "He's not that old. I would've said nineteen, maybe twenty. Much closer to our age."

Kalisha glances up from the small mirror she's holding as she wipes away the makeup from her face. "Wishful thinking, babe. He's definitely older than us."

Laying back down, Gabby frowns at the ceiling. She's usually pretty good with picking people's ages.

Maya picks up the remote and turns on the television attached to the wall on the opposite side of the room. "I have eight minutes before it's my bedtime. Is it okay if I catch up on the news?"

"Sure thing," Gabby and Kalisha assure her, a smile in their voices.

Maya loves information almost as much as she loves routine.

An ad appears on the television screen, showing a good looking man extolling the virtues of a state of the art security system. The camera zooms in on his face as he reveals perfect white teeth in a dazzling smile. "We live in dangerous times. Make sure you keep your home safe."

Gabby frowns. This company is taking advantage of

people's fears following the murders. As clever as it is, it's tasteless.

The image cuts to the news and the grave face of the news anchor. There are no new murders to report, but the other five have happened seven days apart. The man angles his head to the side just a little, his gaze centered on the camera. "Mercy City wants to know. Are there more coming?" he says somberly.

The TV flicks off. "I think an early night might be in order," Maya says quietly.

"Good idea," says Kalisha. "All those murders are just awful. Like, ritualistic or something."

Maya pulls in a sharp breath. "You think it has something to do with those cult murders that happened years ago?"

"No," assures Kalisha. "The cult was dealt with at the time."

Maya sits up, eyes wide. "You think these are copycat murders?"

Gabby rolls over, smiling gently at her. "I think it's some crazy serial killer that the police will catch very soon. We're safe here. Heck, we're locked in every night, meaning everyone else is locked out."

Maya nods, looking as if she desperately wants to believe those words. "Who knew curfew was a good thing, huh?" she jokes weakly.

Gabby smiles wider. "I sure as flip didn't see that coming." The whole idea of curfew is almost draconic.

"Goodnight, y'all," yawns Kalisha. "I can't be the self-appointed representative of ravishing vixens without my beauty sleep."

With giggles and goodnights, they all settle down into their beds. It's not long before Gabby can hear their soft, rhythmic breathing, along with the odd snuffle. She's glad they've fallen asleep so easily.

If only she could do the same.

The number seven has stuck in her mind, like it's significant or something. A murder every seven days. And five have happened so far. The news anchor is right. Will there be two more? A shudder ripples down her spine. Kalisha's also right. They do sound ritualistic. Which means someone is killing in honor of some skewed belief.

Rolling over as quietly as possible, Gabby stares out the window. The gates to the academy are beyond, and she doesn't believe for a second they could stop anyone intent on murder. If she could, she'd wrap this place in a big protective bubble. Then do the same for Mercy City. No one would need to be afraid for their life.

She stills, blinks, then blinks again, hoping she didn't just see what she just saw.

A red sports car is driving toward the gates. A red sports car she recognizes after her fateful first meeting with Colt.

He's leaving?

She tells herself it doesn't matter, but she also doesn't tear her gaze away. Where is he going at this time of the night? And why?

Before any possible explanations can pop into her mind, Gabby gasps. The rear of the car explodes as Colt is wrenched out like an unwilling bullet. The car continues to the gates and burst into flames, becoming a spectacular fireball a breathless second later.

Throwing off the covers, Gabby scrambles down the ladder and out of her room. She breaks into a run, feeling the two lines down her shoulder blades burn as she sprints down the stairs. Her heart is a pounding drum as she reaches the first floor. No one could survive what she just saw.

She stops as she reaches the front doors. She should tell someone, but who? Glancing over her shoulder, she wonders if she should go to the staff quarters, no matter how crazy this all sounds. A guy being yanked out of the back of a car seconds before it turns into a blazing fireball. That's definitely what Maya would've done. Probably also Kalisha.

The sound of screams reach her and Gabby breaks into a run, the decision made for her. The terrified sound isn't something she can ignore.

Her pulse is thrumming like a hummingbird on speed when she reaches the gates, finding two security guards lying on the ground. Gabby kneels down, noting their closed eyes and pale skin.

Please don't let them be...

But then she sees one chest rise, then a second. She sags with relief. They're breathing, so not dead.

"Hello? Can you hear me?" she says, but neither of them make any movement to show they're conscious.

Gabby stands, knowing she needs to decide what to do next. She has no idea whether it was them screaming, especially when they seem unharmed. She glances up, her gaze focusing beyond the open gates.

"What. The. Frig."

The road is empty. Clear. Not even a flicker of flame let alone a blazing inferno.

The car is gone. Not only that. It's like it was never here. Never alight.

Gabby glances down at the two unconscious guards. They can't exactly answer any questions for her.

Wrapping her arms around herself, she takes a few unsteady steps backward. She knows what she saw. She saw the car flame grilled. And Colt—

She glances around frantically, but there's no sign of him. There's no way he could've walked away from an accident like that. And yet, he's gone.

Another few stumbling steps backward and Gabby spins

around. She's suddenly glad she didn't tell anyone what she saw. They'd think she's crazy.

Heck. Right now she's not terribly confident where she sits on the sanity meter.

The security guards are fine, just taking some sort of weird nap. She'll go to her room and do what she's done with every other freaky-ass brain glitch that's happened since she came here.

She'll pretend it never happened.

She's only taken a few steps away when alarm tingles down her spine. She stills, glancing over her shoulder even though there was no sound. It feels like she's not alone.

She leaps back in surprise when she finds she isn't.

The old man standing there arches a brow. "May I ask why you're out here, young lady?"

Gabby quickly takes in the security uniform and the badge over the man's breast pocket. Shit. He's the head of security. "Sorry, Mr., ah, Bishop. I, ah, thought I heard something."

He looks around. "Heard what?"

"Absolutely nothing, it turns out," she says cheerily.

"And yet, here you are," he says, eyes narrowing. "Despite curfew."

Gabby flushes. How has she found herself in this situation, again? Especially after her nice, normal day! "I'm so sorry, Mr. Bishop. I don't normally do things like this."

Well, not until a few days ago.

"You are aware of the rules here, aren't you, Gabrielle? And that they are strictly enforced?"

Gabby glances down at her hands, wondering how he knows her name, but knowing she can't ask. Right now, she needs to get back to her dorm room. "Yes, I do. I'm very sorry Mr. Bishop. It won't happen again."

There's a groan from the gates and Mr. Bishop spins around.

He squints and Gabby hopes that maybe his eyesight is poor and he can't see the security guard rolling on the ground several feet away.

Mr. Bishop spins back to her. "What have you done, girl?"

"It wasn't me, I swear! I thought I saw something and came out here to check. I found those two, unconscious. I promise."

He looks at her for long moments, his face inscrutable in the dark. "You're telling the truth."

The words aren't a question, they're a statement. Gabby holds her breath, unsure of what's coming next. She got a taste of Mercy Academy today, and it was delicious. She wants more.

And it's possible she just jeopardized everything.

Mr. Bishop rubs his chin. "I suggest you return to your room, Gabrielle, and hope no one else sees you. You were obviously in the wrong place at the wrong time. I'll tend to the guards and see if I can get to the bottom of this."

He's going to cover for her?

Gabby's so happy she could almost hug the man. Smiling widely, she has to stop herself from curtseying. They're not in the middle ages, for crap's sake. "Thank you, Mr. Bishop. I really appreciate it."

He smiles back at her, and she's struck by the youthful intelligence she sees in his eyes. Eyes that are almost familiar...

His bushy eyebrows contract and Gabby quickly spins on her heel, not wanting to ruin her good luck by gawking. Hurrying away, she breaks into a run, the sharp rocks digging into her feet in a way she hadn't noticed coming out here. She was obviously too high on adrenaline.

Ignoring the pain, she slips through the front doors without looking back. Within minutes, she's back in her room, glad to find Kalisha and Maya are both still asleep.

Gabby creeps back up her ladder and crawls under the

covers. She settles in, pulling them right up to her chin and rolling over so her back is to the window.

She closes her eyes tightly, as if that will help her fall asleep quicker. She should never have gone out there.

She's only been at Mercy Academy a few days and she's already failing dismally. She's finding herself outside of men's dorm rooms. Male staff members, no less. She's seeing things that aren't there. She's breaking the rules.

Each and every action is another step away from normal.

That's because you're not normal.

Gabby yanks the covers over her head as the words whisper through her mind. But once they've gained form, they don't go away, no matter how much she wants them to. In fact, they settle in her consciousness, making themselves right at home, all righteous and smug.

Because they know they're true.

8

COLT

Colt stands at his window, even though the girl is long gone. Of course she had to turn up, before he could finish everything he needed to do.

He'd checked the security guards, hoping he didn't have to repeat the memory burning spell again. It would mean having to experience every one of their memories again, and one of the men in particular had too many unhappy ones, molded by a life of poverty and drug use. Getting the job as a security guard had been his ticket out of his own Hell.

And these memory spells can sometimes go awry, he's seen it. Colt's been on Earth for too many centuries though, possessing body after body, and has become a master at it. Relieved, he'd found the men's minds were intact, their recollection of Colt and his car now nothing more than a brief blackness.

He'd turned his attention to the car. Lifting his hands with the palms outwards, he'd gritted his teeth. The wreckage rose into the air, mirroring his actions. He'd tilted his hands as he muttered a spell in the guttural tongue of his ancestry. Soundlessly, the car crumpled into itself. He clenched his fists and what was left of the vehicle crumbled to dust, floating peacefully to the ground.

Colt sighs in his dark room. He'd grown fond of that car and it'll take time to find a suitable replacement. He scowls. Especially considering it seems he can't leave the academy grounds.

Someone has cast a spell ensuring he remains at Mercy Academy. He doesn't like the sound of that.

And then, she turned up before the guards could wake.

He'd stood in the shadows as he'd watched her approach. What was the foolish girl doing there, anyway?

Not so much a girl, he admits to himself. He couldn't help but notice the sway of her hips in those short pajama bottoms, or the pale skin peeking above where her tank top didn't quite reach. Every one of her curves is that of a woman.

He frowns. Although she's definitely foolish. She doesn't know when to let something go. She keeps popping up at inopportune times. And she disregards the rules.

She's being very unwise.

"Meshuga," he mutters.

Although he's not sure who he's calling the idiot, the girl or himself. He should've been quicker. There should've been nothing for her to see. He cannot afford for that to happen again.

And she keeps turning up...

Five times since he's arrived at Mercy Academy she's crossed paths with him. The first, she'd argued, unable or unwilling, to acknowledge the error of her ways. The second, she'd turned up at his room looking beautiful and confused, then done it again only hours later. Fourth, she'd shown surprising fighting skills. Then fifth, she had to go and stumble across the unconscious guards.

Fate seems to be playing with him. He met her once, a very long time ago by human standards, but little more than a trifle in the lifespan of a demon from Hell. Nor is it a memory he'd rather revisit. Those Gods are fickle and petty with their own agendas. And he has more pressing matters to deal with.

He needs to know if this Gabrielle Heartley is a threat. She displayed 'more than ordinary' fighting skills back in the class and held her own against him, which is surprising considering very few among mortals can do so. She could just have had a good teacher. Or she could be something else...

He needs to know whether she's a demon tasked with returning him to Hell.

And seeing as he can't leave, he has no other choice. He will find out exactly who, or what, Gabrielle is.

Apart from beautiful. Beguiling. And full of attitude.

Colt grunts as he crosses his arms. Not many have been able to impress him during his time on Earth. Visions of the class he taught that evening float before his eyes. He can see his fight with her as clearly as he would see anything under the sun. It had been almost spellbinding.

All the more reason to suspect she's more than human.

He's about to turn away from the window when something has him looking back out. Colt frowns and steps closer.

The night sky is no longer glittering with stars, it's a blanket of onyx. And yet no storm was approaching when he tried to leave. Narrowing his eyes, he watches. Waits.

And sees what he was hoping he wouldn't.

Plumes of ebony black are pouring down from the sky, twisting and contorting in excitement. Demons. Hundreds of them.

Descending on Mercy Academy.

No doubt here to take him away.

Well, not without a fekking good fight.

Colt's about to turn away, adrenaline flooding every cell, when he sees something that should be impossible. The inky smoke—the demons—hit an invisible wall as if the academy is surrounded by a glass bubble. The demons writhe and thrash, spreading out as they try to get past the barrier.

And fail.

The protection around the academy is absolute.

Just as quickly as they arrived, the demons flee, their attempt to attack thwarted. Colt remains by the window, wondering what in the world just happened. A movement down by the gates catches his attention and Colt realizes he wasn't the only person to see the phenomenon.

Mr. Bishop, the old security supervisor, is standing in the center of the road, his hands on his hips and his neck arched as he gazes at the sky. Colt groans. It's going to be the last thing he'll ever see.

The old man turns around and Colt peers at him, trying to get a gauge of how he's reacted to what he just witnessed. He's probably terrified. About to call for backup.

But Colt's eyebrows shoot up as he's surprised for the second time in just as many minutes.

Mr. Bishop is smiling.

Colt snorts, shaking his head. The old man's eyesight is probably too poor to see the threat that poured down from the sky. It'll be his saving grace. No human can know of the supernatural. It's too dangerous.

Wiping his hands down his face, Colt sits on the bed, his eyes suddenly heavy. He hasn't slept for days, always on edge that some demon might find him. Belphegor wants him. The demons attacking the academy only proved that. But it seems whatever shield is keeping Colt in, is keeping those hordes of demons out. It's actually offering him the most protection he's had in centuries.

He lays down as sleep tugs at his consciousness, refusing to be denied this time. And yet, even as he sinks, despite what he just saw, it's images of the girl that come with him. Like she has no intention of leaving.

The moment he's within the grip of sleep, they finally dissipate.

Only to be replaced with others.

Light trickles into the darkness he finds himself in, its tendrils driving the black away and replacing it with a silvery white. Colt finds himself standing in the center of what looks like a huge banquet hall. The vision is blurry, but he can make out bodies lying on the floor. Horror slices through him, but not because of death itself. He's seen too much of it in his lifetime.

What horrifies him is the way they're laid out on the floor. His gaze follows the design and he registers it's a pentagram. Just as he wonders at the formation, the bodies start to burn. The flames are unusual though, a red center with a flash of bright gold. They're not flames he's ever seen before and definitely nothing ordinary. He can't make out if the fire is celestial or infernal. It looks like it is a blend of both, but he knows quite well how the two don't mix.

This is most certainly a strange dream. When he tries to move, he finds himself stuck, rooted to the spot. He curses and tries again, wanting out of his dream and back into his conscious mind. But his body is not his own.

The vision changes to a forest clearing where seven shady outlines have gathered around a round stone table. Seven dark pieces of stone lie on it, each piece glowing with a strange power that makes it tremble.

Without warning, the seven shady figures burst into flame, twisting and writhing as they die a gruesome death before his eyes. Colt frowns, confused as to why he's seeing this. He tries again, but can't take himself away.

A young woman bursts into the clearing, fire in her hand. She doesn't appear to see him as she waves her flames over each of the pieces. They shiver, then with lightning fast movement, spear to the center of the round table. The pieces collide in a blaze of fire, joining along jagged, uneven lines. In a blink, the pieces merge, forming a black stone.

With an aura that reminds him of the one place he's spent hundreds of years trying to forget. Hell.

The light starts to dull, progressively swallowed by darkness. Yet Colt senses that the encroaching night isn't his dream's making but that of the merged stones. Shadows swirl around it. He can feel its power here, even in the dream plane. Raspy whispers fill the air, yet the girl doesn't appear fazed as she stands there, looking at it.

Who is she and what's she doing in his dreams? There's something about her that's familiar. Blonde curls. Gentle curves.

He calls out to her but she doesn't hear. Curious, he steps closer, her features coming into focus. He groans.

"What are you doing in my dream?" he demands.

Gabby spins around, eyes flaring when she registers him standing not far away. "You're in mine, thank you very much."

He frowns. "I beg to differ. This is most certainly my dream."

"Beg, huh?" she asks, raising her brows. "Sure thing. Go for it."

Colt scowls. "You're very impertinent."

She arches a blonde brow. "And you talk like you're from the dark ages."

"Leave. Now," he growls.

She takes a step forward, her eyes narrowed. "Make me."

He narrows his own eyes. It is she who's come into his dream. Not the other way around. And yet she's standing there, full of attitude.

He'll show her whose dream this is. Colt stalks forward,

thinking she'll step back. He's bigger and stronger than her. It's time she started acknowledging that.

Her blue eyes flare in a way that he's coming to expect as she lifts her hands to her hips.

Shock roots him to the spot for a breathless second. He doesn't understand. He's supposed to have full control over the events in his dream plane. Yet, the girl openly defied him. How is this possible?

He lunges this time, deciding he'll throw her over his shoulder and carry her out if he has to, but she ducks the strike and sweeps his feet out from under him. Landing on his back, Colt winces as pain radiates up his spine. He's about to vault to his feet when she leaps on top of him, straddling his waist with her legs, her hands trapping his above his head.

What the—

Colt struggles, trying to dislodge her. This is his dream. He will not be bested.

But Gabby's too strong. His hands remain where they are, pinned to the forest floor, his hips captured by her thighs.

He stills, unused to the feelings coursing through him. Warm feelings. Ones that are rapidly increasing in temperature.

"Now this is kinda cool," she purrs, sending shivers skittering over his skin.

Colt blinks as his mind agrees without his consent. In fact, it wants her to move closer. To press all of her along all of him.

Suddenly, someone or something grabs Colt by the shirt and pulls him out from under her. "I think that's enough for now," says a female voice.

Back on his feet, Colt glances around, finding Gabby has disappeared. What's more, a swirling white portal opens and an invisible power sucks him into it. The next thing he knows, he's back in the banquet hall.

"You seem to have developed a strange ability, Colt Grayson," says the female voice.

He frowns as a female form cements in front of him. At first, she looks like a stranger, but as her features gain clarity, he takes a sharp step back. It can't be.

"Miss Aimee, what are you doing here?" he whispers.

Guilt flushes through him. He knew her when he was just a new demon in an alien world. She's long dead.

She angels her head. "You see me as Miss Aimee?"

Colt nods, not liking the uncomfortable feeling slithering through him. "Yes."

"That's interesting," she murmurs, her gaze far too perceptive.

"Who the scheisse are you if you're not her?"

She smiles. "I'm called by a lot of names, the most popular being Atropos, Clotho, and Lachesis. Well, at least that's what people used to call me when I was three. Now, I am one and just called Fate."

"Fate," Colt breathes. He hadn't expected to run into her again.

"Yes, that's the response I usually get, as if I get a say in how events unfold. I thread the Loom, nothing else. The fabric of life is woven by choices, not me."

"Why are you here?" he growls.

The woman angles her head. "I haven't seen many who can walk into other people's dreams. You seem to have discovered an ability to be a dreamwalker."

"I really went into that girl's dream?" he asks, disbelief evident in his tone.

"Yes." The woman nods. "What also surprised me is that she was aware of you doing so. Most people are untrained in how much control they have in their own plane. The fact that she can do it is…intriguing."

"That's one word for her." Unsettling is more apt. "What exactly is she?"

Fate shakes her head, smiling. "What she is, I shall leave for you to find out. But I can say that your destiny is linked to her in some way."

Colt sighs at the thought that his future could forever be linked to a girl who frustrates him so much. That's the last thing he wants. Or needs.

And yet, something within him tells him Fate is right. He's connected to Gabby somehow.

"Why are you here?" he asks, trying to change the subject.

Fate's features turn somber. "You need to find the seven stones before they figure out what to do with them," she tells him. "And the girl is the only one who can help you."

"And why would I want to do that?" That sounds very little like lying low.

"The stones are the key, Colt Grayson, which is all you need to know."

With another calm smile, Fate vanishes, leaving behind tendrils of white smoke. He curses. This is exactly something the goddess would do. Leave cryptic messages that raise more questions than have answers and then disappear.

He takes a step forward, about to demand she returns, when his eyes snap open. Colt finds himself in his bed, the beginning of dawn painting the sky beyond the window. Sitting up, he rubs his forehead, trying to make sense of everything he just experienced.

When that proves fruitless, he gets off the bed and opens the window to let the fresh morning breeze in. The desire to leave the academy thuds through his veins. And yet, the need to stay is now rooted in his heart. He's never experienced anything so confusing.

He switches the TV on with his mind, needing a distraction.

An image of a reporter interviewing a young man in his early twenties fills the screen.

The reporter holds out the microphone. "David, what exactly did you see the night before your neighbors were killed?"

The young man ducks his head. "Well, I was on my way to a party with my girlfriend, you see. But all of a sudden, I felt cold. Like, out of nowhere. So, I decided to get a jacket. I was just making my way back when I saw seven red lights hovering above their house." He rubs the back of his head. "But the really weird thing is that these red lights formed a symbol of some kind."

The camera flicks to the reporter, who has an expression that could only be described as a convenient mix of curiosity and concern. "What sort of symbol?

The young man shrugs. "I think it looked like a seven sided shape, a heptagon, but I'm not sure."

With a flick of his hand, Colt turns the TV back off. The media's no doubt trying to fuel the countless conspiracy theories that are blossoming in the wake of the serial murders. It could be nothing but the drunk or drug-fueled visions of a young man on his way to a party.

And yet...

Fate mentioned seven stones. Seven stones that he must find before someone else does.

And now seven lights have been seen in the formation of a heptagon.

The goddess herself would say there is no such thing as a coincidence.

Which means he has to decide what to do about it.

9

GABBY

Gabby juggles the tray carrying her breakfast as she holds her cell phone above, trying to give the camera time to focus. The tray wobbles, and she quickly shuffles until it steadies again.

"What are you doing?" Kalisha asks with a quizzical frown.

"Careful! You could drop it," Maya squeaks, sounding like that would equate with bringing on the apocalypse.

Gabby snaps a photo, then sends the image with one hand. "Relax. I can juggle five balls at once, including with my feet."

"Of course you can, Miss Kick Ass," Kalisha says, rolling her eyes. "What's the photo for anyway? The food here isn't exactly foodstagram material."

Grabbing a hold of her tray with two hands again, Gabby looks around the cafeteria. "You haven't seen my mom's cooking." It seems everyone woke up at the same time and decided to have their breakfast along with them. Every table is full.

A hand rises from the back of the room, waving wildly. "Gabby! I saved you a seat!"

Kalisha groans. "Not Klae again."

"She might be a bit odd, but she has a good heart," says Gabby.

"See how every other table is full, apart from hers? Sitting with her is social suicide," Kalisha says quietly. "We're freshmen. We can't afford to do that."

Gabby's brow wrinkles. She wants to fit in as much as Kalisha does.

But she also doesn't want to be a bitch.

"That's not what Mercy Academy is about," she says. "And we're having breakfast, not dating her."

Maya smiles. "I agree. I say we give her a chance."

"Fine, then," Kalisha huffs. "I could probably give her a few tips about her skin care routine, anyway."

Gabby rolls her eyes and they make their way over. Klae's smile only grows the closer they get, and Gabby knows they made the right decision. She decided a long time ago she'd be someone others could rely on. Stable. Dependable.

Unlike her father.

Pushing the thought away, Gabby sits down beside Klae, Kalisha and Maya sitting across the table. She notes the table is littered with flyers. "Someone's been busy. What are these for?"

Klae beams, her bracing glinting. "Every theater class has to conduct a play each semester." Her smile impossibly grows. "And this time, I'm directing one."

Kalisha leans forward, a piece of toast in her hand as she swipes a thick layer of marmalade on it. "Oh, what's the play about?"

"A love story actually, although I'm still drafting the script."

Kalisha chews her toast thoughtfully. "You need a makeup artist?"

Gabby bites her lip as she contains her smile. Seems Kalisha can see some benefit in befriending Klae.

"I think I've got that part under control," Klae says, flicking her limp hair over her shoulder.

Kalisha's eyes pop open as she chokes on her marmalade toast.

Klae bursts into giggles. "Ohmigod, you should see your face."

Maya is the next to join her, then Gabby. Realizing the joke was on her, Kalisha shakes her head ruefully, also giggling. "You got me."

"I'd love your expertise," Klae says, still smiling. "Your makeup is amazing."

Today, Kalisha's gone for an understated smokey eye and almost nude lips. And yet, everything from her carefully sculpted eyebrows to her subtle blush is perfection. She grins. "I know, right?"

That has another round of giggles circling the table. Gabby jabs her fork into her hotcake, glad she insisted they come to this table. Not only was it the right thing to do, it's turned out to be fun. Normal. Just like college is supposed to be.

All the weird-ass shit that's been happening, just like the way too sexy dream with Colt last night, can go get shoved in the It-Didn't-Happen box.

Klae pushes one of the flyers a little closer to Gabby. "You should totally audition. You'd be perfect for my heroine."

Surprise jolts through Gabby. She glances down at the flyer, noting the abundance of red love hearts on it. "It's a romance?"

"Yeah," Klae says dreamily. "A love story."

"Ah, I'm more of an action girl."

"As in Die Hard action or Chainsaw Massacre action?"

"More of a Pirates of the Caribbean," Gabby says with a grin.

"So fight scenes and special effects," Klae says thoughtfully. "That can be arranged."

Gabby's eyes widen. "Oh, I didn't mean change your play for me! You follow your vision, Klae."

"Not so much changing it, but giving it a new angle," she says, her eyes lighting up. "Most people wouldn't try something like that—too ambitious. But I love a challenge."

"Seriously, don't change this for me," Gabby insists.

"Nah, everyone else is doing romance. You've given me an idea about how to make mine different. Besides, you'd fit the protagonist perfectly."

"Are you sure?"

"Totally sure," Klae says, looking excited. "You'll love playing her."

Now intrigued, Gabby places her chin in her hands. "Okay then. Keep me in mind."

A play sounds fun and dare she say it...normal.

Klae claps her hands. "Awesomesauce!" She gathers up the flyers. "I knew they were missing something. Now I know exactly what it is."

Kalisha leans forward, pointing with her fork. "I think you might be losing sight of what college is all about."

"I am?" Klae asks.

"Boys! And girls! And anything and everything in between," laughs Kalisha.

Maya raises a brow. "As opposed to learning? Or grades? Or academia?"

Kalisha's eyes twinkle. "What are these words you speak of?"

There are more giggles and Gabby's chest warms. This is how she imagined college would be.

She's about to have some of her breakfast, when her phone dings. She pulls it out to see Arielle has replied to the image she sent.

Hotcakes are supposed to be a golden brown color?!?

Gabby grins, quickly texting back. And not frisbee consistency! Who knew??

Mind. Blown.

Another message quickly follows. Telling me this is the equivalent of sending food porn to a gal in the desert! Too cruel!

Gabby chuckles. Her mother has a special talent for turning any food into charcoal, and she does most of the cooking while Arielle's mother, Sierra, focuses on her research.

I know, she types, adding a winking emoji for good measure.

The reply is almost as quick. Revenge is sweet. Particularly when it's swift. This message is accompanied by a devil emoji.

That has Gabby's smile dimming as she wonders what her cousin's planning. Her phone rings a second later, her mom's smiling face filling the screen.

Gabby glances at her friends. "It's my mom. I'll take it outside."

The others nod and Gabby answers, quickly walking to the back door of the cafeteria. "Hey, Mom."

"Honey, Arielle said you were just messaging her about how much you miss my cooking."

Gabby shakes her head at Arielle's genius, even as she smiles. "I was. The hotcakes here are totally undercooked."

Her mother tuts. "I'll make you an extra big stack the next time you come home."

"That would be lovely," Gabby murmurs as she plots her own revenge. The fact she started this is irrelevant.

"How is everything?"

Gabby keeps wandering, the usual warmth blooming in her chest when she talks to her mother. "Great," she says, almost meaning it. "I was just having breakfast with some friends."

"That's wonderful," her mom practically gushes. "I knew you'd make friends quickly. You always do."

A bunch of loud students walk past and Gabby presses her finger to her other ear, slipping through a nearby door. "And I might try out for a play, too."

"Great idea! You'll be amazing."

Gabby rolls her eyes as she finds herself in a small court-yard, although she's not entirely sure where in the campus she is. "You always say that."

"And I'm always right."

Shaking her head, Gabby rolls her eyes a second time. "Good thing you're totally unbiased."

"I know," her mother laughs.

Turning a little, Gabby startles when she finds she's not alone. A large marble statue rests in the center of the courtyard, its canine face carved in a permanent growl. Gabby frowns, stepping a little closer. Taller than her, the large dog-wolf sits on an ornate pedestal, proud shoulders holding up a massive furred head. Its lips are pulled back, revealing canines as long as her hand.

"Honey, you still there?" her mom asks.

Gabby shakes her head. "Yeah, sorry." She turns away from the intimidating statue, unsure what it is or why it's here. Whatever it is, she's pretty sure its name isn't Bunnikins or Snuggles. More like Bulldozer or Meatloaf or Rip Your Leg Off. "And I've also joined a martial arts group."

And had a dream where she took down the instructor, then climbed on top of him, her body alive in a way it's never been before...

"You do love your martial arts. I'm so happy you're fitting right in, Gabby. I'm so proud of you. Your father would be, too."

Gabby's smile falls from her face.

Not only does her mother have no idea what her father thinks of her, Gabby doesn't give a shit what his opinion is.

Her father is the one man Gabby hates. He got her mother pregnant and promptly left, abandoning them like neither of them mattered. Actions like that change people, which is exactly what it did to Shell Heartley.

It doesn't get any higher on the douche-meter than that.

"And how are you going?" Gabby asks, changing the subject. Her mom would be hurt to know how Gabby really feels about her father. She doubts her mom knows exactly how much his leaving impacted her.

"Oh, fine," her mom says breezily. "I got extra locks put on the doors and windows."

The presence of a serial killer in Mercy City would be terrifying her mom. She's always been a worrier, expecting the worst. Gabby suspects her mom wasn't surprised when the man she fell so hard for upped and left her. It just proved there are few guarantees in life.

Which is why Gabby's so determined to be dependable. Stable.

Goddamned freaking normal.

Her mom deserves to see how her loving and nurturing has raised a successful daughter she can brag and boast about.

And when that happens, Gabby's going to point out she did it without the douche who got her pregnant then hightailed it. She couldn't depend on him.

But she can depend on Gabby.

"Good idea," Gabby says, realizing she's gone silent again. "I'm sure he'll be caught soon."

"I'm sure he will be," her mom says, the false brightness in her tone apparent even over the line.

"Did you want me to come home over the weekend? I could—"

"Of course not! Don't be silly. I have Sierra and Arielle, remember?"

"I don't mind—"

"Honestly, Gabby. We're fine. And we agreed that you'd spend the first few weeks on campus. So you could settle in."

Gabby sighs. They had. But that was before she realized how hard it would be to be away from home. Maybe she should've just gone to the local university. Closer to home.

It's just that Mercy Academy is prestigious and scholarships are hard to come by. And her mom was so proud when Gabby was accepted...

"Love you, Mom."

"Oh, I love you, too, honey. You go be your best self. That's all I've ever wanted."

They hang up and Gabby stares at her cell. She wants to be her best self, too. She wants to make her mom proud.

And she wants to prove she's nothing like her father.

The bell rings, snapping her out of her reverie. She looks up to find the statue staring at her. At least she's not seeing things like statues frowning at her again...

Still, not liking the way the overgrown hound is scowling at her, she hurries out of the courtyard. She's just shut the door when a tingling sensation slips down her spine. Stilling, Gabby glances around.

Students walk the corridors, all immersed in conversations or their phones, but across the hall someone is standing as still as Gabby is. Donald, the guy who gave their orientation tour is staring at her with more intensity than the statue, as if he was waiting for her to come out. Except his face is strangely blank.

With a jolt, Donald straightens and shakes his head a little. His gaze quickly slides away and he rushes to blend in with the students.

Unsure what that was all about, Gabby makes her way back to the cafeteria. She has to get to class.

She had a lovely morning with her new friends.

And the phone call with her mom reminded her why she's so determined to succeed at Mercy Academy.

She's damn well going to be the most normal, boring, ordinary girl this place has ever seen.

10

COLT

Colt shuts the book he's reading with a sigh. He's been here, in the academy library, for four days now, any moment he's not teaching. He needs to know the significance of those seven red lights hovering above the house where the people were murdered.

He suspects they were hovering above every murder site.

Because those slayings weren't committed by humans. Which means the police force don't have the capacity to tackle this case. They'll never catch the perpetrators.

He opens the next book, even though his confidence that he'll find anything is waning. He'd go out and investigate it himself, except he's unable to leave the academy grounds.

Someone wants to keep him here. Another mystery that needs to be solved.

He scans the pages, flipping through them quickly. For someone as old as he is, there's very little he hasn't seen or read, and the mythology he's looking at now is no different. Surely there has to be something about the seven red lights in here.

But he finds nothing.

In fact, there are more theories about the origins of the

murders on social media right now. Crazy conspiracy theories from a Bigfoot rampage to a glitch in the Matrix. All that wild postulating has done is feed the panic slowly gripping Mercy City. Colt shakes his head. If only people knew what really lurks behind the veil of human ignorance.

He reaches the end of the book and realizes it's the last in the pile. And there are no others. He's scoured every shelf, explored every obscure mythology recorded in old books tucked in forgotten corners.

And all he has to show for it is a sore tuckus.

He closes the book forcefully, frustration tightening his muscles. The thud draws the attention of a librarian walking past. He frowns, his spectacles slipping down his nose. "Quiet, please."

"Apologies," Colt says dryly. "I couldn't find anything on Bigfoot."

The librarian shakes his head and continues on, leaving Colt to brood over his lack of progress. It's highly likely the killer will strike again. And soon. It's been seven days since the last murder, which means more death may be slated for today. But he has no idea where. And who will be the next victims.

With another sigh, Colt pushes to his feet. The thick carpet muffles his footsteps as he makes his way between the shelves of books toward the exit of the library. He'll go for a run. Maybe that will clear his mind and he'll come up with another angle to consider.

Right now, Bigfoot is looking like his best lead.

He's just reached the end of the shelves when he stops. An aura that's foreign, yet fast becoming familiar, tingles each of his senses. Colt angles his head as he hears the light footsteps. Draws in a lungful of air carrying lily and rose. Then drinks in her breathtaking beauty.

Gabby is walking toward him, carrying a stack of books.

Most of them relate to the history of politics but he's surprised to see a couple on the martial arts of the world. The memory of the dream, where she'd knocked him down, then climbed on top, has his blood heating.

What would she taste like?

Colt jolts at the unwanted thought.

He's deliberately, and rather forcefully, ensured she stayed out of his mind. Researching the murders has given him something to focus on. Although that didn't stop the wily girl from creeping in during moments of distraction or weakness, for the most part, he's been successful.

Avoiding her has also helped.

And yet, the next time he sees her, his mind is considering devouring her.

Gabby approaches him and he finds himself leaning against the shelves. Waiting to see what she'll do. Say. Because the truth is, he has no idea. This girl is an enigma. A mystery. And he thought those no longer existed for him.

Her eyebrows twitch a second before her blue eyes fly to his. She blinks, the jolt of awareness he was waiting for leaping between them. But then her gaze flickers, passes over him, and then focuses ahead on the doors of the library. Within a handful of steps she walks past, continuing toward the exit.

Barely acknowledging him.

Colt straightens, unsure why he's so shocked. He knew she's unpredictable. Capricious.

But still, she totally ignored him? As if he wasn't even there? He's an instructor of this academy if nothing else. One she's inconvenienced more than once.

Frowning, Colt follows her. He'll have a word with her about basic etiquette. Maybe suggest she find a book or two on courtesy and manners.

Gabby exits the library and he stays a few feet behind. He's about to call out when someone across the hall reaches up and waves. "Hey, Gabby! You coming to History of Theatre?"

That would explain the books.

Assuming his opportunity is lost, Colt slips behind a column, surprised to see Gabby ignore the peer.

The guy raises his hand a little higher. "Gabby?"

But her head doesn't even twitch in his direction. Instead, she walks straight past, just like she did with Colt.

The guy drops his hand, flushing as he glances around. Tucking his head, he quickly walks the other way, obviously hoping no one noticed his rejection.

Colt rubs his chin. To be honest, Gabrielle doesn't seem to be someone who is outrightly rude like that. She's certainly never backed down from an altercation with him.

Which would suggest she's acting strangely.

Stepping back into the hallway, Colt follows her again, this time watching far more closely. He knows he should turn around and ignore this. There's enough unusual khara going on right now, and he doesn't need to add more shit to the pile. He's spent centuries avoiding piles of khara.

And yet, he does anyway.

There's a voice within him telling him to stay. To get to the bottom of this. Maybe then he'll be able to understand the pull she has. One he's never felt before.

If she's a demon, then it's a powerful spell, indeed. If she's something else, he needs to know what he's dealing with. All supernatural beings leave a trace, but he senses nothing magical about her. If she can mask herself that well, then it's not a spell that's dangerous. It's her.

Then there's the protection spell around the Academy, the one that's preventing him from leaving.

And Belphegor and his demons. Someone warning him from within the Academy.

And the murders.

Gabby takes a sharp right, and Colt continues to follow. Where does she fit in all this? And why does Fate believe their destinies are tied...

Gabby continues to walk, her gait steady and unwavering, and Colt realizes they're heading to the gymnasium. That wouldn't be unusual if she wasn't supposed to be in class.

Colt's eyebrows hike up as she enters. And if there wasn't an all male class going on.

A few of the young men stop the game of basketball they were playing, whistling and catcalling. Colt stands in the doorway and crosses his arms, frowning deeply. The men instantly stop, one or two flushing that they've been caught by an instructor. It's days like this Colt's glad for the glamor spell that makes him look a few years older.

One of them scuffs the floor with his sneaker. "This is a guy's session. The girls are supposed to be in the other gym."

Having shown no acknowledgement of the catcalls, Gabby walks straight to a table beside a white board. She puts the books down and picks up a couple of whiteboard markers.

Colt takes a few steps further into the gym, wondering what she's doing. Her actions are shifting from peculiar to downright bizarre.

Stepping up to the whiteboard, she begins to draw long, straight lines, each one intersecting the other. When that's done, she changes whiteboard marker. With quick flicks of her wrist, she adds some scribbles to her strange drawing.

Finished, she steps back, as if to survey her creation.

There's a squeak of sneakers and a shout from the basketball game and Gabby jolts. She spins around, the red on her cheeks apparent even from this distance. Crossing her arms and ducking her head, she rushes out the opposite door.

Baffled, Colt walks over to the whiteboard. He should've walked away. This girl isn't supernatural. She's just plain crazy.

His eyes fall on the drawing and he draws in a sharp breath. How is this even possible?

Stepping closer, his gaze roves over the seven intersecting lines. A heptagon. With each point made distinct with red circles.

It's exactly what the eyewitness described to the police.

Colt glances at the door the girl exited through.

Who is this Gabrielle Heartley?

And what does she know?

II

GABBY

Gabby stands on the other side of the gym door, frowning.

What. The. Actual. Fuck.

How had she ended up in the gym space during a boy's basketball class? She scours her memory of the last few minutes, only to find nothing. As if that period of time never happened.

In fact, the last thing she remembers is carrying books through the library, in a hurry to get to History of Theatre. She'd glanced up and seen...him.

Colt was standing beside some shelves, casually leaning against them, looking unassumingly hot. She'd glanced up, her gaze connecting with his.

And saw seven lights shifting in some strange formation, deep in his brown gaze.

After that, there's nothing.

She looks down at her hands, finding them empty. Where the hell did she put her books? Maybe in the gym. She glances over her shoulder, knowing she can't go back in there. She's acting one clown short of a circus as it is.

Nor is she going to class, late, without her reading material.

Which leaves her standing here, waiting. Once class is finished, she can go and look for her books. And then next Theatre History lesson, she'll return, as if nothing's happened.

Because nothing did.

She leans against the wall, crossing her arms over her churning stomach. She was doing so well. Why did she have to go and have another memory lapse?

This isn't the first time weird shit has happened...

Tightening her arms, Gabby ignores the annoying voice in her head. Everyone does weird things at times. And there are memes everywhere about people entering a room and forgetting what they were there for.

You're not eighty. Or on drugs.

Great. She has an hour to kill, listening to this.

If her mom were to find out any of this is happening, she'd freak the flip out, and that's the last thing she needs right now. Gabby wants—intends—on being the stable, dependable part of her mom's life.

Her hands clench. There are other things that have happened, long before Mercy Academy, and when she ignored them long enough, they went away. This won't be any different.

"Here are your books."

Gabby pushes away from the wall at the sound of the familiar voice. Of all the people to turn up...

She turns, finding Colt a few feet away, wearing dark slacks and a dark blue shirt. He's an instructor at the academy, she reminds herself. Even if he looks far too young to be one.

And he's cranky and surly and keeps turning up when she has a brain glitch.

It doesn't matter how good he looks. He's off limits.

She lifts her chin. "Oh yes, my books. I'd just left them..."

Colt raises his brows as she waits for him to finish the sentence. "In the gym?" he volunteers.

"Yes, in the gym," she says on a relieved exhale. "That's where I put them."

He tucks the books against his hip. "You don't remember, do you?"

"Of course I do," she says quickly. "Why else would I be standing here, waiting? I was going to collect them once the class was finished."

"I'm curious," he says, his dark eyes alive with interest. "Why did you go in there in the first place? It was a boys' class, after all."

A traitorous flush creeps up Gabby's cheeks. Shit. Crap. Dammit. "If you'd just give me my books, I'll let you get back to your work."

Colt's hand tightens around them. "What were you doing there, Gabby?"

Her name on his lips startles her. It sends a delicious shiver down her spine. "I was just..." Her words fade away. She has no explanation.

"And why did you draw that symbol on the whiteboard?"

Her eyes widen. "I did no such thing. I'm terrible at art."

His eyebrows hike in challenge. Pulling his cell from his pocket he swipes the screen and turns it around to show her. "You drew this. A heptagon with seven red points."

The photo he shows her is exactly that—a seven-sided figure with seven red circles highlighting each point. And yet, she's never seen it before in her life.

She startles as she realizes that's not the truth. She has seen that before. Seven lights in a circular formation.

In Colt's beautiful chocolate eyes.

What is it with this guy? "Look, I don't know what your problem is, but I did not draw that."

His eyebrows hike up in surprise, then instantly slam down in a frown. "You most certainly did."

She places her hands on her hips. "Could I have my books back, please?"

Watching her as if she's a grenade about to go off any second, Colt holds them out. "This would be much easier if you just told me the truth."

Gabby grabs them, making sure to avoid her hands touching his. "I'm not lying," she snaps. "I didn't draw that."

She spins on her heel and stalks away, clinging to righteous indignation. Sure, she overreacted, but this is all far too confusing, and that's not a nice feeling. Anger, no matter how misplaced it is, is far preferable.

Plus, he's really annoying.

Turning a corner, she blends in among the throngs of students, not bothering to glance back. The chatter around her fills her ears and mind, a blissful distraction from whatever just happened back there.

"I know, it's terrible. I can't believe it happened again."

Gabby slows her steps, falling behind the group of three students in front of her. The note of horror in the girl's voice is unmistakable.

"Yeah," says her friend. He shakes his head. "Seven people were killed this time."

Gabby suppresses a gasp. Seven people this time?

And this massacre brings the total to six. All exactly a week apart. Surely the police know that the next will happen in seven days time.

She shakes her head, knowing there's nothing she can do about it. But the awful feeling coating her insides doesn't go away. So many deaths. And there's more to come.

"Disturbing, isn't it?"

Gabby's head snaps up, finding Mr. Bishop, the security

supervisor, standing next to her. She was so deep in thought, she didn't hear him approaching.

She nods, feeling a little sick. "It really is."

Despite the noise and bustle around them, he keeps his gaze steady on her. "I think we should talk."

Startled, Gabby pulls up a quick smile. What would the head of security want with her? "Now's not a good time, I'm afraid. I have classes—"

He spins around, heading down the hall. "This way."

Glancing around, she realizes she has little choice but to follow. Mr. Bishop weaves his way through the students and along the corridors of the academy. Gabby rushes to catch up, glancing at him from the corner of her eye. He's moving far faster than she's seen before. Maybe he took his arthritis medication or something.

"Have I done something wrong?" she asks. Has she had another brain glitch and ended up in the staff quarters again?

"Not that I'm aware of," he answers, quickly glancing at her before looking ahead again. "I need to talk to you. Privately."

He reaches a door and Gabby recognizes it as the courtyard she'd been in earlier today when she spoke to her mom. Mr. Bishop pushes it open and steps through, indicating for her to follow. She does, uneasiness churning in her gut. What would the head of security want to talk to her about, in private?

Inside the courtyard, Mr. Bishop walks over to the statue of the large wolf-thing. He turns to Gabby. "Do you know what this is?"

Stopping a few feet away, Gabby clasps her hands in front of her, wishing he'd get to the point. "A dog who popped too many steroids?" she says with a weak smile.

But Mr. Bishop doesn't seem to find the joke funny. "Have you heard of hellhounds?"

That wasn't what she was expecting to hear. Gabby shrugs. "Sure. They're creatures from Hell."

"They were created during the first era of Hell, molded from the flames of the Underworld itself. Stories have it that Lilith had a hand in their creation, but there is no definitive proof."

Not sure what the mythology lesson is all about, Gabby nods. If Mr. Bishop likes to read about this sort of stuff, then good for him.

He indicates toward the statue. "Although, this isn't a hellhound."

"I'm sure it's relieved to hear that," Gabby says, once more trying to lighten the mood.

But Mr. Bishop's face remains firmly in the land of the serious. "This is a celestial hound, created by the divine fires that burn in the furnaces of Pearl City."

"Pearl City?" This story is getting weirder and weirder.

"You probably know it as Heaven. We don't call it that, we refer to it as Pearly City."

"We?" squeaks Gabby. All of a sudden, she wants to be anywhere but here. And yet, her feet are rooted to the spot.

Mr. Bishop smiles. "Angels, of course."

Gabby takes a stumbling step backward. She should've insisted she go to class. This man is crazy. "Look, I don't know what you're trying to tell me, but—"

He takes a step forward, recovering the ground she created between them. "You don't believe in angels?"

"Well, yes, I do." She straightens her shoulders. "I just don't believe you're one."

"I see."

There's something in Mr. Bishop's tone that has Gabby stilling. As if she just issued him a challenge.

He pulls back his shoulders and raises his chin, his gaze

holding hers even though she desperately wants to look away. Walk away.

Before she can even blink, two white wings unfurl behind him. Every cell in Gabby's body freezes in shock. The wings are massive. The color of luminescent ivory. And absolutely stunning.

Surely they can't be real...

"Who...who are you?" she says, her voice barely more than a breath.

Angels can't be real, let alone here on Earth, standing in front of her.

"Can't you tell?" Mr. Bishop asks. "Can't you peel through my masks and see for yourself?"

Of all the confusing answers to give her! She frowns. There has to be a reasonable explanation for this. "No," she replies, shaking her head.

"Then you really have much to learn," he says, sounding almost disappointed. "I thought just being here would bring the angel out in you. But when it didn't happen, I thought seeing the truth would be enough."

Gabby wrings her hands together, pulling hard enough that it hurts. "I don't know what you're talking about."

With a sigh, Mr. Bishop's wings retract, much to Gabby's relief. The feeling that she's slowly, surely going crazy diminishes a little.

"Seventeen years ago, a witch's spell created a Tear opened between the dimensions of Hell and Earth. Demons started pouring through without being summoned, and they are definitely planning something, possibly as serious as an apocalypse."

Apocalypse?

"We angels have always sought to protect humanity from the scourge of demons, but we are hard-pressed to defend the innocents. There are too many of them, and too few of us. So we formed a club of sorts. A union of supernatural creatures who train and hone their powers to protect vulnerable humans."

"A club?" she squeaks, surprised to find she spoke out loud this time.

He nods. "A secret supernatural club that runs in secret rooms beneath the Academy." He points to the celestial hound. "This statue protects the entrance."

Gabby takes another step backward. She doesn't know what parallel universe she's just stepped into, but she needs Dorothy's red shoes so she can tap, tap, tap the fuck out of here. She's about as far from normal as a girl can get.

"Why are you telling me all this?" she asks.

"We have been aware of you being supernatural as soon as you stepped into the academy," he answers, those intelligent eyes of his watching her closely. "Although I've been aware of you for much longer than that..."

"What do you mean, longer than that?" She's never seen this man before she came to the academy.

"I've been watching," he says. "Waiting to tell you the truth."

Gabby swallows. This is the moment to run. To stop something she should never have let get this far.

And yet, she's as still as the statue. Her gaze doesn't leave the old man's. "What truth?" she whispers.

"That I'm your father, Gabrielle."

12

COLT

Colt watches Gabby walk away from the gym, her movements stilted in a way he hasn't noticed before. He turns and walks in the other direction, deep in thought.

His accusation angered her. And yet, she looked confused.

As if she genuinely had no recollection of what she did.

Taking the curved staircase to the second floor, Colt heads back to his room. Now that he thinks of it, she almost seemed in a trance as she walked toward the gym, ignoring the guy who called out to her, then the catcalls of the boys playing basketball. He's heard of such things happening with mortals—amnesia, fugue states where the mind doesn't recollect what the body has done.

He frowns as he opens his door, the image of her drawing flashes through his mind, not needing the photo he took on his cell phone. It was a vivid rendition of the eyewitness' statement to the police, which doesn't make sense. Maybe she saw the same news report he did.

Or does she know more about these murders than she's letting on?

Not that he should be thinking about this at all. The strange actions of an erratic girl shouldn't be his focus right now. He should be focused on where the killer might strike next. The sixth murder was just committed, as he predicted. He curses under his breath, shutting the door a little more forcefully than he intended. If the academy wasn't protected by a supernatural barrier, he would have gone outside and investigated.

Although the barrier has protected him from Belphegor's demons. He's not sure if he should shake or thank the one who created it.

Sitting on his bed, Colt takes his shoes off as he mentally turns on the TV. The news channel runs on the small screen, the reporter speaking about the killer having struck again just like the students were in the hallways. This time, it was a club. Another pair attacked in a public establishment, their blood surrounding them in a ring. No doubt in the shape of a heptagon.

But unlike the past murders, others there were brutally massacred as well. They were potential witnesses to the crime, and so they were eliminated.

Flicking his hand, Colt turns the TV off. He doesn't want to hear more conjecture and conspiracy theories. He needs the truth.

If only he could visit the crime scene. He could get a real understanding of what's happening.

He almost shoots to his feet as an idea leaps in his mind. There's a spell that could allow his conscious self to visit the crime scene without having to leave the Academy. Bi-projection. He can go investigate, without ever leaving the grounds.

Smiling a little, he conjures a piece of chalk and draws a circle large enough to hold him inside it. He sits in the center and focuses in his mind on the name of the club. His lips move, forming words in a silent monotone. An ancient language, a tongue long forgotten.

But one that yields immense power.

His eyes drift shut as his consciousness separates from his vessel, dividing mind and body.

He opens them a moment later, finding himself inside the club, yellow 'Do not Cross' tape behind him. The place looks like a converted warehouse, bare and expansive with industrial pipes running the length of the roof.

The crime scene has been cleared out. In place of the bodies, there are nothing but outlines drawn in white chalk. The smell of bleach and death tickle his nose, making his stomach turn.

Ignoring it, Colt looks around. He came here, determined to find answers.

In the center of the floor, only a few feet away, a heptagon has been drawn on the ground. He walks to its center and stands quietly, eyeing every direction. The club's empty. The entire establishment, which was crowded and full of revelry only hours ago, now stands eerily quiet except for a radio in the distance. Colt breathes in deep, registering the faint scent of sulfur.

And yet, it's not the usual scent he associates with demons. Interesting.

He bends down and touches the ground with his hand. It's cold, colder than usual. Definitely supernatural.

His lips move in an incantation, muttering a spell. Time passes, and yet nothing happens. Colt's brow compresses. It almost feels as though his spells aren't working.

Cursing, he tries again, this time pressing the ground harder. Words tumble out of his mouth again in a soft whisper, the demonic language flowing with unwelcome familiarity. He avoids using his native tongue after forsaking Hell and choosing to stay on Earth, but there's no choice. Whatever ritual has occurred here could have been a summoning. And if it was, whatever was called forth will pose a great threat to this world.

Flames appear at each point of the heptagon, shooting out in fiery lines around him. Colt stills as faint visions of pyres appear at each apex. There are bodies on them. And they're burning.

Shrieks and screams assault his ears, full of agony and tortuous pain. He winces, but he cannot help them. All he's seeing is what has already occurred.

Within seconds, the entire heptagon is alight with crimson fire and more lines form. These ones spear from each apex diagonally into the center, meeting beside Colt's feet. Curious, he places a finger on the flame-colored circle that forms.

Instantly, pain grips his arm. His veins bulge, red and angry, the heated color exploding across his skin. Fire, hot and painful, surges through his body. He throws his head back, refusing to lift his hand as he squeezes his eyes tightly shut.

Just as suddenly, the pain disappears. Colt opens his eyes again to find he's still in the club, the expanse of the warehouse stretching out around him. And yet, it's different. There are no chalk outlines, no fiery heptagon.

And there are people here.

Some are stacking wood in order to build the pyres, while others haul logs from a truck parked at a loading dock at the other end of the large room. Colt moves cautiously, taking in their strange, stilted movements and blank faces. He has no doubt they're under a spell of some kind, compelled to complete this grisly work. He calls out to the person nearest him, a strapping young man, but he goes about his tasks mindlessly. Colt sighs. He didn't really expect an answer.

He's gone back further in time, to right before the murders.

Once the pyres are built, the victims are dragged in and hoisted onto them. Weird symbols have been etched on their foreheads. Symbols Colt has seen before, although he doesn't remember where. He's about to take a closer look when seven tall men in black robes appear from behind the truck.

They enter solemnly, their face shielded by a silvery-white mask partitioned in the middle with a bold black line. "Light the fires," they intone simultaneously.

The hapless workers nod and rush to fetch oil and matchsticks. As they get busy, the tall men spread out and raise their hands, muttering an incantation in a language Colt doesn't recognize, which is surprising. Still, whatever they're saying, it's not good.

He stills, conscious he made an assumption. Are the bodies in the robes human? Or something else?

Moving forward, Colt focuses on the closest one. There's no supernatural aura around him, yet there's something off. It has uneasiness braiding through his spine.

The robed man lifts his arms again and throws his head back. Colt focuses all of his energy into his hand. If he channels his powers in just the right way, maybe he'll be able to knock the mask off and learn who, or what, he is.

He pulls his arm back, preparing to strike, but a powerful gust of wind hits him in the chest. With a grunt, Colt's thrown high into the air. His body sails across the warehouse then slams into the cement floor, sliding across the smooth surface.

The fiery lines of the heptagon disappear. The pyres vanish.

Colt's alone again, rolling on the cold ground in pain.

He waits for long seconds, blinking through the agony. Luckily, the healing works quickly, sucking away the pain as his body mends. He stands up shakily, clutching his chest. The burst of wind had felt like a wrecking ball. Keeping his breath shallow, he looks around. Whoever struck him could still be here. All he finds is silence. Eerie silence. Even the radio has stopped.

As the seconds stretch out, Colt realizes he's alone. Clenching his hands, he curses. He was a split-second away from discovering the identity of the man.

A sharp noise has him spinning around, then spinning back when another echoes from high above. The windows several feet above are opening and closing repeatedly.

Colt slowly turns, eyes narrowed. Maybe whatever attacked him is about to show itself.

This time he'll be prepared. He'll fight back.

He watches, wired and ready, as a white light pours through the now open windows. As it enters the room, it grows brighter. Larger. Becoming the size of the sun.

Colt retreats, trying to understand what he's up against. Lightning flashes within the giant orb, creating flares of white light. He lifts his arm to shield his eyes. The light is blinding.

The energy coming off the ball is overwhelming.

As he watches through squinted eyes, the large mass divides into seven, smaller circles. And yet, the threat feels just as ominous. Each one crackles with furious energy, undeniably focused on him.

Even as Colt braces himself to fight, he acknowledges he's outnumbered and outpowered. And he has no idea what he's facing. He raises his hands, calling forth the flames of Hell, his only real defense.

But his hands stay cool. No flames leap from his palms.

He swallows. His powers are gone.

The seven white lights move, floating in closer both to him and to each other. Arcs leap between them, creating a pulsing net of energy.

A pulsing net of death.

Colt staggers backward, preparing to run. The act of cowardice isn't one he chooses easily, but he'd prefer to stay alive.

And out of Hell.

The circles move before he gets a chance. With the same speed as the lightning clashing within them, the white balls of fury attack. The light blinds him. Pain blinds him.

Colt screams, the agonizing sound torn from his throat against his will. But the white fire coursing through his body is too much. It's incinerating him from the inside out.

He falls to his knees, back arched and mouth still pouring out a scream. At least his death will be quick.

As fast as the pain starts, it disappears. Colt opens his eyes, looking around cautiously.

The warehouse is dark again. The orbs have vanished.

Swaying a little, he looks one way then the other. "What the..." he mutters.

The sound of footsteps jolts him out of his surprised stupor. The police must be back. A quick scan and he sees three large crates in the corner of the room, disco lights sitting on top of them. Colt rushes over and slips behind them. He crouches down, peering through the crack to see who's arrived.

It turns out, it's not the police. Two women enter, surveying the scene.

They walk to the chalk outlines and the black-haired woman squats, her fingers brushing the concrete floor. She frowns. "A powerful ritual has taken place here, Sierra," she says. "Maybe something's been summoned."

Colt narrows his eyes. Who are these women, and how did this one know about the ritual?

He focuses on the dark-haired woman first, sensing a supernatural aura radiating from her. It's familiar... The other one doesn't give out anything, which means the one named Sierra is human.

"What do you think's been called?" Sierra asks.

The dark-haired woman straightens, looking around

uneasily. "It's impossible to tell, but power was created here, and it's a force to be reckoned with."

Sierra looks around too, as if she expects it to jump out any moment. "Can you find it?"

"I could, but I'm not sure I want to come face-to-face with it."

Sierra chews her lip, not looking like she likes that response.

The dark-haired woman slowly turns around, her gaze unfocused. "But there's another power here that might be able to face it," she says.

Colt stills. Surely she's not talking about him. He hasn't twitched a muscle.

But then he recognizes the woman's aura.

Sierra frowns. "What are you talking about?"

Blaise stops her slow spin, unerringly facing Colt's hiding place. Her sharp gaze stares directly at him even though he's barely visible.

Shaking his head, Colt stands. Sierra leaps back as he moves around the crates and approaches them. "Well, well, well, if it isn't young Blaise."

13

GABBY

Gabby isn't sure whether she's angry or furious. She decides to settle on plain old pissed.

"Liar," she spits.

This man is claiming to be her father. And for what? To get her to join some club? Well, if this is how far someone is willing to go, they should've done some research first. Her father is the one person she hates. He left Gabby and her mother, not even hanging around to see her born. Claiming to be him would never endear her to anything.

The old man shakes his head. "I have no cause to lie. I am your father."

"I'm not buying it," she snarls.

"Why is this so hard to accept?"

"My mother told me everything. He looked like me, for starters." And even after nineteen years, he wouldn't look like he's got one foot in a nursing home. She puts her hands on her hips. "Who are you? Tell me the truth."

The old man smiles. "My name is Gabriel. Archangel Gabriel."

Gabby rears back, already shaking her head. He's trying to

tell her she's not only the daughter of an angel, but of an archangel? Before her foot has landed, Mr. Bishop's features change. Smooth out. His body grows taller and fills out.

A man stands before her, handsome and strong. Gabby blinks.

With blond hair just like hers. Blue eyes just like she has.

One word escapes her numb lips. "Why?"

Why now?

The man—Gabriel—lifts his hand. "I've never been far away, child. Not long after you were born, I sensed a Tear open between Hell and Earth. For seventeen years, demons have been pouring through it, ones even stronger and higher level than the last." His hand drops. "I had to protect you."

Gabby's lost the ability to move. She doesn't even blink. Her entire being is focused on trying to process the words hanging between them.

"All these years I've been keeping you safe. From demons who would want to end the daughter of an archangel." He smiles. "Like a guardian angel."

Something moves on Gabby's face, and she realizes it's a tear. It tracks down her frozen cheek, although she barely feels it. The pain in her chest is far too overwhelming.

"When I heard you were applying to this academy," he continues, "I ensured your application would be accepted."

That has Gabby snapping out of her agony. "I studied hard for that scholarship!" In fact, she studied her ass off so much, she's surprised she has one left!

He nods in acquiescence. "It was a strong application. But you didn't know about the Tear. That demons are among us. And that they're here, in Mercy Academy." He takes a small step forward. "Or, that it would bring out your powers."

"I...I don't know what you're talking about."

"Your drive will be to protect, Gabrielle. Your angel side will be clamoring to come out. That's why I suggested the club. It'll help you control your powers. Accept the angel inside of you."

Gabby shakes her head. "I don't want this. I want to be normal."

It's all she's ever wanted.

"I can understand that. You were raised among humans like no angel ever has. But there is untold power within you, power you're not equipped to control." He must see something on her face, because he sighs. "Have you experienced anything unusual? Any blackouts, time you don't remember?"

Gabby doesn't say anything. She doesn't like that the answer is yes.

"That happens when something triggers the angel within you and it comes out to protect, either yourself or those around you. Just like you did with the supernatural barrier around the academy."

"No," she breathes. More lies.

"Like I said, I have no reason to lie to you. You don't remember, but I saw you create a powerful barrier to stop supernaturals from entering or leaving this place."

The memory of the car bursting into flames, the same car that disappeared as if it never existed, flares in her mind. The guards, they were unconscious.

She shakes her head. This can't be true. It just can't be.

"These powers need to be controlled, Gabrielle. Otherwise, you are a danger to you and others." The man lifts his hand again and extends it, palm out. "Join the club. Let me teach you what it means to be an angel, daughter."

The final word slices through her like a white hot blade. Gabby draws in a sharp breath through her teeth. How dare he...

She pulls herself up, the pain washed away by a fiery wave of fury. "I'm no angel," she snarls. "And I'm not your daughter.

Even if any of this was true, you think you can come in here now, and have some touching reunion? As if you never fucking left us?" Her voice rises with each question. "Thinking I'll believe that you've cared all along? Could you be any more arrogant?"

His hand drops, followed by his shoulders, but he doesn't answer.

Gabby takes a step back. "Well, you can shove it——" She angles her head. "I assume angels have asses. They need somewhere to jam their bullshit ideas."

His eyes narrow, and she knows she's gone too far, but she doesn't care.

If he's not her father, she's angry that he's trying to manipulate her just so he can recruit her to some screwed up club.

And if he is her father...then she's livid. He screwed her mother over, in more ways than one. She doesn't care what he claims to be, she will never, ever forgive him.

Gabby draws herself up. "The answer is no. Now, I'm going to leave this courtyard and join my friends. I'm going to go to classes and complete assignments. I'm going to live a normal, human life." She spins on her heel. "Stay away from me."

She's at the door when his voice reaches her, despite its softness. "You'll need me, daughter. It's only a matter of time."

She yanks open the door, storms through and slams it closed. The bang isn't nearly as satisfying as she'd hoped it would be. A part of her wants the whole building to collapse down on that man.

She never wants to see him again.

Back out in the corridor, a chill sweeps over her. Rubbing her arms, Gabby looks around. The hallway is empty. Quiet.

Too quiet.

Where has everyone gone?

The window high above shows it's night time. How long

was she talking to that man? A movement to her left has her spinning around. There, at the end of the wide corridor, two crimson eyes stare back at her. The moment it registers it's been found, the being turns and runs, just like it did in the dining hall.

One word hisses through her mind. Demon.

She shakes her head. They're just as real as angels. And she doesn't want any part of it.

She's going straight back to her room to pretend none of this ever happened.

HANDS CLENCHING INTO FISTS, Gabby turns and sprints after the dark figure as it shoots into the assembly hall, heading for the stairs. She hunches her shoulders, determined to catch up.

But the being doesn't step onto the stairs. It leaps, black wings exploding from its back, and it propels itself to the second floor. She takes the stairs two at a time, heaving air into her lungs, cursing that it just got more of a lead on her.

Because it has freaking wings!

Crimson-eyes angles down a corridor, half-running, half-flying as it tries to get away. Gabby injects everything she has into her muscles as she sprints after it. The need to end it is overwhelming.

The chase takes her down the silent, empty corridor, a sharp left, and down another, up more stairs. She can feel her heart pounding harder and faster as her focus lasers on the creature of the night ahead. Two sharp lines of heat burn down her back.

Crimson-eyes glances over its shoulder, scowling when it sees she hasn't given up. It takes a sudden right and darts up a narrow set of stairs. Huffing, and knowing she can't keep this up forever, she follows. With each step, crimson-eyes pulls farther away.

He's trying to tire her out.

And it's working.

Leaping off the top stair, she finds herself in a wide hallway in what must be the top floor. And crimson-eyes is already at the other end, a large arched window ahead. He stops and turns, his red eyes flashing as he grins. Gabby puts her head down and runs, trying to make the most of his cockiness.

A second of her feet propelling her over the parquetry floor passes. Then another. The creature expands his wings, then angles himself at the window. A last look over his shoulder tells her he knows he's going to escape her. That this lung-bursting chase has all been for nothing.

Because he's going to jump right out the window.

Like Hell he's getting away.

He leaps, lifting his arms to protect his face as he crashes through the window. Glass explodes, glinting in the evening light as shards spray outward. The moment he's passed through, his wings expand, holding him midair.

Gabby doesn't stop running. All it takes is a thought. A flicker of acknowledgement. Permission to be free.

And her wings unfurl.

She leaps, satisfaction spearing through her when crimson-eyes sees her coming after him, wings and all. She slams into him, their bodies colliding and wings tangling. Gabby uses the opportunity to land as many punches as she can. Her fists connect with face and chest and air each time he ducks. He throws his own punches, but she's spent years training at her local dojo. She knows how to evade and block as well as strike.

If only there were time to glory in using her martial arts skills. But she can't. Not when the ground is coming at them.

They land with a thud that seems to tsunami through Gabby. She's thrown off crimson-eyes, rolling in a tumble of limbs and feathers. She leaps to her feet the first chance she gets, finding the creature has already done the same.

They face off, several feet between them, shattered glass like crystal confetti sprinkled on the lawn. They're at the back of the academy, nothing but night witnessing this.

The creature shakes and black mist falls off it like layers of skin, revealing a middle-aged man sporting the hell-colored eyes. "Angel," he spits.

Before Gabby can respond, his wings spread wide, onyx-colored with each feather tip a deadly red. Then contract. A gust of air hits her in the chest, making her stumble backward. The creature flaps his powerful wings over and over, his eyes glowing brighter as he focuses all his strength on pushing her away. With each one, Gabby loses a little more ground.

"Not happening," she grinds out.

Drawing in a deep breath, she pulls her fist back, then punches the layers of storm coming at her. The force fractures the waves and they dissipate, dispersing into little more than a gust. Gabby leaps, using her wings to cover the distance between them and she lands on the creature's chest, knocking him to the ground. She slams her knees onto his arms, straddling him so he can't move.

"What do you want?" she demands.

The monster's lips twist in a sneer. "Ooh, we have a newbie."

She shakes him. Power is thrumming through her veins. Power she's never felt before. "What are you? I won't ask again."

"Demon!" he snarls. "I'm a demon."

Shock ripples through Gabby, even though it shouldn't. It was obvious all along.

The demon takes advantage of her surprise, bucking up and

knocking her off. He leaps to his feet with lightning speed, then viciously kicks her in the ribs. Pain detonates as a crack echoes through her chest. Gabby rolls on the grass, groaning as she holds her torso.

But then she's pushing herself to her knees. Biting her lip as she plants one foot on the ground and comes to a stand. It hurts to breathe. To move. To think. But she's not staying down.

She finds the demon walking toward her, the sneer twisting his mouth is back. "A newbie angel? That's dared to stand up to me?" he spits. "I sensed power in you. In fact, I ran because I thought you were old, but here I find you, clueless about our worlds. Helpless. Weak." His gaze rakes her body. "Waiting for yourself to heal. An angel who knows what they're doing wouldn't do that. They would attack despite the pain."

Without warning, he lands a punch across her cheek. And fucksticks, it's a hard one. Gabby buckles, her head snapping to the side. Once again on all fours, she spits blood onto the ground. A couple of her teeth feel loose. At least the fire in her ribs seems to have abated.

"You don't even know how to fight," the demon mocks. "Not well, anyway."

He draws back his foot and slams it into her shoulder. Then her thigh. Then her ribs. The series of cracks and pops draw a groan out of her, and she stays on all fours by sheer force of will. The demon said she can heal. If only she could get a chance to…

She braces herself as he winds up for another kick. This one is aimed right at her abdomen. It connects with such force it feels like her insides were just liquified as she's propelled into the air. She slams into a nearby tree, agony splintering down her spine. Her vision swims and darkens. Her consciousness starts to slip from her grasp.

"You're an embarrassment to all angels," the demons sneers. "I assumed you were all tougher than that after the way you've systematically removed my friends from the academy." He leaps, wings flapping, and lands in front of her. "I don't suppose you know who those angels are, do you?"

He kneels down, his red eyes studying her.

She turns and spits, even though it misses. "Go screw yourself."

He snorts. "I don't think you know," he muses, calling her bluff. "Why would they put a newbie here? Especially when everyone knows there have been no new angels since the time of Jesus Christ. You are a mystery." His lip curls. "But not one important enough to solve. Your death might just be the thing to send the annoying angels a message."

He roughly grabs her hair and yanks, making her eyes sting, then jerks her head to the side, exposing her neck. He lifts his other hand, clenched in a fist, ready to bring it down and snap her neck.

Gabby draws on her last reserves of strength, on the little healing that's happened in her battered body, and sweeps her leg through his. The demon topples with a cry and she quickly gets out of the way. Picking up a handful of dirt, she whispers words she's never heard, in a language she's never used. She blows softly and the soil particles fly out, spraying over the demon's face.

He howls in pain, clawing at the speckled mask as the smell of burning flesh hits Gabby's nostrils. She stands where she is, clueless to how she did that, but glad for the reprieve. She can feel her body repairing.

"Seems you may have underestimated me," she mutters. Her body still hurting, but no longer broken, she jumps, using her wings to gain height and momentum. Then powering forward, she slams her foot into the demon's face. His head snaps to the side, his body following a split-second after. He twirls and tumbles, landing on the ground. She strides over and lifts him up, punching him in the face once. Twice. Three times.

He groans, blood dripping from his mouth and nose.

"Why are you here, at the academy?" she growls.

The demon's crimson eyes flash with annoyance. "None of your business."

She slams her fist into his cheek. "Tell me," she growls.

"This academy," the demon pants. "It's...a battleground."

Alarm slithers up her spine. "A battleground? What sort of battleground?"

"Between angels and demons...Heaven and Hell." His gaze rises to glare at her. "And you'll lose."

Gabby raises her fist to hit him again, but his hand comes up and grabs it before it connects. He twists, and the pain radiating up her arm has Gabby releasing him. As he spins, he brings his onyx wing around, and plows through her.

She stumbles back, finding the demon has followed her. He sprays her with punches. Some she blocks. Others, she doesn't. She gets a few strikes in herself, but the demon barely acknowledges them. The determination on his face screams of the need for blood. Her blood.

Crap. She should've ended this while she could. She made the same mistake he did—talk, which allowed him time to heal.

No! This isn't going to be a repeat of the battering that happened a few minutes earlier. And this demon has the advantage—he's a strong fighter, and he knows his powers. But Gabby just did something she didn't know was possible. She blocks a strike to her face, then dodges an uppercut to her jaw.

Actually, two things. Fly. Then turn dirt into a weapon.

Tapping into the instincts that had those two feats happening, she lifts her hands, palm out.

A scorching fire glows in her hands.

She swipes at the demon and he jumps back, but her finger brushes his shirt and it catches alight. He screams, first in frustration, then, in pain. She steps forward, deciding it's time to finish this, but the demon leaps into the air.

He lifts his arms in a wide arc and the shattered glass of the window they crashed through rises into the air, returning to the window frame high above returning to its original intact smoothness. With a last sneer, he clicks his fingers and disappears.

"Get back here, you piece of chicken shit!"

But the night sky gently twinkles at her, calm and serene. With the window fixed, it's like none of this ever happened.

She bends over, her hands resting on her knees as she breathes deeply. What just happened? Surely not everything Gabriel said is true.

Her father.

Pain slices through her, jagged and piercing. It's like an old wound is being torn open. Then someone's throwing salt on it. Then acid.

Then taking her writhing, sobbing self and putting it through a grinder.

Her wings retract, and she chokes back a sob. She can't do this. Not here. Not now.

Not ever.

Straightening, Gabby wipes the hair from her face, shoving down the pain into some dark corner of her mind.

It's simple. She won't do this.

"Well, you certainly drove him away," says a male voice behind her.

Gabby spins around to find. Mr. Bishop approaching, his walking stick sinking into the soft ground. She frowns. "Drove who away?"

He arches a gray, wiry brow. "Who do you think?"

Gabby glances around, surprised to see scrape marks on the ground, even singe marks on a nearby tree. It looks like something big just went down. She shakes her head. "I have no idea what's happened here."

In fact, she's not even sure how she got here.

Mr. Bishop narrows his eyes. "You're going to tell me you don't remember fighting off a demon?"

She startles, taking a step back. "What in the world are you talking about, Mr. Bishop?"

"You just defeated a demon, Gabrielle."

Tired of his manipulations, she glances around again. "I don't see a demon."

"That's because you defeated him," he says, this time snarling the words.

"Huh." She shakes her head. "And I came out unscathed?"

"You healed."

"That's convenient. And no one else saw this fight?"

The old man's eyes narrow. "I placed a cloaking spell on you and the demon. Humans cannot know we exist."

Gabby crosses her arms. "Also convenient."

Mr. Bishop's hand clenches and unclenches around his cane. "Your determination is...impressive." His lips settle into a thin line. "But your angel is coming out, faster and stronger than I expected, Gabrielle. And you're becoming a magnet to our enemies. It's imperative that you accept it, rather than repress it."

Suddenly, she's no longer willing to humor the old man. "Look, you believe what you want to believe, Mr. Bishop. But don't try and drag me into your dungeons and dragons world, okay?"

Turning around, she finds herself angry. Far angrier than she should be.

Drawing in a calming breath, Gabby walks away, her pace increasing the closer she gets to the doors of the academy.

She's not sure what happened back there, but she knows one thing.

She doesn't want any part of it.

14
COLT

It was centuries ago that the witch Celeste Jourdain summoned Colt to her small village in medieval France. She'd been his ticket out of Hell because the moment he was out, he decided he wasn't going back. In thanks, he'd vowed he would protect her bloodline for the generations to come.

Over the years, Celeste's descendants rose through the ranks of the witch community, becoming some of the most powerful witches ever known. Colt had watched and whenever one was threatened, he was there to help.

As he steps around the crates, he draws in a deep breath, inhaling the familiar scent of the witch's bloodline. Blaise is this generation's descendant.

She blinks in surprise. "Colt, what are you doing here?"

He stops in front of the two women. "Same thing as you, I suspect—investigating what really happened, and who could be behind these depraved murders."

Blaise nods, looking around. Today, her long hair is black, either designed to blend in, or to tap into the color's association with protection. "Demons, you think?" she asks.

"Perhaps," he says thoughtfully. "You were saying that you believe something has been released here?"

Blaise looks at the other woman, Sierra. "We think the killer is after something. These ritualistic murders, I don't think they're random."

Colt nods grimly. "I agree."

Each of the murders have been seven days apart. Then there was the seven lights above the last murder scene. Seven people were murdered here.

And the recurring heptagon.

"Yes," Sierra says. "But there are some...inconsistencies."

"Inconsistencies?" They're usually as telling as a pattern.

"The smell of sulfur for example," Blaise answers. "We've visited almost all of the crime scenes and found the smell to be present at each one. But it's not the kind of sulfur demons leave behind. There's something different about this."

Colt glances around the warehouse. He'd noticed the unusual scent of sulfur, too.

Blaise narrows her eyes. "Yes, it's almost like they want any supernatural investigation to come to the conclusion this is the work of demons. We think someone's trying to frame them. "

As much as he detests his kind, the thought of demons being blamed for something as awful as this has Colt angry. "The number seven certainly seems significant. The eyewitness said he saw seven lights. And it was seven white lights that attacked me." He glances around. "I believe there were seven killers."

Blaise frowns. "We noticed that, too, but haven't come up with anything. Can you? Why the seven lights? Or the heptagon? Demons favor a pentagram for their symbol."

"My lead is tenuous at best," Colt says, frustration simmering deep in his gut. "There's a girl studying at Mercy Academy. I saw her drawing a heptagon with these seven lights, but I'm not sure she remembers doing it. Some sort of amnesia, possibly. I think she knows something about these murders, especially her alter-ego."

"Mercy Academy, you say?" Sierra asks, frowning. "What did you say her name was?"

"Gabrielle," he replies. "Gabrielle Heartley."

Sierra gasps, her eyes widening. Her response has Colt focusing his gaze on her. Sierra looks both shocked and yet like she dreaded this was coming. "Do you know her?"

She nods. "She's my niece."

Colt stills as surprise jolts through him. Sierra is human, but she's working with Blaise. He wouldn't be surprised if she's an Archivist, just like the witch, an ancient sect of people committed to documenting and chronicling the supernatural.

Which means Gabby may know of the supernatural, too.

Or, she's part of it.

Colt's about to demand some answers, when his surroundings flicker. He determinedly tries to maintain his presence in the warehouse, but the spell falters. With his next blink, he's back in the familiarity of his room.

"Skata," he mutters.

He was about to find out more about Gabrielle. In fact, Sierra may have had all the answers he needs. Realizing he's still sitting within the chalk circle, he closes his eyes again. He must go back.

But his head swims so ferociously his body sways. Colt's eyes fly open and he reaches out to grip the bed. The spell sapped his strength, along with the attack. He won't be going back tonight.

Colt tries to stand only for his legs to give out. He lands heavily on the bed, shaking his head. He hates feeling weak. Almost as much as he loathes feeling vulnerable.

He pulls his cell phone out of his pocket. Hopefully Blaise will contact him.

As if she heard his request, there's a ding on his phone.

Can you send me any pictures of what Gabby drew? Thanks, Blaise.

Colt scrolls through and finds the image file then attaches it to his reply. The file appears, small lettering beside it. 777 KB. He shakes his head. The number seven is most certainly becoming a theme in this investigation.

He sends the message and waits, hoping Blaise can make something of it. Nothing in the academy's libraries have told him anything about the seven bright lights and he can't leave the academy physically.

Two green ticks appear beside the image, followed by a quick reply. Thanks. I'll keep you posted if I learn anything.

Colt waits to see if there's anything more, but his phone remains quiet. Eventually, the screen goes black. Frowning, Colt quickly types.

Who or what is Gabby?

He watches his screen with focused intensity. Surely Sierra knows. This time, the message arrives quickly.

She's not a threat. That's all we can say.

He's spent centuries protecting Blaise and her ancestors. They've never lied to him before. But Colt's been alive long enough to know that everyone has their own agenda, and people will go to extreme lengths when it comes to those they care about.

There's no way of knowing if Blaise is telling the truth. All he does know is that she and Sierra won't be giving him any more information.

With a frustrated sigh, Colt slams his phone on the bedside table. It seems Gabrielle Heartely is the greatest mystery of all.

He rubs his face, exhaustion tugging at his muscles. Within

the space of the next breath, the need for sleep crawls through him, burying deep in his bones. He's not sure which took a greater toll—the projection spell or almost being burned alive by seven white lights.

He lays down, his head pressing into the pillow, his eyelids heavier than they have been in a long time. Two thoughts struggle to rise through the darkness enveloping his consciousness.

There are many inventions that man takes for granted, and soft furnishings are one of them.

And maybe this will all make sense in the morning.

COLT OPENS his eyes to find soft light bathing his room. He sits up, surprised. He slept the whole night through? Another first in a long time. The knowledge of the protection spell surrounding the academy has obviously reached his subconscious.

Feeling more refreshed than he has in decades, Colt heads to the window. Drawing aside the curtains, he sees that dawn is here, even the small sliver of sun enough to bathe the academy grounds in a peachy glow. Birds flit from the trees and land on the grass below, pecking at any crumbs they missed the day before. There were never any views like this in Hell.

The sound of dogs barking draws Colt's attention and he sees two greyhounds running and leaping across the lawn. They chase each other, tongues lolling and tails wagging. Colt smiles.

Hellhounds never played. They were too likely to kill each other.

"Rocko! Tommy!" calls a familiar brusque voice.

Colt turns to see the security supervisor, Mr. Bishop, approach the canines. The dogs quit their playing and run to him, their tails wagging even harder.

"Come on now, off to your kennels," the supervisor orders. "It's breakfast time."

The dogs yip with excitement, one spinning around and around on the spot. In silent agreement, they race away, no doubt headed to the supervisor's cottage that sits a little apart from the academy. Mr. Bishop watches them leave, but rather than follow, tilts his head up.

His gaze connects unerringly with Colt's.

Colt suppresses a frown. He assumed the old man's sight wasn't that good.

"Morning, Mr. Grayson," Mr. Bishop greets him from below.

"Morning." Colt returns the greeting automatically, unsure what this means.

With a short salute, the old man leaves, off to feed his dogs. Colt shakes his head. He'll keep an eye on Mr. Bishop, but there are more pressing matters to focus on.

Quickly changing into shorts and a t-shirt, he makes his way outside. His morning run will help clear his head.

Leaving the academy building, Colt breaks into a jog, enjoying the feeling of the gentle breeze on his face. Hell didn't have those either. Just a constant infernal wind eating away at your skin. If you stayed still for too long, it started to blister.

He rounds the corner and picks up the pace. The rear of the academy is largely lawn and trees, opening up a straight line to the rear boundary. A few laps will keep this human body strong.

He's only a few feet away when his nose wrinkles. He quickly registers the scent of demon.

And of blood.

There's been a fight. A brutal one.

Following the smell, he finds himself at the corner of the building. To his left one of the towers of the academy looms, a stained glass window glinting high above, but it's what's below that has his eyes narrowing.

Gouges have been dug into the grass. Two sets of footprints have crushed the fragile blades. A nearby tree has been scorched.

Colt does a slow turn. Two fought here, one of them a demon, but he can't get a sense of what the second is. The trace is masked. Powerfully masked.

He bends down and presses his palm to the ground, muttering an incantation. Flashes of what happened flicker through his mind.

There's fire. Black wings with red tips. Snarling lips and crimson eyes. He draws in a sharp breath.

And pearl-white wings, gilded with silver.

Angels! How is it they're here on Earth?

Colt stands slowly, a heavy weight settling in his gut. The presence of angels does not bode well for this world, especially with so many demons pouring through the Tear. It means war is coming.

He closes his eyes again, sifting through the images more carefully. Maybe there is something else to be learned.

This time his shock has him taking a short step back. Blonde curls flash behind his closed eyelids. Lush lips pressed in a determined line.

Gabrielle was there!

His brow creasing, Colt tries to untangle the fragments of images, but they're too fleeting and disconnected. In fact, they dance away, as if they don't want to be seen.

His eyes snap open as the frown deepens. Could Gabby be an angel?

Because if she is, that makes her the enemy. One just as

dangerous as Belphegor and his demons, and the mysterious beings committing the murders.

Spinning on his heel, Colt returns to the academy, his run forgotten. One of the greatest threats he's ever encountered is possibly here, in the academy. He needs to decide what to do about it.

Back in his room, he quickly showers and dresses. Breakfast is three granola bars he has in his bag seeing as he's always ready to flee. He doesn't feel like sitting with the other staff members in their separate cafeteria. His mind is too busy planning.

He needs to keep a much closer watch over Gabrielle. Learn exactly who or what she is.

That will decide his next steps.

Leaving his room, he makes his way through the academy with determined strides. He weaves his way up the spiral staircase to the second floor so he can watch over the Assembly Hall. Students are starting to gather, some calm and laughing, others looking harried at the prospect class is only a few minutes away. Colt scans the growing numbers. There's only one face he's looking for.

He finds Gabby the moment she enters, the two friends she had with her in the martial arts class on either side. She's smiling, but there's a tension about her shoulders, as if she's gripping her books to her chest a little too tightly.

Just like the last time he watched her, she stills as if she can sense it. He goes to take a step back into the shadows, but this time, her gaze shoots straight up to his. It finds Colt unerringly, as if drawn to him like a magnet.

Or as if she's aware of her sixth sense in a way no human is.

Colt stills, his hands gripping the railing. Gabby stares at him, as unblinking as he is. The noise of the academy fades away and his hands tighten. He forgets to breathe for long seconds. The pull to go to her is strong.

A shrill bell slices through the spell weaving between them and Colt abruptly steps back, frowning.

The connection between them is undeniable. Powerful.

Confusing.

And a complicating factor he doesn't need right now. Especially when he's more and more sure Gabby's supernatural.

And possibly an angel.

15
GABBY

Gabby drags her gaze away, surprised how much willpower it takes. Colt's not even there anymore and she wants to keep staring. To keep getting lost in the electrifying energy that had shrunk the entire academy and everyone in it to just the two of them.

"For crap's sake," she mutters under her breath, annoyed with herself.

She should've been the one to look away first. Does she have no pride? She has enough going on right now without adding the enigmatic complication of some hot dude who does little more than scowl at her.

Her muscles lock as something strikes her. All the weird shit started happening at the same time she met Colt. In fact, she's been having all these blackouts and lapses in memory since she met him. None of this has ever happened before. Gabby adjusts her shoulders, releasing the tight clutch on her books. No wonder Colt Grayson irks her.

The best thing she can do is avoid him.

"Hey, is everything okay?"

Gabby snaps out of her thoughts, finding Maya looking at

her, a small furrow behind her glasses. "Sure," she says with a smile. "I was just thinking."

Maya's concerned frown doesn't shift. "Are you sure? You've been a little...distracted lately."

Kalisha moves in a little closer. "Is it a guy? I've noticed the way Donald's been watching you."

"What? No!" Although it's disquieting to know that Kalisha's also noticed Donald staring. "It's not a guy."

"You've disappeared a few times, that's all," says Maya.

And Gabby has no recollection of what happened. So far, the best explanation she has is the ramblings of a crazy old man.

Saying he's her dad and she's a freaking angel.

"I'm fine," Gabby assures with a smile that she does her darndest to look as genuine as possible. "Seriously. There's just so many assignments, and so soon!"

Kalisha's mouth twists. "Tell me about it." She brushes back an imaginary strand of hair. "I might need one of Maya's schedules just so I have time to do my makeup."

Maya shifts from foot to foot. "We'd better get to class."

"Isn't being late the eighth Sin?" teases Kalisha.

"It should be the first," Maya says primly.

With a quick giggle, they go their separate ways. Kalisha has Fashion Design, while Maya said something about Academic Integrity, which sounded a bit like death by 'thou shalt nots.'

Gabby's looking forward to her second class of Creative Writing. She hurries down the corridors, making a point of smiling at anyone she might make eye contact with. She's always tried to be friendly, and she really wants to fit in at the academy. With everything that's happened, she's going to have to work extra hard on that.

Nothing a bit of determination won't fix.

Inside the class, Gabby slips into her seat about halfway

down and pulls her books out. She, and the rest of the class, quickly learned Mrs. Keelin's class isn't one you want to be late or unprepared for. Although she dresses smartly in dark skirts and collared blouses, it's possible she stepped straight out of a medieval boarding house. She's stern, unsmiling, and strict.

Zach, the guy who sat behind her last class, passes and Gabby smiles. "Hey, Zach."

His blond eyebrows twitch. "Now you pretend to know me?"

"Huh?" Gabby frowns, unsure what he's talking about.

But there's no time to ask because Mrs. Keelin enters, her sturdy heels rapping over the floor and slams her books down on her dais. The class is instantly silent, every face turned forward. "Now, we won't be having a repeat of the last lesson, will we?"

Only a few people are brave enough to nod assent. Gabby smiles at the dour faced woman, hoping some warmth might crack the ice facade, but Mrs. Keelin's gaze barely settles on her as she scans her students. Gabby isn't sure she knows anyone's names.

"If I mention the Save the Cat moment again while discussing the structure of a story, I do not, I repeat, do not, want to hear meowing."

In any other class, there would be a few chuckles, maybe the guys who said it giving each other a jostle, but there's just more silence. Mrs. Keelin nods, satisfied with the response.

Gabby wonders if there's a Mr. Keelin, or whether he was frozen by that glare years ago.

Mrs. Keelin walks stiffly to the whiteboard and picks up a marker and scrawls in bold, flowing writing, Point 1: The Back Story.

Gabby quickly writes it down in her notebook, absentmindedly noting Mrs. Keelin's beautiful handwriting. Unlike its owner, it's quite soft and feminine. It seems to suggest there might be warmth under all that armor.

Mrs. Keelin turns back to the class. "The seven point structure is the lesser-known format of story, but one of my favorites."

It must be, Gabby muses. Mrs. Keelin almost, like, smiles.

"The first point is the backstory. What's driving your character, and your story? What wound do they carry? What are they driven to do? It's what will mold their behavior. Their choices."

Gabby writes quickly, frowning.

Good thing this isn't about her. Being normal would make for a boring story, but it's all she wants.

"The second point is the catalyst," continues Mrs. Keelin. "This is when a new problem presents in the story, pushing your character off balance."

Like a hot, red-haired martial arts instructor...

Gabby frowns even deeper. She's not going to lose focus in this class.

She's going to be the best boring, normal person this academy has ever seen.

"GABBY!" Mrs. Keelin's strident voice pierces her ears.

But she ignores her, scribbling furiously in her notebook. She needs to get this down. She has to.

Mrs. Keelin's heels rap out an annoyed staccato. "Gabby, I'm talking to you."

Gabby turns the page, the last one now full of drawings and strange letters. Doesn't this teacher realize they're running out of time?

"I will not be ignored, young lady," snaps Mrs. Keelin.

She snatches the book from Gabby's desk so quickly that her pen gouges into the wooden surface.

Gabby shoots to her feet. "Give it back," she growls.

"I beg your pardon." Mrs. Keelin draws in a deep breath and expands her chest. "Sit down, right this instant. And never, ever, speak to me like that again."

Gabby drops her chin. This woman has no idea who she's up against. "Give. Me. Back. My. Book."

"The dean will be hearing about this," snaps Mrs. Keelin. Clutching the book to her chest, she spins around and stalks back to her dais. "Get out of my class."

Anger explodes through Gabby. She needs that book! Lives depend on it.

"No!" she screams, her hands hot fists by her sides.

A gust of wind rockets between the desks, knocking Mrs. Keelin over. She falls down, face first, the book flying out of her hands.

Gasps echo through the classroom as Gabby strides toward her.

"She's about to be expelled, for sure," someone murmurs behind her.

But Gabby doesn't care. There are more important things than enrollment at Mercy Academy.

She walks straight past the sprawled woman, hearing others rushing up behind her. They can take care of the teacher. She needs her book.

She's just squatted down to pick it up when a hand reaches out and snatches it. Gabby spins around, finding Zach standing there, holding it against his chest. "You need to calm down, Gabby. You just attacked a teacher, for fuck's sake!"

A little part of Gabby admires his spunk. It almost makes her smile. Then again, he doesn't know he's facing an angel.

Well, he's about to get an indication.

All it takes is a barely perceptible narrowing of her eyes and Zach goes flying. He slams into the wall to her left, the window beside it rattling with the impact. Frustrated that she's had to do this, Gabby strides over and picks up the book he'd dropped. It's laying open, a heptagon with seven circular points scrawled on the pages. Thick, dark-lined symbols are etched around it.

Clasping it to her chest, she walks out of the room, not looking back.

GABBY BLINKS, finding herself outside the classroom. How the flippity flock did she get out here? The last thing she remembers is Mrs. Keelin talking about catalysts...

Gabby turns around, determined to go back in when she stops. The small, square window in the door frames a scene she doesn't understand.

Mrs. Keelin is sitting on the floor, looking disheveled in a way Gabby didn't think was possible. Several students crowd around her, their faces tight with concern. Most of the others are several feet away, standing around something else.

The crowd parts and Gabby realizes it's not a something, but a someone. Zach is sprawled on the ground, the wall a few feet above him cracked and dented. Someone helps him up and he looks around, confused.

Gabby's lost the ability to breathe. What happened in there?

Zach's gaze stills as he sees her, watching him through the window. His eyes widen, and it's undeniable he looks terrified. "Keep her away from me!"

The students turn around, one or two going pale with shock. "Quick! We need to call someone! She's freaking crazy!"

No...

Mrs. Keelin. Zach. Surely she didn't do this!

Her heart hammering painfully against her ribs, Gabby spins on her heel and runs. She sprints down the corridor, her hand clamped over her mouth in horror. She'd never hurt anyone! She wouldn't jeopardize her scholarship at Mercy Academy!

Careening around a turn in the corridor, she slams straight into a body. A tall, strong, muscled body.

Colt's hands shoot out to catch her before she falls over. "Gabrielle," he murmurs.

The sound of her name in that deep timber of his is the last thing she needs right now. She's off kitler enough as it is. She steps back, noting he's barely even winded even though she came around that corner like a hurricane. "Ah, sorry."

"Of course," he says. His eyes narrow as he looks at her more closely. "Is everything alright?"

Of all the times for him not to be rude and surly! She shakes her head, then promptly contradicts herself. "I'm fine."

Stepping around him, she breaks into a run again. She has to get away. From him. From the destruction in the classroom.

From herself.

Gabby reaches her dorm room and she pushes through the barely opened door, shutting it quickly behind her. She gets as far as the bunk beds before she collapses on the lower one. It's Kalisha's bed, but as fast as the adrenaline spiked, it plummets.

Gabby's back slumps. Her lower lip trembles.

What is happening to her?

She almost yelps when the door opens again, half-expecting men in black suits and Kevlar vests to come storming in. Kalisha and Maya stop, the door shutting quietly behind them.

"Ah, is everything okay?" asks Kalisha.

Gabby tries to smile. "Did you finish class early, too?"

Kalisha and Maya glance at each other. "Class just finished," says Maya, the concerned wrinkle in her brow back.

Well, this time, it's justified.

Actually, it also was the first time. Gabby's been a walking disaster since she arrived here.

"What are you doing here?" asks Kalisha. "Don't you have another class now?"

"I think...I think I may have done something bad," whispers Gabby.

The two girls rush over, sitting on either side. "What's happened?" Maya asks.

"I, ah...probably won't be using the top bunk much longer." Gabby drops her face in her hands. "I think I may have attacked a professor. And another student as well."

"Oh honey," says Kalisha. "You wouldn't do something like that."

"What do you mean, you think?" asks Maya.

"Well, everything seems to indicate I did." Gabby looks at the two of them. "But I don't remember doing it."

Kalisha frowns. "You don't remember?"

Gabby nods, relieved to finally be talking about this. "I have no memory of doing it. It's just a blank space in time. I don't even know why I did it." She sighs, staring at her hands. The hands who attacked a woman and a fellow student. "It's not the first time it's happened either. I've had other memory lapses."

There's silence and Gabby can't bring herself to look up. She shouldn't have said anything. They're going to think she's certifiable.

Maya clears her throat. "My aunt, she's a psychiatrist. She's got all sorts of stories. This stuff happens to people sometimes."

Gabby's head drops into her hands again. "Great. I am crazy."

"No, that's not what I meant," assures Maya. "It means there's an explanation for what's happened. Like people with dissociative disorders."

Gabby's gaze shoots to hers. "You think I have a split personality?"

Maya pushes her glasses up. "I wouldn't go that far. But maybe you're showing some of the symptoms or something."

"Wow, Maya," says Kalisha. "You're quite the psych!"

She blushes as she ducks her head. "I'm going to make it my major."

"Really? I don't remember it on the subject list."

"It's new," says Maya, eyes sparking with excitement. "The debut year at the academy."

Gabby clears her throat. As great as Maya's career choice sounds, she's having a bit of a crisis here. "So, you think I have this...disorder?"

"It would explain what's happening. Maybe you should talk to a counselor or something?" Maya shrugs. "These things are usually triggered by our minds trying to escape something painful. We want to pretend it never happened."

Gabby's gut churns. Flashes of bright red and luminescent white rise in her mind but she shakes her head. "I don't want to talk to a counselor."

"But—" says Maya.

"No," Gabby says firmly. Something within her knows that's a bad idea. "I can't talk to a stranger about this."

And yet, she attacked two people today. Maybe she should. This is becoming about others' safety.

"I just need to get this under control," Gabby mutters.

Somehow.

Maya adjusts her glasses. "To do that, you'd need to accept the part of you that you're denying. Your alter-ego."

Gabby blinks. "My alter-ego?"

"This alternative self. That part that keeps taking over."

"I want to stop hurting people," Gabby whispers. "I can't even remember what happened."

"So Gabby needs to face this part of her. How does she do that?" Kalisha asks, now watching Maya closely, too.

She flushes a little under their scrutiny, glancing down at her fingers as they fiddle with the hem of her top. "Hypnosis has been used successfully."

"You know about this," says Gabby, her suspicion confirmed when Maya flushes an even deeper red.

"Hypnosis is a personal interest of mine. I've been... dabbling in it."

"So you could do it? You could hypnotize me?"

Maya's eyes widen. "Goodness, no. I'm not experienced enough, and things can go wrong if it's not done properly."

Kalisha smirks. "You could end up clucking like a chicken every time someone says egg."

Gabby slumps again, the hope there's a way forward quickly snuffed out. "Oh."

"I mean, you could—"

Maya's words are cut off by a knock on the door. Gabby's heart lodges in her throat, making her feel nauseous.

Kalisha sends her a strained smile as she gets up to open the door. "Maybe someone found the mascara I lost. It cost me more than my best lipstick!"

But the boy on the other side isn't holding a tube of mascara. He can't be. He's too busy wringing his hands. He clears his throat, flicking dark hair out of his eyes. "The dean requires Gabrielle at his office. Immediately."

His gaze darts to Gabby, then quickly away again. She

thinks he may have been one of the people she smiled at on her way to class. Her gut clenches as she realizes he's scared of her.

Because she's the crazy chick who attacked a teacher and a peer.

She pushes to her feet, dread like a lead balloon in her too-tight stomach.

There's no time for answers.

It seems today is her last day at Mercy Academy.

16

COLT

The news of the attack in Mrs. Keelin's room spreads through the academy quickly. At first Colt assumed it was the rumor mill that had attached Gabby's name to it, but he soon realized her name was the only one being bandied about.

Gabby attacked a teacher and a student. Over a book. And then she ran away.

Colt leans against the wall, tucking himself further into the shadows of the little enclave he's chosen to wait in. The administration building is across the wide expanse of floor, a tinkling water fountain in the center. If what the students are saying is true, then Gabby will be coming by this way shortly. On her way to see the dean.

Because her time at the academy is at an end.

Fate must've been wrong. His destiny isn't tied to hers. She's far too erratic, a loose cannon as humans like to say. What's more, she's a magnet for trouble. These stones Fate spoke of won't be found, no matter how vital she believed they were.

And yet, the thought tugs at his chest. Almost painfully. And his mind rebels. He is tied to this girl, somehow. He can feel it in his marrow.

But she can't stay. Not after what she did.

And he can't leave.

Which means none of this makes sense.

Two students wander past, gossiping that the attack was probably a product of drug use. Colt almost snorts, but refrains. He's cloaked himself within the shadows of the alcove, not wanting to be seen. Bringing attention to himself will have people wondering where the sound came from.

Gabby doesn't strike him as the sort to use drugs. Being supernatural is the best explanation for all of this, especially after he saw flashes of white, silver-tipped wings. But the research he's done suggests otherwise. Gabby was born human. She has a birth certificate. No angel has one of those. They bring their true forms with them to Earth, unlike demons who must possess a human vessel. Colt's always envied that about them.

Although, there are other supernatural species with wings. He's heard that some dragons have silver wings, except he hasn't seen one for decades.

Colt clenches his jaw. All this conjecture is getting him nowhere. He needs answers.

He straightens when he sees her enter the foyer. Gabby crosses the length, then passes the fountain. Her chin is held high, but her shoulders are low. He can sense her heart thundering in her chest.

She's scared.

And yet she walks with determined steps, willing to face the consequences of her actions he notes with grudging respect. No wonder he's so fascinated with her. She's a woman of contrasts and contradictions.

And mysteries galore.

Gabby raps on the door, waits a moment and Colt hears the faint voice of the dean.

"Come in."

With a fortifying breath, she does, closing the door behind her.

Colt finds he's no longer leaning against the wall. He's upright, alert. His gaze locked on those doors.

As if he cares what happens next. He frowns. As if he wants to go in there and stand beside her as she faces the dean.

A faint movement from the corner of his eye has Colt angling his head. Mr. Bishop is diagonally across the foyer, staring straight at Colt. No. Glaring at Colt.

When he shouldn't be able to see him.

His suspicion confirmed that there's something not human about Mr. Bishop, Colt takes a step out of the alcove. He'll demand some answers from the old man—

A black sack is shoved over his head, then strong arms wrap around his torso. Colt struggles, calling on his magic, only to find he can't access it. Like a cord has been cut, its power is strangely out of reach.

"Release me!" he demands, fighting against the hands holding him.

His only response is cackling laughter. Then another voice, sounding very much like Mr. Bishop.

"He's about to learn who's really in charge."

And then blackness.

WHEN THE SACK is yanked off his head, Colt's surprised to see a young man somewhere in his mid-twenties before him. His black hair has been fashioned into a long spike down the center of his forehead.

Colt's seen him around the campus, most recently less than an hour ago. He'd watched as this young rooster strutted toward the girls' dormitories. Gabby had exited only a few minutes later, heading toward the administration wing. This was the man who delivered the dean's summons.

"Release me," he growls, yanking at the chains holding his wrists above his head.

The young man smiles, his dark eyes roving over Colt's bound body. "Not so powerful now, are you, demon?"

Colt stills his struggles. So the boy knows demons exist. And that Colt is one. "What do you want with me?"

"Now, now, Colt," the young man purrs. "We're going to be the ones making the demands." He glances at the chains around Colts wrists and ankles. "You're nothing here."

There are a few chuckles and Colt focuses beyond the filth who's captured him, seeing several bodies skulking in the shadows beyond. He's in a room, a large one, most likely within the academy. Whoever this bastard is, he must be supernatural to have cut off Colt's magic. And if he's not human, then just like Colt, he'd be unable to leave the academy thanks to the mysterious protection spell.

He glares at his captor, turns his head and spits.

The young man in front of him grins, almost looking pleased with the action. "I do like seeing you angry, demon." He steps a little closer. "Especially when there's nothing you can do about it."

"Who are you?" Colt growls. This weasel is starting to get on his nerves.

Veins appear along his temples as his face flushes red. Rage flares in his eyes. "I'm the one asking questions here," the man roars. But within a blink, they disappear along with the florid color. He tugs at the sleeves of his shirt, breathing calmly once more. "But I think I'll answer this one. Takes our relationship to the next level, don't you think?"

Colt waits, glaring at him. A name may give him an idea of what he's dealing with.

The man lifts his chin, the tip of his black hair almost touching his nose. "I am Samandriel."

Colt raises a brow. He's heard of the name, but nothing comes to mind.

The smug expression falls from Samandriel's face. He looks...disappointed.

Colt curls his lip. It appears Samandriel has an ego. "Never heard of you."

Samandriel's dark eyes flare with fury again. He not only has an ego, but a short fuse. "Liar. Everyone knows my name."

"Not everyone. I'm guessing you haven't spent much time in Hell."

Samandriel's lip curls, just as Colt thought it might. "Of course I haven't," he spits. "I'm not lower than the scum of the Earth, unlike some."

He steps back, looking at Colt in disgust. He throws out his arms in a dramatic gesture, and two white wings snap out behind him. Even in the gloom of whatever place they're in, they glitter with a gentle alabaster glow.

Samandriel is an angel.

For the first time since he was captured, a frisson of nervousness trickles down Colt's spine. So angels are here, on Earth. But what do they want with him?

Unless they're working with Belphegor...

Either way, he's wanted dead.

"What do you want, Samandriel?" he snaps. "I don't have time for show and tell."

The angel retracts his wings as his eyes narrow. He stalks

back to Colt, a tinge of red staining his cheeks. "I've seen you following Gabrielle Heartley. And that makes me unhappy."

So, the angel is interested in Gabby. The question is, why?

Colt shrugs, the chain around his wrists rattling. "She's pretty. This body is only human, after all."

Samandriel sneers, as if he expected a response like that from a demon. Colt keeps his gaze on him even as he notes his surroundings. It's hard to tell how many others are in the gloom beyond, but it's a safe assumption that they're more angels. Strong ones, judging by their energy signatures. Almost as powerful as Samandriel's.

His thin lips curve up. "You have no power here, Colt the Stalker."

Colt raises his eyebrows. Did this angel just quote a popular cult movie?

Samandriel straightens, smoothing down his already smooth hair. "Pretty good, wasn't it? I'd make a better Saruman in Lord of the Rings, if I do say so myself."

Colt doesn't respond. Samandriel may be a powerful demon, but he's also deranged. That makes him unpredictable.

Samandriel waits but Colt remains silent. He's in more danger than he realized.

With a sigh, the angel steps back. "Boring, Colt Grayson. That's what you are. Boring. I expected more, to be honest. Aren't you demons all about free will, after all?"

Colt still doesn't answer. Maybe if he lets Samandriel talk, he'll get to the point.

"Fine then, let's get down to business, shall we? You, vile demon that you are, are to stay away from Gabby. She's off limits." Samandriel crosses his arms. "I should send you back to Hell, which I assume isn't your residence of choice. That's the reason you've been on Earth so many centuries, isn't it?"

Colt simply watches and waits. This angel likes the sound of his own voice.

"And if you've been roaming so long, then I'd bet my pearly feathers that awful Belphegor is looking for you. He'd be longing to roast your nuts over the infernal fires downstairs. Which means if I kill your body and send you back to Hell, I'm giving him what he wants." He tuts. "And making Belphegor happy doesn't make Samandriel happy."

Colt has to bite his tongue. He doesn't give a skata what makes him happy.

Samandriel angles his head. "And I can't send you away so you can take your demon stench elsewhere, thanks to that pesky barrier spell. Which means..." he grins as if he's telling a story that has everyone on the edge of their seat. "That I'm going to let you live." He claps his hands, twirls on his heels and throws his hands out. "Ta da!"

Yes, this angel is most definitely deranged. It means Colt puts little trust in the promise to spare his life, but he watches and waits. All he needs is for these bonds to be loosened for a second...

Samandriel's bright smile drops as he stalks back to Colt. "But you stay away from Gabrielle. She is none of your business."

The threat has Colt finally breaking his silence. "This girl is important to you," he observes.

"That is none of your damned business, demon," Samandriel snaps, all joviality gone, as false as it was. His gaze turns thoughtful. "Although maybe you should know exactly what you're up against. It really is in your best interests to back off."

Once more, Colt waits. Samandriel is turning out to be a wealth of information.

The angel leans in close as if they're now co-conspirators. "Gabrielle's the daughter of an archangel scheming to overthrow our lord from the Silver Throne. We followed the traitor to Earth, only to find demons. A lot of demons. And many of them found hosts, here, at Mercy Academy. Personally, I was surprised demons cared about something as intellectual as an education, but then I discovered the academy is built over several ley lines. Powerful ones." He smiles, and this time it's almost genuine. "Not that it helped them. We sent a lot back to Hell, although they kept coming. I suspect there's a Tear somewhere."

Colt keeps his face impassive, hiding his surprise that the angels don't know about the Tear. It's been seventeen years since the witch's spell opened it up.

Just like he hid his surprise at hearing Gabby's father is an archangel.

As far as he knew, angels don't sire children on Earth. Her mother is human, making her a half-angel. So if this is true, it makes her an abomination in the eyes of all other angels. They will want her dead.

Just like demons will.

She's surrounded by enemies.

And Samandriel is scared Colt will befriend her. And use her power against the angels.

It's possible he's planning on doing the exact same thing—using her power to further his agenda.

He must see something on Colt's face because he nods slowly. "Yes, I'm pleased to see you understand." He bares his teeth. "So stay away, demon. Or I'll be forced to rethink my generous offer not to kill you."

He steps back and clicks his fingers. Someone approaches from Colt's left, and he knows that he's going to have to take his eyes off Samandriel to understand the threat.

Except Samandriel is possibly an even greater one.

When darkness engulfs him again as the sack is pulled over

his head, Colt tries to fight it, even though it's useless. He's at these angels' mercy.

Not that the vile beings have any.

Within the space of a breath, blackness engulfs him once again.

17

GABBY

The dean's office is just as big and intimidating as Gabby expected it to be. It even has a freaking chandelier hanging high in the arched roof. She half expects to see cupids carved into the plasterwork.

Her feet sink into the plush maroon carpet, the Mercy Academy crest proudly woven into the center. A part of her wonders if she should skirt around it, just as a show of respect.

The dean is behind his desk, facing the large window behind it, his hands clasped behind his back. He knows she's here—he called her in.

But he's making her wait.

Maybe he's trying to make up for the fact his height is far from intimidating. Well, it's working.

Gabby walks up to the two leather chairs facing the large mahogany desk but doesn't sit down. She clears her throat, anxiety gnawing at her gut. "You asked to see me, Mr. Roberts?"

He spins around, his lined face somber. "Ms. Heartley."

Her stomach clenches at the way he says her name. Like he's greeting her at a funeral.

"I just wanted to say, I'm so sorry, Mr. Roberts. I have no idea what came over me and I regret—"

His hand shoots up, stopping her. "I'm the one talking here."

Her mouth snaps shut. For a brief second, tears sting Gabby's eyes, but she blinks them away. She's here to accept her punishment with grace and pride. She can fall into an ocean of tears after she's been chewed out.

And expelled.

"I'm very disappointed with your choice of actions, Ms. Heartley," he says. "Very disappointed."

Gabby nods, her shoulders dropping. The dean sounds more pissed than anything.

"Mercy Academy is proud of the high standards it expects of students. Our reputation is founded on it. Attacking a professor after she brought you to task for not following directions is uncalled for and unacceptable."

Gabby nods again, chewing her lip so hard it hurts. This is the first time she's learning exactly what it is she did.

"And then when a peer tried to stop you, you shoved him into a wall."

Sweet venus, that's what she did, too?

"Expulsion is the standard consequence for such actions."

"I know," she whispers. "I really am very sorry."

Heavy silence hangs in the large room, and even with the chandelier twinkling high above, the place feels dark and somber. Maybe that's just her mood...

Letting out a weighted sigh, Gabby turns to leave.

"But I've reviewed your application and academic transcript, Ms. Heartley." She freezes, unsure how this is relevant. "It was quite impressive. The foundation of the type of student we welcome to the academy. Then there's your extra curricular activities—accomplished at martial arts, lead roles in high school plays, and a handful of short stories published in magazines."

"Yes, sir," says Gabby, at a loss of how to respond.

Mr. Roberts pushes his glasses up. "And it appears someone on the board believes you have potential. Therefore, it's been decided to give you a chance."

She draws in a sharp breath. Those aren't words she expected to hear during this conversation.

"In response to your actions, you're being suspended for a month. You will be required to leave Mercy Academy for that time. We expect a written, sincere apology and for your family to reimburse any medical bills and property damage."

Gabby nods, her head bobbing the fastest it ever has. She's not being expelled!

"And I'd advise you to meet with the academy counselor to work through your, ah, anger management issues. Mrs. O'Rourke is very experienced. You can be on academy grounds to see her, or for select extracurricular activities, nothing else."

"Of course, Mr. Roberts." Gabby blinks. "Thank you, sir."

The dean harrumphs. "You're very lucky, young lady. Any future misdemeanors will not be tolerated. It will be an automatic expulsion."

"Of course," she says again, conscious she's starting to sound like she has a limited vocabulary. "It won't happen again. I promise."

Somehow, she'll make sure of it.

"Well, I'll be watching you to make sure it doesn't. One step out of line, and you're out." Mr. Roberts sits at his desk, picking up a gold-plated pen. "That will be all, Ms. Heartley."

Gabby almost executes a curtsy. "Thank you, Mr. Roberts."

She'll do whatever she can to make sure he doesn't have to follow through on his threat.

Quickly leaving the room, she closes the door quietly behind her. There, Gabby pauses.

She's been suspended, not expelled.

She has a slim second chance.

Hurrying away, she knows she needs to make this work. Which means getting on top of the blackouts.

And booting her alter-ego out.

She's only taken a few steps when she sees Mr. Bishop standing beside the water feature. He's staring at her intently, as if he's waiting for something.

Gabby turns away, frowning. Strange images flit through her mind, a doll levitating in her old bedroom back at home, a piece of paper spontaneously combusting, the snarling face of someone she's never seen before, his eyes glowing red. She closes her own eyes tightly for a long second, pushing them away.

Whatever the crazy old man told her isn't true. It can't be.

In fact, it's probably the stress of everything he's said to her that's triggered these blackouts. His words threaten everything she's ever wanted.

Lengthening her stride, she hurries back to her dorm. She needs to make this all go away, and then she can get back to normal.

Kalisha and Maya shoot to their feet the moment she enters.

"Well?" asks Kalisha. "What happened?"

Gabby opens her mouth, only to find the words lodge in her throat. The reality of what's happened hits her.

She attacked two people.

She's been suspended.

Her future is hanging by a gossamer thread.

She closes the door, trying to steady her breathing. Panic is crawling up her ribs, trying to choke her.

"Shit," says Kalisha. "You've been expelled."

Maya whacks her arm. "Don't jump to conclusions." She turns back to Gabby. "Tell us, Gabs. We're here for you."

Gabby walks to Kalisha's bunk and sits heavily. "I've been suspended. For a month."

"Wow," says Kalisha. "Someone upstairs is looking out for you."

Maya sits beside Gabby. "I know this sucks, but that's actually good news. You haven't been kicked out."

Gabby nods forlornly. She knows it's good news. But the next month is now stretching out before her, bleak and full of guilt.

"When do you have to go?" Kalisha asks quietly.

"Now. I'm not allowed to stay another night."

Maya glances out the window at the darkening sky. "You've organized someone to pick you up? Before curfew?"

"Yeah, sure," Gabby lies. "All over it."

She stands and gets her suitcase out of the wardrobe. How odd to think it was only a week ago that she unpacked it, so full of excitement and anticipation.

"I'll help," offers Kalisha.

But Gabby shakes her head. "It won't take me long." She hadn't been organized enough to unpack everything, anyway.

She grabs her clothes from her section of the cupboard, throwing them haphazardly into the suitcase. The inside quickly fills with multi-colored material and toiletries, the mess representing how her life feels like right now.

She's just finished when Maya appears beside her, holding out a book. "A little light reading for you."

Gabby takes it, reading the title. Self-Hypnosis for Beginners: Unlock your true self. "Thanks, Maya."

"I figured you could read up if you wanted. It might help."

"And you've got time on your hands," adds Kalisha, winking.

That has a smile dancing along the edges of Gabby's lips. "I'll be an expert by the time I come back."

The fledgling smile quickly dies as her words reinforce the fact Gabby's leaving. She still can't quite comprehend how this has all happened. She tucks the book into her suitcase, wondering if it really can help her get to the bottom of this.

Maya's face softens. "We'll take notes and send them to you, so you don't fall behind."

"Thanks," says Gabby, her throat thick. "You two really are the best."

The next thing she knows, she's being engulfed in a double hug. She embraces them back, holding on just as tightly as Kalisha and Maya are.

"We're gonna miss you," says Maya, wiping away a tear from behind her glasses as they pull apart.

Kalisha nods, her own eyes moist. "The room's going to be quiet without you."

"I'll be back before you know it," Gabby promises. "And all back to normal."

Kalisha arches an eyebrow. "Not too normal, I hope," she jokes.

"I'm going to be so normal I'll blend into the brickwork."

They all chuckle and Gabby knows it's time. She just hadn't thought it would be so hard. The friendship she's forged with Kalisha and Maya was stronger than she expected.

Turning, she grabs her suitcase and wheels it to the door. With a last smile and goodbye, she exits the room. She hurries down the corridor, swallowing the lump forming in her throat. Why the hell did she have to go and screw this up?

Heading to the main building of the academy, Gabby passes a few students, probably on their way to the cafeteria for dinner. She goes to smile at them but they glance down at her suitcase, then away, quickly whispering amongst each other.

Gabby's keen hearing catches a handful of words as she walks past.

"Crazy."

"Dangerous."

"No doubt expelled, after only a week."

Each one stings, stabbing a little deeper than the last. Tightening her jaw, Gabby walks past, pretending she didn't hear. She even lifts her chin, only to find holding her head high is hard under the weight of humiliation.

Walking faster, she makes her way out of the academy. Today has to be the worst day of her life.

She's just reached the large doors, the same ones she walked through, excited at the prospect of her future, when she pauses.

She hasn't called anyone, so there's no one to pick her up. Gabby closes her eyes, fighting the tears all over again. She's going to have to call her mom.

The thought shreds her. How is she going to explain what she did? That she's suspended for an entire month. Her mom is going to be so disappointed. And worried. Two emotions Gabby wanted to protect her from. Her mom's experienced enough of both of them.

Her whole body feeling like it's a gazillion times heavier, Gabby pushes open the doors. She'll get away from prying eyes and then make the phone call. Hopefully she can keep the tears at bay until after that.

She steps outside and stops. Someone is standing beside one of the large columns holding up the balcony above.

"Sierra?" Gabby gasps in surprise. "What are you doing here?"

Her aunt smiles as a second woman joins her, long purple hair draped over her shoulders.

"Blaise, you're here, too!"

Blaise nods and Gabby tries to understand what's happening. Why are her aunt and her best friend, two women who've been second mothers to her, doing here?

But before she can ask, a third person steps from behind the column. Gabby blinks, wondering if she's having another 'moment.' Except she's not supposed to remember them.

"Gabby, I believe you've met Colt," says Blaise. "He's a... friend of mine."

Colt's dark eyes glint as he regards her, as hot as always. As compelling as always.

And just as confusing.

He knows Blaise?

What the hell is going on?

18

GABBY

"He's what?" Gabby demands.

Gabby looks from Blaise to Sierra. Both women seem to be wondering what's amiss.

There's no way they could know Colt's the grouchy, surly guy who's been there every time she had a glitch.

Gabby blinks. It's true. From the time she turned up at his room, to the attack in the classroom, Colt's never been far away.

Does that mean he's the trigger?

She looks at him, frustrated with that inscrutable gaze of his. Why is he loitering around, always there when something happens? She'd say he's bad news if Blaise and Sierra weren't standing so casually beside him, claiming to be friends.

Speaking of her aunt, the dean must've called home. Thank flock it was Sierra who answered. It means she can have this conversation with her mom, face to face. It's going to suck enough as it is. Maybe Sierra could help out, try and keep her sister calm...

"Is everything okay?" Sierra asks, watching Gabby closely.

"What?" says Gabby, yanked out of her thoughts. "Sorry, I was just surprised to see you, that's all."

Colt crosses his arms. "I thought you might have been having another of your episodes."

Gabby glares at him. Did he have to go and open his big, delicious mouth?

"Her what?" asks Sierra.

He turns to her. "You don't know?"

Sierra arches a brow at Gabby. "Don't know what?"

Colt frowns, possibly flushes a little now that he's dropped her in hot water, shrugging sheepishly. And damn if it's not endearing.

A thought strikes Gabby as she turns back to her aunt. "If you're not here because of the...episodes, then why are you here?"

It's Sierra's turn to shift uncomfortably, which instantly makes Gabby uneasy. This is one heck of a weirdass coincidence.

Blaise sighs. "I think she should know."

Gabby freezes. She's just about had enough of learning new and startling facts.

Sierra nods, her gaze returning to Gabby. It's hesitant and sure all at once. "We've been investigating something. We got a lead and it brought us here."

"Investigating? A lead?" Gabby knows she's parroting, but she can't help herself. Something about the way Sierra's saying this tells her there are layers to her words. Layers Gabby isn't too keen to peel back.

"We're tracking something," says Blaise. "Something dangerous."

Sierra's lip thin. "A demon."

GABBY GLANCES AROUND, frowning. How the flippety-flock did she get here?

She's beside a tree, the gates of the academy not far away. A quick spin around reveals the building itself yards behind her.

Not again...

Gabby's stomach bottoms out as she realizes she had another black out. The last thing she remembers is talking to Sierra and Blaise, Colt standing in the background. Sierra and Blaise were telling her they were investigating something.

Demons.

Gabby grabs the tree to steady herself, digging her fingers into the bark, feeling nauseous. She's slowly, inexorably going bat shit crazy.

Sierra can't be part of this insane talk of angels and demons. That would mean Mr. Bishop was telling the truth.

He's her father.

And she's an angel herself.

Gabby clamps her hand over her mouth. Right now, being suspended is the least of her worries.

She turns around, finding her aunt and Blaise, Colt, too, only a few feet away. They must've followed her. Seen everything.

"What's going on?" she asks, sounding like a lost child.

Sierra approaches her, the Heartley blue eyes soft with compassion. "You've finally come into your powers."

Blaise joins her. "That was most definitely impressive."

Gabby looks around, having no idea what they're talking about. A part of her wants to walk away, pretend this isn't happening.

But she suspects that's been part of the problem.

"She doesn't remember," says Colt, approaching a little more cautiously. "My guess is she just had another of her episodes."

"Episodes?" Sierra asks sharply. She frowns in concern. "What episodes?"

"I've, ah, been doing things and not remembering them," confesses Gabby. "It's happened a few times now." Her voice drops to a whisper. "I don't know what's going on."

The only explanations she's been given have been impossible to believe.

Her aunt engulfs her in a hug and Gabby clings to her. Her whole world is progressively turning upside down and inside out.

"I know what's going on," Sierra says quietly. She pulls back. "The truth is no longer willing to be denied."

Gabby's stomach clenches painfully. "What truth?"

"You're not human, Gabby," says Sierra gently. "You never have been."

She's instantly shaking her head, denial clamping around her mind. "Of course I am."

Sierra's eyes are calm and sure. "I'd always suspected. Little things that gave it away as you were growing up. But now I know. You're supernatural."

Blaise nods. "And that part of you is obviously wanting to come out. To finally be acknowledged."

Gabby shakes her head again. But that would mean...she's an angel.

"Which would explain the episodes," says Sierra. "That part of you is taking over."

"I've heard of it happening before," agrees Blaise. "It can be difficult to accept."

Gabby frowns, stepping away from them. "How can you be so sure?"

Blaise smiles, her eyes twinkling. "We just watched you remove the barrier surrounding the academy." Her smile grows. "Thanks, by the way. I wouldn't have been able to leave."

Gabby takes another stumbling step back. Mr. Bishop said she'd erected the protection shield.

It can't be.

She can't be a freaking angel.

Archangel Gabriel can't be her father.

The ass who abandoned her and her mother all those years ago.

"I've always sensed this about you," says Blaise.

"Sensed?" asks Gabby. Is Blaise going to tell her she's an angel, too?

"I'm a witch," she says, pride tinging the words.

"I see," Gabby responds, unsure what else to say. What's next? Vampires? Werewolves? Fairies? She turns to her aunt. "And what are you?"

Sierra lifts her hands. "Plain old human, I'm afraid. I learned about this all a long time ago and have been researching it ever since. Blaise and I are Archivists, our role is to document the supernatural."

"Right." Has anything been as it seems in her life?

Sierra's a history professor, or so Gabby thought. Turns out she's chronicling everything that should be impossible in this world.

"So, what's been happening with these episodes?" asks Blaise.

"I've, ah, been doing things." She clears her throat. "Earlier today, I shoved a teacher and a student during class. Pretty hard from what I saw afterward. I've been suspended for a month."

Sierra gasps. "You're lucky you weren't expelled."

Gabby hangs her head. "I know. And I could've really hurt them."

"It's vital we figure out what's going on," says Blaise, frowning. "You need to accept your supernatural side."

"Whatever that is," murmurs Sierra. "Your mom is human like me. That means this has something to do with your father."

Gabby flinches.

"You know, don't you," says Colt, speaking for the first time. He takes a step forward. "You know who your father is."

Gabby's gaze snaps to his. Does he have to take this moment to be so freaking perceptive?

"Gabby?" asks Sierra, the frown back. Blaise is looking unsurprised.

"I do," she confesses, not quite believing these words are about to come out her mouth. "He's here. He's an angel."

Sierra gasps while Blaise nods knowingly. Colt watches Gabby, silent and still, and for some reason, she's kinda glad. He's acting calm in a way she's not feeling right now. It's just what she needs.

Sierra goes a little pale. "Whatever you do, don't tell your mother any of this."

Gabby nods. "Of course." There's no way her mom can know.

"So it's your angel side you need to accept," says Blaise. "Not doing so is getting you in trouble, and I know how much Mercy Academy means to you." She frowns. "It's just there's little we know about angels."

Colt nods. "True. They don't come outside of their precious pearly gates, content to watch over Earth."

For the first time, Gabby wonders what his role is in all of this. He obviously knows about the supernatural, just like Blaise and Sierra do. Is he human? Maybe a witch, too?

"That's our understanding as well," says Sierra. "But we have evidence that suggests angels have been here on Earth for a long time now. With the demons here thanks to the Tear, that doesn't bode well."

"We also think demons are the ones behind the murders," says Blaise. "That they're sacrifices of some kind."

Gabby resists the urge to rub her temples. She's just trying to get her head around being a half-angel and her aunt and Blaise are talking about demons, Tears and sacrifices. Her whole body feels like it's going to burst, there's so much emotion and information clashing within it.

"Maybe we talk about this more at home?" Sierra suggests gently. "This is a lot to take in."

Gabby frowns, unsure whether being at home is going to make this any easier to process. "Didn't you say you were tracking a demon?"

Blaise rests a hand on her. "We can come back for the demon. Besides, Colt can look into it now that he knows."

"He can?"

Colt subtly raises a brow but keeps his lips tightly shut. He's not going to explain how or why he knows about any of this.

"Yes, he can," says Blaise. "That's why we came here. We tried to call once we realized where the trace led us, but we couldn't get hold of him."

She glances at Colt whose lips tighten even more. "Yes, I was...indisposed."

Indisposed? Does anyone use that word nowadays? Is that why Kalisha and Maya think he looks older than he is?

"We should go," says Sierra. "The dean won't be happy that you're still here."

"Yeah, he was pretty clear that he wanted me off the premises," says Gabby heavily.

Blaise turns toward the academy. "Come on. My car is in the parking lot."

She and Sierra start making their way across the lawn, and

Gabby follows. She hesitates as she's about to pass Colt, then stops.

She looks up at him, his wine-colored hair a deep burgundy in the evening light, his eyes their own shade of shadowy twilight. "Who are you, Colt Grayson?"

Something flares in his gaze. "Your only priority right now is to figure out who you are, Gabrielle Heartley."

As true as that is, she recognizes the artful deflection. "Does anybody know?"

She's only ever seen him alone. He doesn't say much. And seems determined to give off 'stay the hell away' vibes.

"They're best off if they don't find out," he growls.

He's warning her to back off.

She steps a little closer, a smile tugging at her lips. "And yet, you're here. Helping. Isn't that interesting?"

His mouth clamps shut but Gabby's already turning away.

He's right. She needs to figure out what to do with all the mind screwing information she learned today.

But finding out about Colt Grayson may actually be fun.

19
COLT

Colt watches Gabby sashay away, trying to keep his gaze from roaming her curves and failing.

Cursing himself under his breath, he turns his head. He shouldn't feel this way. Especially now that he knows she's part angel. One who some very powerful beings are interested in.

Is that why Blaise tracked a demon back here?

Colt glances around the dusky grounds. If a demon did come through the barrier and to the Academy, he would have sensed it. Even though demons can mask their aura or scent, the magic's not absolute. Colt would've detected it.

Just what he needed. More mystery.

He hears Blaise's car in the distance as it makes its way down the academy driveway. The flare of challenge in Gabby's blue eyes flashes through his mind. It's a good thing she's going away. He needs some distance from her.

And yet, he finds himself watching the car leave. A small jolt of pleasure streaks through his chest when he sees Gabby looking back at him through the rear window of the car.

Cursing again, he jams his fingers through his hair. He's spent too long on Earth. He's starting to act like a mortal.

Not that he plans on ever returning to Hell. That reminder has him striding away, but not toward the academy. He makes his way to the boundary of the grounds a few yards away. To the place the barrier once existed.

Colt shakes his head, still surprised it was Gabby who created it. But he most certainly watched her remove it with little more than a flick of her fingers. She's definitely powerful, particularly for a halfling.

Bending down on one knee, he presses his hand to the soil where the barrier crossed. He closes his eyes, focusing inward as he mouths a spell. The barrier not only kept the supernatural from leaving the academy, it also stopped them from entering. He saw it himself when demons rained down and were stopped. The same could be for angels, too. Yet Blaise believes the demon she was tracking came here. How could it get through the barrier?

Images quickly appear in his mind of demon after demon who tried to breach the barrier. But to Colt's surprise, there are several angels, too. And they fail just like the demons do. Which means the barrier spell denied entry or exit to celestial or the infernal species. It didn't affect any earthly species. That's why Blaise was able to enter without repercussions.

Yet there's no vision of any demon entering the barrier in the recent days. As far as Colt knows, only an ancient demon could breach such a powerful barrier. Yet, if an ancient demon had appeared on Earth, Colt would have known. Just like he had sensed trouble when the Tear had opened up seventeen years ago.

He dusts off his hands, frowning in thought. Whatever it is, Blaise is tracking something strong. And dangerous. And he's sworn to protect her, just like he has every one of her ancestors. To keep her safe, he needs to find this demon.

Which brings him back to his original question—what brought it here? He doubts the murders in the city are demonic, and Blaise and Sierra came to the same conclusion. Yet they came upon a demon at one of the crime scenes and followed it here. Colt stares at the leaf littered soil as if it has the answers he's seeking. Was the demon also investigating the murders?

He pushes to his feet. The only way he'll get answers is by finding the demon and questioning it. And if it's an ancient one, that's not going to be easy. He sets his jaw resolutely. That won't stop him.

He turns and staggers as a surprising pain spears through his head. Pressing his fingertips to his temples, Colt glances around. He's not alone.

A young woman is walking toward him, a cold smile icing her lips. Her eyes smolder with silver hatred.

"Demons," she spits. "You're all abominations, and fast becoming a pandemic on Earth."

Colt narrows his eyes. Did the girl just equate him and his kind to a pathogenic virus wreaking havoc on humankind?

"I don't have time for this," he snarls.

"Too bad," snaps the woman as two huge white wings sprout from her back, each tip a shimmering silver.

Colt sighs. He has a demon to track. And now an annoying angel is trying to pick a fight.

Angling his head as he keeps his gaze on her, he unfurls his own wings, black and crimson tipped. The rush of power suffuses his body. It always feels good to reconnect with his true self.

The angel drops her chin and they slowly circle each other.

"Samandriel should've killed you when he had the chance," says the angel. "Instead, he showed mercy and made a deal with you. One you couldn't keep. That makes the agreement null and void."

Colt's lip curls, his own hatred for this celestial being just as strong. "I won't let anyone be a pawn in the wars you angels fight among yourselves."

"A demon caring for an angel," she sneers. "You expect me to believe that?"

"I don't care what you think."

She laughs. "What do you think her archangel father would say if he heard? Even though she's an abomination, part of her is an angel. Celestial blood. He'll annihilate you. Especially after you broke the deal." Her eyes rake over him in disgust. "Not that such a thing as honor can be expected of you and your kind."

Colt arches an eyebrow. "Quite the talkative angel, aren't you? Are you hoping you'll bore me to death?"

Fury flashes through her silver eyes. "If you want a fight, you'll get a fight, scum."

With a powerful thrust of her wings, she launches at him, quicker than he expected. He's heard angels can fly faster, but he hadn't expected her to be that fast. Colt somersaults backward as she lands where he was standing a second ago in an explosion of dirt. The tips of her wings spear into the ground, having formed into daggers.

The angel straightens, snarling. Colt grins at her.

Just as he expected, it angers the angel. She runs at him again, but this time he's prepared. He blocks her punch, and the next strike and the next. As the next punch aims for his head, Colt ducks, spins and executes a kick to her shin. She screams as it connects and seeing his chance, he follows through with a punch to the cheek.

The angel drops to the ground, blood trickling from the corner of her mouth.

"See?" taunts Colt. "All talk."

Teeth bared, the angel flies upward, her fist connecting with his jaw. The strike is so hard and fast that it sends Colt arching upward, pain exploding through his head as his teeth rattle. The taste of metallic blood fills his mouth.

He lands several feet away with a thud that echoes straight up his spine.

Colt's struggling to get back to his feet when the angel's kick lands on his chest. He's thrown again, tumbling over sticks and stones until his body hits the rough bark of a tree. Leaves flutter to the ground as the impact draws an involuntary groan out of him. He's pretty sure several of his bones are broken.

Once again, he tries to stand. He grips a nearby branch, hauling himself up with shallow breaths. He can't afford for the healing to take too long.

The angel stalks toward him, triumph lighting her features. "You're getting rusty, demon," she sneers. "Consider me sending you back to Hell a favor. It's there that you'll learn to fight again." She chuckles coldly. "It's a win-win situation."

Still leaning against the tree, Colt glares at her. "You won't kill me."

She snorts. "Why would you think that?"

"And steal the honor from Samandriel? I doubt he'd be very happy about that. You wouldn't want to anger him."

"That's not an assumption I'd encourage you to make."

"You would've killed me by now if that was your intention," he points out. He has no idea whether he's talking the truth, he just needs a little more time to heal. "You wouldn't be stopping to have these little chitchats."

With one quick movement, she's before him, her hands clamping around his throat. Colt struggles, but his still-broken body doesn't have the strength to throw her off. He flails with his hands, but she uses her wings to keep them away. Next, he tries his own wings, but the angel's already using her own to cocoon them, creating a shield of death.

His own.

"Does this feel like I won't be able to kill you?" she demands.

Colt couldn't answer even if wanted to. His throat is being progressively constricted, his airways painfully crushed. His lungs burn as his head pounds. It feels like she's going to snap his neck in half.

Unless he does something.

Calling on what little strength he has left, Colt digs his heels into the tree trunk behind him. And pushes.

The angel's eyes flash with surprise as she stumbles backward. It's the opening Colt needed as her hold on his throat loosens. With a short, sharp movement, he knocks her hands away.

But it's not the reprieve he was looking for.

The angel spins and kicks. Her foot plows into his chest and he's launched backward. She follows using her speed and kicks again before he can land. This time, Colt's launched into the air, branches and twigs snapping and cracking as his body powers through them.

He lands several feet away with enough force to knock the air out of his lungs. Before he can stand up, the angel is above him, holding him by the shirt.

"I do not answer to Samandriel," she snarls. "I'm going to enjoy sending you back to Hell."

Colt glares at her through the haze of pain. She's right. He misjudged her. He forgot Samandriel and Gabriel aren't working together.

They may both be angels, but they're enemies.

The angel's wings extend to their full breadth. Even in the gloom, they glow like an ivory moon. As he watches, the silver-tipped feathers turn into pointed shards. Preparing to impale his body.

He'll never be able to heal from that in time to save himself.

He's about to be sent back to Hell.

And if he thought infernal damnation was bad before, this time it will be worse. He's escaped his captors for centuries. That's hundreds of years of planning their vengeance.

The angel's eyes flare with excitement. Her body contracts toward his.

Colt closes his eyes, accepting that the next time he'll open his eyes, it will be in Hell.

A tortured shriek assaults his ears. His eyes fly open, shocked to see a hand protruding through the angel's chest. Her face is just as shocked. Her mouth opens and closes like a fish who just found themselves out of water.

Steadily, the light in her eyes dies. Blood pools in her mouth and tumbles over lips. She drops to the ground, the hand that impaled her still clutching her heart.

Colt pants as he watches her attacker stand there, holding the organ as blood seeps between his fingers, dripping to the ground in heavy, red globules. He staggers to his feet, instantly recognizing that he's facing a demon.

An ancient one.

"I heard you and your friends have been tracking me," the demonic figure says in a raspy whisper.

"I don't have any friends," Colt says through gritted teeth. His body's still healing. And yet he needs all the strength he can muster. "Who are you?"

The demon cackles as his features mold and shift.

Colt freezes. "Mr. Roberts," he whispers in shock.

The dean of Mercy Academy is an ancient demon?

"That is one name I go by," says the dean. He steps forward, dropping the angel's heart as if it's nothing but a piece of rotten meat. "But you know me as someone else."

The demon's mask melts away, exposing the truth beneath. Colt takes an involuntary step back as he recognizes the face.

He wasn't scared of the angel. Even when it was sending him back to hell.

But the enemy now standing before him sends a cold shiver of fear down Colt's spine. "Belphegor!"

G abby wipes her hands down her skirt, once again wishing it was a little longer. She needs a whole lot more material with the way her palms are sweating. She glances at the front door of her house, then the suitcase by her side. She really doesn't want to tell her mom what she's done.

A hand lands on her shoulder and she glances over to see Sierra there, her eyes full of sympathy. "It's going to suck but you have to do it."

Gabby's mouth twists. "I'm eighteen years old," she says, knowing she sounds petulant. "I'm old enough to make my own decisions."

AKA mistakes.

Sierra arches a brow. "Good point. Because being an adult means not running away from the consequences of our...decisions."

Gabby sighs. Running away was exactly what she was considering doing. To somewhere in Uzbekistan. "She's going to be so disappointed," she says quietly.

"She loves you, Gabs," says Sierra. "And yes, this is going to be a shock, but you haven't been expelled. Seems even the dean knows this is out of character for you. It'll blow over eventually. Especially now that you know why it happened."

Gabby frowns internally. She does know why this happened. Because a self-centered archangel thought he'd pop down to Earth and get some random woman pregnant, then flap his pearly wings and fly away like it didn't matter.

If it wasn't for him, Gabby wouldn't have anything to suppress. None of this would've happened.

And Gabby wouldn't be so compelled to protect the woman he'd abandoned.

Shaking her head, she readjusts her shoulders and tightens her grip on the handle of her suitcase. Her aunt is right. She has to face this.

She opens the door and enters her house. The familiar scent of the potpourri her mom loves so much and burnt anything-that's-edible fills her lungs. It wraps around her like a comforting hug. Under different circumstances, it would've been good to be home. A welcome grounding after a rocky start to college.

But she's here because that rocky start turned into a boulder avalanche.

Her mom enters the living room Gabby's standing in and stops in surprise. Her gaze flickers down to the suitcase beside her daughter. "Gabby? What are you doing home?"

Gabby opens her mouth to speak, only to find her throat is tight and constricted. How is she going to explain what she did to her gentle, loving mother?

"Gabby?" she asks, taking a cautious step forward. "Is everything okay?"

"I'm, ah, going to be home for a month."

Her mom's hand flutters to the neckline of her strawberry apron. "I'm not following."

Gabby clears her throat. "I accidentally hurt someone," she confesses. "A professor, and then a student who got in the way."

"You did what?" her mom asks, aghast.

Gabby takes a step forward, her heart cracking at the horror on her mom's face. "I didn't mean to, and no one was seriously hurt. But yes, I did. I've been suspended for a month."

Her mother's face hardens even as her eyes develop that hurt, watery look they do when she's overwhelmed with emotion. "Tell me what happened."

Shame scorches through Gabby. "It's all a bit of a blur. But the teacher took my book and I shoved her to get it back. She fell over. Then I did the same with a guy who tried to intervene and he crashed into a wall."

And then looked at her, terror in his eyes.

"You did what?" Her mom frowns, red tinging her cheeks. "Gabby, I expected better of you!"

She winces. "I know. I'm really sorry. Nothing like this will ever happen again."

She'll do whatever she needs to make sure of that.

"Hurting someone?" her mom says, her voice rising. "You've always felt things strongly, but this?"

"I know. I shouldn't have done it."

Her mom's anger dissolves as quickly as it flares. She's never been one to stay angry long. Gabby's chest tightens. That means the worst part is coming next.

Her mom drops to the nearby sofa, studying the carpet as if it has the answers. "I tried so hard to do this right. Where did I go wrong?"

"This isn't on you, Mom. This was me, acting without thinking. It's not your fault."

Her shoulders droop. "What would your father say?"

Sierra's hand shoots out and grabs Gabby's arms. An

acknowledgement of how much those words anger Gabby. A warning.

Her mother can't know that her father is the one who's caused all of this.

It only reinforces that Gabby wants nothing to do with him, no matter what supernatural taint flows through her blood.

From the corner of her eye, she sees Arielle come down the stairs, no doubt hearing the drama below. She stops on the bottom step, behind Gabby's mom. "What's going on?" she mouths.

Gabby doesn't answer. Even if she could, she wouldn't want to say the words that just flashed through her mind.

The future she dreamed for herself is progressively being destroyed.

Her mom's gaze returns to her, full of the pain Gabby's caused. "Maybe you're better off at the local university. Closer to home."

Gabby reels back. She worked her butt off to get into Mercy Academy, ironically, to make her mother proud and prove to her that she's a kick ass single mom. Although she briefly thought the same, that she should transfer, her mind instinctively rejects the idea. She has to go back.

Surely her father will move on once he sees she wants nothing to do with him. That even an archangel can't build a bridge over the chasm between the two of them.

She'll go back and do this properly.

"Shell," Sierra says. "Let's not make any rash decisions."

Gabby's mom spins to face her sister. "She's been suspended, Sierra! From the most prestigious academy in the state, possibly the country!"

Sierra takes a step forward. "I know, I'm not saying it's not serious. I'm just saying we need to think this through."

Gabby's mom draws in an indignant breath. "You think I'm

being overprotective again, don't you?" She doesn't give Sierra a chance to answer. "I let her go, didn't I? Against my better judgment, I might add. And look how that turned out!"

"Some...rough patches were inevitable." Another step forward, and slightly to the side, and Sierra's partially blocking Gabby.

Her mom throws her hands up. "Of course you'd take her side," she cries.

"I'm not taking sides, Shell." She steps more fully in front of Gabby, tucking her hand behind her back and waving for Gabby to move away. "I know you're worried about her. She's your daughter. You love her."

Gabby hesitates, realizing her aunt is gesturing her to leave. It's just that she's not entirely sure that's the right thing to do. This is her mess, she shouldn't leave Sierra to clean it up.

Her mom's back bows as she covers her face with her hands. "I really do love her."

Sierra quickly walks over and sits beside her sister, wrapping an arm around her shuddering shoulders. "I know you do," she says gently. "With all your heart." She glances up at Gabby and flicks her head toward the stairs.

She's telling her to go.

But Gabby still hesitates. Her mom's hurting, and it's all because of her. She's never felt more awful.

Her mom leans into Sierra. "I just want her to have the world."

"I want the same for Ari," Sierra says with a small smile.

Gabby realizes Sierra's the best person to be there for her mom right now. Her sister. And a fellow single mother.

Arielle seems to think the same, because she waves her hand for Gabby to join her. Reluctantly, Gabby picks up her suitcase and scoots around the couch. Her mom doesn't seem to notice. Gabby's just reached Arielle on the bottom step when Sierra's quiet words reach them.

"It's just that Gabby can't have the world if she's stuck at home."

"She also can't beat up anyone who doesn't agree with her," Gabby's mom snaps.

"We've all had moments when emotions got the better of us," Sierra points out.

Gabby's mom huffs, but doesn't respond. Only someone else who also fell pregnant as a teen could say that to her.

Sierra's definitely the right person for this right now.

Gabby grabs Arielle's hand and they sneak up the stairs to their room. Inside, Gabby leaves the door ajar so she can hear whether she should return. There's nothing more she wants than to make amends with her mom.

"It'll be over soon," Ari assures her as if she just read her mind.

Gabby nods as they sit on their respective beds. She's surprised Arielle didn't move Gabby's out the first moment she could.

Picking up her pillow and wrapping her arms around it, Gabby hopes Sierra can help her mom calm down. Despite everything that's happened, she doesn't want to leave Mercy Academy. It's her one chance at really making something of herself.

Someone her mother will be able to brag about to every person who looked down their nose at her for being a teen mom.

Her mom's voice wafts up the stairs. "I just think this is a sign. She's not coping there."

Arielle's face twists in an attempt at a smile. "You know she's a worrier. It'll be fine."

Gabby's face flops onto the pillow. She knew her mom was worried about her going to Mercy Academy.

And now she's added fuel to that shitfire.

All because her father thought he could pop into her life.

She's never hated the guy, and everything he stands for, more. It doesn't matter that he's an angel.

She'll never be like him.

"So, what are you going to do about it?"

Gabby's head snaps up. "What?"

"The cousin I know doesn't bury her face in a pillow. She deals with it."

Gabby's about to say it's not that simple when she stops herself. Ari's right. She's a fighter. Even when the going gets tough.

She jumps off the bed and grabs her suitcase. Inside, she pulls out the book Maya gave her. Arielle joins her, reading over her shoulder.

"Your solution is self hypnosis?"

Gabby opens the book, quickly skimming the table of contents. "I need to find out what's going on when I'm blacking out. This is one way I might be able to do it."

"You've been blacking out?" Arielle asks, concerned.

Gabby waves her hand. "Long story. But I think this can give me the answers I need."

Arielle leans a little closer as Gabby skips the introductory chapters and heads straight to the Hypnotize Yourself section. "Is it safe?"

"I won't do it properly yet. I just want to see what's involved."

She wants to feel like there's a way forward.

Gabby finds the link to a guided self-hypnosis track and she types the website into her cell phone, taps on the big blue Play button, then connects to the small speaker on her bedside table. Soft music fills the room, followed by a soothing male voice.

"Now that you've read all about self-hypnosis and made the informed choice that it's right for you, welcome. You're about to embark on a journey of self-discovery."

Arielle shifts a little. "I'm not sure you've made an informed choice?"

Gabby shushes her as she lies on her bed, wriggling a little until she's comfortable. "I'm not going fully under. I'll just listen for a bit."

Maybe if she can remember what she did, she can have a sense of how to control the part of her that's taking over. A part of her she has no doubt has to do with her father.

"Do not listen while driving or operating heavy machinery," continues the man in a gentle cadence. "Now, close your eyes and focus on your breath."

Gabby does as she's told, her body softening into the mattress. The man's hypnotic voice has her progressively relaxing, her breathing becoming deep and slow. She quickly discovers exactly how much tension's been stored in her body. Possibly enough to power Texas. As her muscles loosen and unwind, Gabby almost smiles.

Even if it doesn't work, she'll certainly feel refreshed afterward.

The man's voice fades away as she floats in a state of half-consciousness. Idly, she wonders if she'll fall asleep as she drops further and further into pleasant nothingness. It feels like she's falling, dropping, sinking.

Suddenly, the darkness around her seems to change. As if it's gaining substance.

It's no longer nothing. It's something.

A door appears in front of her, locks and chains clamped to just about every inch of. Gabby approaches it, no longer feeling quite so relaxed. She stands before it, knowing the answers she's seeking are on the other side.

Except there are dozens of padlocks and bolts all over it, maybe hundreds. Is she supposed to unlock every one of them?

Drawing in a steadying breath, Gabby reaches a hand out. She came here for a reason. She doesn't want to keep hurting people. The moment her hand brushes one lock, it fades away. The instant disappearance spreads over the door swiftly, dissolving the remaining contraptions keeping the door closed.

In a blink, it's bare. Exposed. Waiting to be opened.

Moving before she changes her mind, Gabby reaches out and touches the door handle. It swings open, blinding light exploding from within.

Gabby raises her arm to shield her eyes, but the burst of light is short-lived. As she lowers her hand, she sees the door's gone. That there are pulsing balls of energy floating around her, flickering images within.

Her memories. Waiting to return to her awareness.

She hesitates. There was a reason they were behind a heavily locked door. Telling herself her alternative is to bury her face in a pillow, Gabby steps forward.

She quickly retreats when something streaks past her with enough speed to blow her hair across her face. She shoves it away, eyes widening when she finds a solid black wall in front of her. Looking left and right, it spans as far as she can see.

It obscures everything. Including the memories.

Gabby presses her hand against it, surprised to feel how solid it is. Nor does it dissolve and disappear just like the locked door did.

"You can't get past it," whispers a barely perceptible voice.

Gabby takes a few steps back, turning one way then the other. "Who's there?"

"Who else would it be?"

A bright light appears high above, growing as it gently floats down to eye level. Gabby stands where she is, heart thumping, but not backing down.

This is what she's here to face.

But as the bright light takes shape, she takes another step backward. That face. The hair... She's looking in a mirror, at her reflection.

"Who did you think you'd find?" her replica mocks.

Gabby shakes her head, confused. "I...I don't understand."

"Surely you saw this coming." Two giant wings snap out behind her, glittering in the darkness. "I'm the angelic part of you."

Gabby narrows her eyes. "How do I get rid of you?"

She chuckles lightly, sounding exactly like Gabby, but colder somehow. "We are one. You think we're separate, but we're not."

"No," Gabby denies vehemently. "This is not me. It will never be me."

"I've been protecting you," says her doppleganger. "I wouldn't have to do it this way if you accepted this."

"But, you hurt people!"

"I do what needs to be done," snaps her angelic self. "What you're too human to do."

"They're the ones I should be protecting," shouts Gabby. "Not relegating them to collateral damage!"

Gabby takes one more step back. No wonder her father's so heartless. There's no way she's accepting this part of her.

"This is far bigger than a professor or a student," snarls her angelic self. Her wings arch high, a stark contrast to the black wall behind her. "I am the power you need to defeat the demons. War is coming."

"I'm not terribly sure angels are the good guys here," retorts Gabby. "I won't be some pawn in your game."

Her winged reflection straightens and lifts her chin. It's a familiar enough action that Gabby knows a challenge has been issued.

Which is fine by her. She's not some cold-hearted being who doesn't care who gets hurt in the name of winning.

She takes a step forward. "Get out of my way. I'm going to tear that wall down."

"You built the wall," snaps her angelic self. "It's where you've tried to contain me all your life. But I'm stronger."

"Then I need to get rid of you."

"Impossible. You need to accept me, not deny me. If you don't, your blackouts will keep happening. I will do what needs to be done."

"I won't let you," snarls Gabby. "If I contained you for eighteen years, I can do it again."

"You're about to find out how wrong you are."

Before Gabby can retort, her reflection runs at her, becoming a burning ball of white light. She crashes into Gabby and is instantly absorbed.

Gabby arches as power fills her.

"GABBY, WAKE UP!" Gabby opens her eyes to find Arielle shaking her. "Thank goodness!"

She shoves her cousin's hands away. "I'm fine!"

Arielle takes a step back, frowning. "You were under pretty deep. And then you started thrashing around everywhere."

"I said I'm fine." She pushes to her feet. "Now get out of my way."

Arielle narrows her eyes. "There's no need to be rude."

"I don't have time for this," Gabby growls. She stills, realizing maybe this girl is the best way to make her point.

With one swift movement, she shoves Arielle away. The force sends her cousin across the room. Arielle lands on the bed, her head slamming against the wall. She blinks groggily before her eyes flutter closed and her body goes limp.

GABBY BLINKS, finding herself standing beside her bed. Frowning, she realizes she just had another black out. Right after the angel within her jumped into her.

The door's shoved open and her mother bursts in, Sierra right behind her. "What happened?"

Gabby glances around, confused by the alarmed look on both women's faces. She gasps.

Her knees go weak.

Arielle is sprawled on her bed, unconscious.

21

COLT

Colt stands very still. Fight? Or Flight?

Neither is likely to end well for him.

When he was in Hell, Belphegor was the only demon who was stronger and more powerful than him. And faster.

"Long time no see," says Belphegor with a smile.

Centuries, in fact.

The last time Colt had seen Belphegor was after a failed mission. He'd been summoned, the same antsy uneasiness crawling between his ribs as now. Colt was tasked with scoping out a rival demon faction led by Asmodues. He was supposed to find out what he was up to. His covert spying had paid off, though, when he'd learned Asmodeus was preparing his demon army to attack one of Belphegor's castles in the third circle of Hell.

Armed with this information, Belphegor had deployed most of his forces to protect it that very same day.

Except Asmodeus had attacked the second circle of Hell, somehow bypassing one of the most dangerous and protected Gates.

It was only thanks to Blaise's ancestors that Colt had survived the rage that would've followed. Belphegor blamed Colt for the loss of his minions and castle. And every drop of that fury would've been channeled into torture, deep in the bowels of the Underworld. Blaise's ancestor summoned Colt just in time.

The Tear opening up had made him uneasy. He'd come to Mercy Academy because he thought it was safe.

Seems he was very, very wrong.

Colt crosses his arms, not answering Belphegor. He needs more information before he runs or fights for his life.

"You should be scared," says Belphegor, his hard smile growing. "You've escaped me for centuries, both in Hell and on Earth. That's quite the feat. The mentor in me wanted to applaud you for a job well done." The smile drops faster than the temperature around them. "But I was too fucking furious."

Colt tenses. Hopefully his ability to fight Belphegor will be as effective as his ability to elude him.

Belphegor sighs, his own body unwinding. "But that was a long time ago. I'm not angry any more."

Colt doesn't relax. Belphegor isn't someone to let go of grudges, especially after the way Colt inadvertently let him down, then ran. It must be a trick. Although why a demon far more ancient than him would resort to that is beyond him.

"After you were summoned, I thought my chances of finding you were slim, Colt. But seventeen years ago, the borders between Hell and Earth thinned and a small part of the inter-dimensional fabric tore." Belphegor's eyes blaze. "I was in the outermost circle of Hell and I felt it. Such a rush! Such wonderful news! Demons could now be let loose on Earth, off to carry out the Great Lord's bidding."

Surprise jolts through Colt, although he doesn't show it. He thought that quest was nothing but legend.

Belphegor extends his arms. "We can now free humanity from the yolk of the angels, to open their eyes to their so-called divine being." His hands drop and his gaze blazes with crimson fire. "I found power where I could, channeling the dark objects I inherited from Mother, and came through the Tear. Although I was following another demon who betrayed me, I realized I had the chance to find you. So I took the dean's body—as unsavory-looking as it is—and learned everything I could about you from my demonic informants." His smile returns, devious and triumphant. "Imagine my joy when you accepted the invitation to join the academy. You came to me!"

Belphegor laughs, the sound raking down Colt's spine. The ancient demon is right. He walked straight into a trap.

"And here we are," says Belphegor, his face settling into a satisfied grin, any sign of the mild-mannered dean long gone.

"Indeed." Colt unwinds his arms, ready to move. "Now that you've found me, you can stop killing all those people."

Belphegor snorts. "You think I'm behind those ritualistic sacrifices?" He shakes his head in disgust. "You've been hiding for far too long, Colt. You're oblivious that there's a war going on. Angels and demons have been fighting it out while you've skulked in the shadows, playing at martials arts instructor. And we're losing."

"I don't care about your war. And I don't believe you about the sacrifices. Someone tracked you here after you'd been to one of the murder sites."

"Ah," says Belphegor. "Are you making friends, Colt?"

Colt doesn't answer. He makes alliances and agreements, not friends.

"I wanted to know who was murdering humans and trying to blame demons," says Belphegor. "If others believe this, an army of angels will descend. It will be a full fledged war, Colt.

There's no way to count how many lives will be lost. We don't want that. Not until the Gates of Hell are opened."

It's Colt's turn to snort. "The Gates of Hell can never be opened. That lore is long forgotten."

"Says who?" snaps Belphegor. "The Great Lord wants them opened, and he will make it so. Soon he'll be able to project his thoughts into this world, rallying the Sins to his cause." His face lights with fervor. "What a glorious day that will be, Colt, when all the Gates of Hell are open and the cage that imprisons the Great Lord is destroyed."

Colt shakes his head. Belphegor is talking of fairy tales. "The cage was forged with ancient and powerful spells. Lucifer hasn't been able to break free of it."

"Except the spell only exists while the archangel Michael rules the known dimensions."

"And Michael cannot be defeated," Colt points out. "Not even by Lucifer. We all know what happened during the Rebellion."

Only the lucky ones survived.

"We will succeed this time," promises Belphegor. "Lucifer will come to Earth as its lord, and all those who serve him will be welcomed into Paradise."

"I never picked you for a dreamer, Belphegor. Lucifer is trapped. There is no one who can take down Michael."

A slow, wide smile spreads across the ancient demon's face. "Yesterday I came across a young woman. I instantly recognized her for what she is. An angel. Or rather, an angel-human halfling with immense power." The smile lights Belphegor's red eyes. "Unlike anything I have ever seen."

Colt freezes. Then scowls. "Why are you telling me all of this, Belphegor?"

"Because you know her, Colt. She's the one you can't take your eyes off. Gabby, isn't it?"

"She means nothing to me," he snaps.

"Oh please," says Belphegor, rolling his eyes. "I've been watching you. My men have been watching you. You may tell yourself it's curiosity, but you're fooling no one but yourself. You seem to have forgotten you're a demon and she's an angel. Sworn enemies."

"I hold no feeling for her," insists Colt. Belphegor isn't telling him anything he doesn't know.

"Sure you don't," says Belphegor with a sly wink. "I'd think this disgusting affection you're cultivating is a terrible idea, if it wasn't so useful. In fact, I'm going to encourage it. This girl is close to solving those murders."

"She knows nothing about the murders," growls Colt. For some reason, the need to have Gabby out of this conversation is overwhelming.

Belphegor gives another arrogant roll of his eyes. "She knows more than you think. Those episodes have been happening more than you realize." His focus lasers in on Colt. "I need you to be there when they happen. We need to find out who is carrying out these murders and blaming them on our kind. You don't want a war on Earth, do you?"

Colt's about to reiterate that this has nothing to do with him, but he stops himself. Gabby is caught up in this in ways she doesn't realize.

He holds Belphegor's gaze. "A war between angels and demons will mean nothing but disaster and devastation to humankind," he says, pretending this is what he's concerned about. "They've had enough of that in recent decades."

Satisfaction softens the lines on Belphegor's face. "Then you'll do what you're told. Like a good soldier."

Another jolt of surprise tugs at Colt's insides. Belphegor's recruiting him again? After he failed him with Asmodeus?

Belphegor isn't known for showing mercy or second

chances. In all of Colt's centuries, he's never heard of it. And yet here he is, asking Colt to spy on Gabby and learn what he can about her supposed investigation in the serial murders.

Even though he's seen nothing to suggest that. When has she had a chance?

"You'll need to be careful, though," says Belphegor as he watches Colt mull over the offer. "There are at least two angel factions here as far as I can tell."

Colt arches a brow. "You mean Samandriel?" he asks, showing he's not as ignorant as Belphegor has taken him for.

"You know them?"

"They paid me a visit," says Colt, omitting that they'd captured him. "Samandriel asked me to stay away from the girl."

"Interesting," muses Belphegor. "I've had my demons keep watch over you since the moment you arrived. No one reported anything like that."

"They could have masked themselves. Or taken care of those demons."

"Possibly. And they just let you leave?" Belphegor asks doubtfully.

"They did."

"Also interesting. Clearly, there's infighting among the angels. I suspect this faction wants to use Gabby as a weapon or a pawn against the other faction."

"Against her father, Gabriel." The moment the words are out, Colt regrets them. He doesn't trust Belphegor. Who knows what he'll do with this information.

Just as Colt suspected, the archdemon's eyes flash. "That makes sense. She's powerful, especially for a halfling. Her father being an archangel would explain that." He angles his head. "And yet, you haven't stayed away from her."

Colt's lips thin. "She's as innocent as any human in this," he snaps. "And deserving of protection like any other human."

Belphegor stares at him, one eyebrow raised, but Colt refuses to squirm or look away. He may not have involved himself with humans for hundreds of years, but that doesn't mean a thing.

His old master turns and begins to pace, rubbing his chin. "So Samandriel wanted to scare you away from the girl. Why?"

Colt doesn't respond. He's known Belphegor long enough to know he's not expected to. The ancient demon is thinking. Scheming.

"One thing we've noticed is that Gabby's episodes are triggered, usually by you." Colt frowns, not liking the sound of that. Belphegor doesn't notice and he continues to walk several paces, then turns. "I suspect the supernatural triggers them. And if Samandriel wants you staying away, then maybe he doesn't want Gabby having these episodes." He frowns, thinking even more deeply. "He doesn't want her angel coming out for some reason. To keep her vulnerable? Or for some other reason?"

Colt waits and listens attentively. Belphegor has existed for millenia. His theories are worth considering.

"And yet, they didn't kill you," he says, stopping back in front of Colt. "Why?"

That has Colt's lips twitching. "He didn't want to give his arch enemy a reason to smile."

Belphegor chuckles. "He thinks I'd rejoice in your death, does he?"

Colt snorts. "Of course you would. I failed you."

"That's true, you did. And I was furious."

Colt glances at his old mentor. He's talking in past tense.

"Even when I came through the Tear, I wanted vengeance. But once here on Earth, I started to remember you were my most promising student. One who exceeded all my expectations. Your death would not bring me joy, Colt. And I no longer intend on returning you to Hell." His lips twist. "At least not for now. We have work to do if we are to avoid a war before we're ready."

So Belphegor has a use for him. After centuries of being hunted, Colt has a reprieve. It's a novel feeling. One that has his body feeling lighter than he's ever remembered.

Except, this freedom comes at a price.

"Focus on Gabby, Colt. Follow her. Find out what she knows and tell me everything." Belphegor's face hardens in a way that's all too familiar. "Do not fail me, demon. I won't be merciful the second time around."

Ice winds around Colt's spine. The fury that Belphegor once felt for him is banked deep within his mentor's eyes.

Be a hunter, or be hunted. That's his choice.

Colt nods, a differential motion that's also familiar. "I will do as you ask."

Belphegor stares at him for long seconds, as if assessing the truth in those words. He steps back with an acknowledging nod. "Excellent. Now, I must go." He grimaces. "We have a staff meeting tomorrow. Humans do love to listen to their own voices."

With a flick of his fingers, Belphegor vanishes, leaving Colt standing alone in the dark, an ugly feeling churning in his gut.

He should never have come to the academy.

22

GABBY

Gabby curls up tighter into a ball, guilt and shame devouring her from the inside out as the faint lines of dawn caress the curtains over her bedroom window.

She hurt Arielle. She's like a sister to her. Gabby holds her stomach even tighter. She's out of control. A danger to those she loves.

All because there's an angel inside of her with something to prove.

A tear trickles down, joining the others in the soaked patch on her pillow. Arielle's soft breathing fills their shared room, only making Gabby feel worse. Arielle had come-to quite quickly. She'd insisted she was fine, her love for Gabby stronger than anger.

"You need to deal with this," Sierra had hissed under breath. She'd gone to her daughter and wrapped her arms around her. "Let's get some ice on that lump, shall we?"

Gabby's mother had looked like her heart was breaking. She'd said nothing, then left.

Gabby bites her lip, trying to contain a sob. Arielle had tried to act like nothing was wrong. But she'd winced when someone spoke too loud. She'd not quite met Gabby's eye when she said she was going to bed early.

She'd rolled over when Gabby came to bed, her feet heavy and her body aching with regret, pretending to be asleep.

Gabby needs to fix this. Self-hypnosis hadn't worked. Sierra and Blaise don't know enough about angels to help.

Which leaves one person.

You'll need me, daughter. It's only a matter of time.

Gabby pushes up and brushes away the strands of hair stuck to her cheek. As much as she doesn't want to, as much as the thought makes her sick, she needs to talk to her father.

Creeping out of bed, Gabby silently dresses, then slips out of the house. She catches a ride about a block from her house, ignoring the curious glint in the driver's eye as she climbs into the back seat. There's no way he could ever guess why she's out so early. She can just imagine the conversation.

"I'm off to see my dad. He's an archangel who abandoned me before I was born. What a douche act, right? Anyways, my inner angel keeps taking over and doing bad shit, so I need to find out how to get her under control. He's the only one who can help me."

The driver would immediately change direction and head to the nearest loony bin.

He drops her off beyond the gates of Mercy Academy like she asked him to. She needs a few moments to steady her nerves. She's about to do something she never thought she would.

Ask her father for help.

Gabby approaches the gates, her heart sinking when she sees they're closed. Of course they would be this early in the morning. Except they open the moment she approaches them. Walking through, she sees the guards asleep within their little office. Gabby stops where she is. Are they exceptionally lazy, or is something else going on?

Is her angel about to come out and run the show again?

A short, sharp honk sounds behind her, making Gabby jump. She spins around, her hands to her chest, seeing a black Ford Mustang idling behind her. Colt's behind the wheel.

Of course he is.

This time, though, Gabby steps aside. She doesn't want an argument. She sure as flock doesn't want to bring attention to herself.

The rumbling car moves forward and Colt pulls up beside her. He hooks an arm through the open window, the rolled-up sleeve exposing a tanned forearm. "Want a ride?"

Mr. Rude and Surly is offering her a ride? Gabby looks around, unsure of this alternate universe she just stepped in. "Ah, I'd rather walk, but thanks."

He arches a wine-colored eyebrow. "And give the dean a reason to expel you?"

Her spine stiffens. "I'm allowed here for counseling sessions, thank you very much."

Colt glances out the windshield. "This early in the morning?"

Damn his smart mind. "I didn't want to be late," she snaps.

"You sure?" He revs the motor a little, filling the air with deep purring. "This way you won't have prying eyes watching you enter."

Against her will, Gabby's eyes glance at the passenger side seat. She shakes her head, just as much to get her to snap out of it as to communicate her answer. "No, thanks."

"I don't bite, you know," he says, his own voice a pleasant rumble.

Gabby's pulse leaps. He's not only being nice, he's flirting with her? That's the last complication she needs.

"If that's the case, then what's the point?" she says before she can stop herself, her voice husky in a way she would never intend.

Colt laughs, the sound just as pulse tripping as the sexy promise. He looks up at her, the early morning light finding burnished highlights in his dark red hair. "See you around, Gabby."

With a last lingering look, he drives away, leaving her wondering what just happened. Did Colt just flirt with her? And did she just flirt right back?

Shaking her head again, but this time with a little more vigor, she makes her way down the driveway. Maybe her angel side is trying to take over again. All the more reason to meet with her father.

Gabby makes her way to the academy, regret tugging at her heart. She's only been gone a day and she already misses the place. She misses Kalisha and Maya and the friendship they've forged. She misses the sense of belonging she'd always craved. She misses the future she was looking forward to so much.

Which she can never have.

Gabby slips through the front door, realizing she's not sure where her father would be at this time. Or any time for that matter. He's a stranger to her, and pretending to be the head of security at Mercy Academy. Finding him may take longer than she'd hoped. Maybe she should try the cranky dog statue first.

Walking a little faster, she rounds the corner of the corridor, and crashes straight into someone. The young woman lets out a squeak as a glazed donut is mushed into her face.

"Klae," gushes Gabby. "I'm so sorry!"

Klae smiles, wiping away at the pink icing surrounding her mouth like lipstick a four-year old has put on. "Good thing it's delicious." She frowns. "You're not supposed to be here."

"I'm here for my counseling appointment," says Gabby quickly.

Klae nods sagely. "I knew what happened wasn't like you. I'm glad you're getting help."

Gabby smiles. This girl has a generous heart. "Thanks." She shifts a little, hating letting her down. "And about the play, maybe you're better off finding a replacement. I can come in for extra curricular activities, but—"

"Oh, that's great news," Klae beams, still wiping pink icing from around her mouth and on her braces. "I thought I was going to have to delay it by a month."

"What? You don't need to do that!"

"You're my leading lady, Gabby. Of course I was going to do that."

Gabby impulsively gives her a hug. "Thanks, Klae."

She's flushing as she pulls back. "Of course." Her gaze slides away. "It's not like there were people lining up to take your place."

Gabby suspects even if there were a hundred people vying for the role, Klae would've turned them down. She's that type of girl. "Thanks, anyway. You're a good friend."

Klae flushes even deeper then quickly turns away. "Anyway, I'd better let you get to your appointment." With a quick wave, she rushes off down the corridor.

Feeling a little bad for lying about why she's here, Gabby sighs. Her whole life has been a lie. She'd better get used to having to hide far more than why she's at a place at any given time.

She makes her way to the small courtyard, stopping the moment she steps through the door. Her father is there, as if he knew she was coming. Gabby stills, a riot of emotions exploding through her.

He was expecting her. She hates that.

He instantly unfurls his wings, displaying everything he is.

And he's no longer under the guise of Mr. Bishop.

His strong features are topped with golden curls. His eyes are the same blue that's stared back at her from a mirror all her life.

He's most definitely, undoubtedly the man who fathered her.

He glances at the creepy-as-heck statue he's standing beside. "It's so peaceful, so still. And yet it holds great power. Just like angels." He looks back to Gabby. "Just like you."

Gabby crosses her arms. "Whether I like it or not."

"It's a blessing," her father assures her. "You carry a part of Heaven within you. It is what all angels must harness when they come into their power."

Gabby frowns, taking a cautious step into the courtyard. "I thought all angels were born that way."

"In a way. God created Grace, divine fire that is pure light. Angels are those who carry that Grace." Her father inclines his head. "As do you."

Gabby thinks of the alternative self she met under self-hypnosis. The Grace living within her.

"Angels born in Heaven are able to accept their angelic part easily. You were born on Earth and raised among humans. And your mother is human. It seems you haven't...accepted your angelic part as yet. That's why you've been having your episodes, and I suspect they're becoming more problematic. That's why you're here, asking for my help."

Gabby's eyes narrow ever so slightly. "I haven't asked for your help, yet." Ari's unconscious form flashes through her mind. "But yes, the episodes are becoming an issue."

"Angels are protectors. It is our role in Heaven and on Earth. The angel within you is coming out at times you've been in danger. And not just from demons. There are others who want to hurt you."

"Except she attacked my cousin," Gabby snaps.

Her father doesn't look surprised. "Angels also do what needs to be done. She's trying to show you what could happen if you don't accept this."

The angelic part of her, powered by Grace, will just take over anyway. And Gabby will have no memory of it, yet still live with the consequences.

"The sooner you accept your angel, the sooner the episodes will end," her father adds. "You'll be able to control your powers."

Gabby crosses her arms. "And I'll do what needs to be done, no matter what?"

He nods again, looking proud that's exactly what she'll become. "It is what angels do. We protect."

"So if I do this, it's my angel side who will run the show?" she asks, needing to confirm this.

"Humanity is what makes you weak. Emotional. No doubt impulsive. A war is brewing, it will only get in the way. You must accept your angelic side."

The same being that could father a child and leave before she was born.

It's everything she never wanted to be.

And yet, she can't continue to have these black outs. She's a danger to everyone like this, including those she loves. She can't live like that.

Her father watches her closely. "If you want to protect those you care about, and countless other lives who are in danger, then this is what must happen."

Gabby's arms fall to her side, her stomach clenching so hard it makes her nauseous. She has no choice.

It's possible she fought this too long as it is.

Her gaze rises to connect with her father's. "Let's do this."

His lips twitch as if they want to smile and something warms in his eyes. He's proud of her. Except the knowledge doesn't spark any reciprocal warmth in her. Her father's pride means nothing to her.

If anything, it makes her only more ill.

He turns to the celestial hound statue and places his hand on it. "We will do it within the safety of the club."

The club he mentioned. The one he wanted her to join.

The one she just agreed to become a part of.

"Apertum," he murmurs.

The statue's eyes blaze with light and then silently but swiftly it shifts backward, exposing a rectangular hole in the ground. Gabby steps forward and peers down, seeing a stairway leading into the bowels beneath the academy. She glances over her shoulder, wondering if it's too late to back out.

"Don't worry, I cast a spell. No one can see us," her father assures her, misreading her apprehension. "The moment I touched the statue, an illusion was cast over us. Anyone who might see us will just think it was a trick of the mind that we were here at all. It's the same for demons. This place is cloaked from those abominations."

He spits out the last word, his hatred apparent. She supposes they're born in Hell, making them angel arch enemies.

He waves his hand over the opening. "After you, daughter."

She stiffens, not liking him calling her that. She strides past him, her spine so straight it feels like it might snap. "I may be accepting being an angel, but you do not have the right to call me that."

She was raised by humans because he left her. She's dealing with all of this because of that. She'll never forgive him.

The staircase is a little longer than she expected, but she

quickly sees why. The area that opens out is huge. A strange mix of modern and ancient, there are monstrous stone columns holding up the high ceiling, an expansive granite floor, and yet an area to her left looks like a state of the art gym, another has couches with a large flatscreen TV, and another has a bank of computers.

"Wow, this place is massive," she says before she can stop herself.

"I've dedicated most of my time to establishing this place. A haven for supernaturals. A place for them to meet on neutral ground. Many friendships and alliances have been forged within these walls." He walks forward, his arm waving to the left. "The club spans the entirety of the academy. There are training grounds, entire wings dedicated to supernatural species, common rooms, gymnasiums, meeting rooms."

"And you built it?"

"Mostly. As an archangel, I felt it was my responsibility."

Gabby wonders at that. He didn't bother to care for the woman he impregnated or his child, and yet here he is, building a safe haven for who-knows-how-many. He's either more heartless than she expected, or he has an agenda of some kind.

He leads her through the area, their steps echoing in the expanse, then opens a door to his right. Inside is a room, two chairs sitting in the center. Like he's been planning for this.

"Take a seat," he says, his tone almost warm. "Let's get this underway."

Gabby does as she's told, despite the unease coiling through her. She doesn't want to be here. She doesn't want to do this.

She's about to lose everything about herself she was actually proud of. She's about to lose her humanity.

"Take a deep breath," her father instructs. "Relax."

"Last time I did that, it didn't end so well," she mutters.

He glances at her as he takes the seat beside her. "You did this on your own?"

"I tried some self-hypnosis. The angel took over to prove how strong she is."

He nods sagely. "The wall you've built to contain her, along with all the memories of what you did while she was in control, has no doubt left your angelic self frustrated. Self-hypnosis would have allowed her even more control."

And the first thing she did was attack Ari to prove a point.

This is the person Gabby's about to become.

"But once you accept your Grace, you'll also have access to your powers. You'll be able to protect those you care about. War is coming."

And she can protect them from herself.

Gabby nods sharply. "Let's do this," she says again as she settles into the chair and closes her eyes.

"I will help you reach your subconscious. It's quicker than human ways."

Gabby opens her eyes to look at him, maybe point out humans aren't as inferior as he thinks, but she finds herself in the blackness of her mind. Shit. She's already here.

The door appears in front of her, no longer decorated with locks. Waiting. No longer a barrier.

Throwing back her shoulders, Gabby steps through. She's not looking forward to it, but there's no other option.

The wall appears on the other side, her angel in front of it. Winged Gabby angles her head. "Back so soon, huh?"

"You hurt Arielle!"

"I did what needed to be done to protect you. Because you've pretended I don't exist, along with everything else behind that wall."

"Protect me?" snaps Gabby. "You got me suspended and hurt the one person I consider a sister!"

Winged Gabby shakes her head. "And you think that is the worst that is happening? What about the murders happening in Mercy City? Demons pouring into the world. And powerful forces with dark and evil intent." She hikes her hands on her hips. "That's what I'm trying to stop."

Gabby clenches her jaw. "You want to control me. To take over."

"In return, I will protect you. Give you powers you could only dream of."

Gabby looks away. None of that was ever on her Santa list. "Will I feel anything at all?" Her reflection looks at her in confusion. "If you take over, I'll lose my humanity, won't I? I've seen what my father is like. What you're like. I actually have emotions."

"Emotions?" she scoffs. "They only make you weak. They'll make us vulnerable."

"Sometimes," Gabby agrees. "But they also mean I care about others. Those I'm protecting," she points out archly. "Isn't that kind of important?"

There's nothing she won't do to protect those she cares about. The fact she's standing here is proof of that.

"And yet, you can't protect them without me."

Check. Mate.

Gabby glances at the wall behind her angelic self. Her very own Grace. "You expected to be in control from the beginning, didn't you?"

"I was willing to wait," she says archly. "But as you grew, you rejected me. The more I tried to reach out, the more securely you built that wall. And now you can't get to your memories, or the powers I would gift you with."

"And you only started breaking through recently," Gabby says thoughtfully.

"You're in danger now."

Gabby lifts her chin, staring at her mirror image. She's just realized she loves her family too much not to fight for this. "I'll let you out, or in, if that's what it takes, but I won't give you total control."

She reels back. "That's not how it works."

"I refuse to give up my humanity. You're welcome to come along for the ride, but I call the shots." Gabby holds her steely gaze even though she has no idea whether this is possible.

"Your humanity is your weakness," her angelic self spits. "You won't have the strength to fight me."

"So, if I stay in control, you agree?"

"If you stay in control, you have earned that right. I will grant you your powers and access to your memories."

Gabby doesn't point out that if she pulls off this impossible feat, her angelic self won't have a choice. The moment she accepts this, the wall will come crumbling down.

It's whether Gabby will still be herself that's in the balance.

She opens her arms wide. "Come on in, bestie."

Her angelic alter-ego nods resolutely and walks toward her. As she moves, she morphs back into a blazing white ball. In a blink, she shoots toward Gabby's chest, impaling and diffusing all at once.

Gabby arches as power surges through her, both euphoric and overwhelming. She feels it spread through her torso. Explode up her spine.

Streak straight for her mind.

And she welcomes it, just like she said she would. The time for fighting is over.

The time for accepting her truth is here.

White light bursts behind her eyes as she's filled with Grace. It saturates her. Engulfs her from the inside out.

But she doesn't let it overwhelm her.

Instead, she welcomes it with warmth. She connects with it.

And wraps herself around it in the same way it is her. She allows her humanity to be what greets her angelic self.

At first, her Grace fights it, tries to dominate. Only to find there's nothing to dominate. Gabby can't win this with strength.

But she can meet it with what makes humans strong. Love.

How can someone truly protect something, fight for it, when it doesn't deeply care about the outcome?

She senses the Grace's surprise. Initial resistance. But then it melts. Welcomes the novel feeling.

It seamlessly, beautifully becomes a part of her.

With a startle, Gabby looks around, not quite believing she did it. She'd been fighting this all along, when all she needed was to embrace it.

The wall is gone. There are far more memories behind it than she ever thought and they bombard her mind. Shapes and images, places she's never seen before, become part of her mind.

Gabby's eyes fly open with a gasp.

And they hold the answers to the murders.

23

GABBY

Gabby stands in the corridor, watching students walk past. Everything looks normal. The odd burst of laughter, a few harried frowns, the eclectic mix of fashion she's come to associate with Mercy Academy.

And yet, everything is different.

There's a fire banked within her, waiting. Impatient to explode in all its glory.

At the same time, she's calm in a way she's never been before. Whole. A piece she didn't know was missing has been found.

She's an angel. Well, a half one. But she can sense already, a powerful one.

Zach wanders past with a couple of friends and Gabby tenses. He was a victim of her split persona and as much as she wishes she could change that, she can't. But he smiles at her as he passes. "Hey, Gabby."

"Ah, hey, Zach."

He continues on as if she didn't plaster him to a wall. "What the..."

"I took the courtesy of wiping their memories of what

happened," her father says beside her, once more under the guise of Mr. Bishop. "You're still suspended, but only those you want will know what happened."

Gabby clears her throat. "Thanks."

Now he's making a show of looking out for her?

And yet, the same hatred she felt has gone. A part of her understands why he did it. Her angelic part. Not that she forgives him, or is planning on hugging him or anything cutesy like that, but she's not bitter anymore.

"One day you'll be able to do the same," he says. "I'll teach you that and much more. Once you tell me why we're standing here.

"Like I said, we're waiting." One of the first things Gabby did when she came out of her trance, was send a couple of text messages. Her father had watched silently, obviously aware things hadn't turned out like he expected them to.

"For what? Or whom?"

"For us," answers a female voice to their right.

Gabby instantly smiles at the sound of Sierra's voice. It grows when she sees Blaise with her. Then falters when she registers the person standing behind them.

Colt.

He smiles a little, a delicious warmth flickering in the depths of his chocolate eyes. Her own lips tip up in response, almost instinctively. Now that she's being honest with herself, she can admit she's drawn to him. And he obviously knows about the supernatural. Is he one himself, like Blaise? He's definitely not angelic—she'd be able to sense that. Or is he a human who's learned there's far more moving in the shadows than most people realize, like Sierra?

"Why are they here, Gabby?" her father asks tersely, glaring largely at Colt.

"Because there's something I need to share with all of you."

She spins on her heel and walks across the corridor, heading to the Assembly Hall.

She doesn't speak as she opens a door just before it and slips down the narrow corridor. At the end is a stairway and Gabby continues down it, all four of the others throwing her puzzled glances. She just smiles and continues on.

The basement at the bottom is dark and gloomy, and rather musty, with a door ahead. Gabby steps through, entering a small room with little more than a few piles of old papers and several spider webs.

Sierra wrinkles her nose. "We couldn't do this somewhere else?"

Gabby grins. Her aunt's fear of spiders is deeply entrenched. So deeply she passed it onto her daughter, Arielle. "The good news is, we're not staying." She walks to the center of the room and looks down. "The bad news is, these arachnids are the ones who escaped."

Sierra's eyes narrow as she follows Gabby's gaze. "Escaped from where?"

Gabby squats, her finger tracing a barely perceptible symbol on the tiled floor. One in the shape of arched wings.

Instantly, a square area of tiles disappear as if they were never there. Gabby straightens. The Gabby of earlier today would've been shocked and amazed. But now that she remembers everything, she knows she's done this several times.

In fact, far more times than she could've guessed.

"What I want to show you is down here," she says, descending this next set of stairs.

"Urgh," mutters Sierra. "I hate going into these places."

"It's better than descending into Hell," says Colt under his breath.

Gabby frowns as she continues down. What does he mean by that? She can sense there's something more to Colt, but surely he's not familiar with Hell itself. Would she sense if he's a demon?

With a quick shake of her head, Gabby pushes the thought aside. She's accepted her angel side. She'd feel if he was dangerous, just like she did when she sensed the demon she chased and fought. He's most likely human but with far too much magnetism.

She reaches the next floor down, a basement beneath a basement, the smell of stale, damp air tickling her nose. It's dark, but Gabby already knows what this place looks like. She's the one who did all the interior decorating.

"What is this?" her father asks.

She flicks the light switch. "Apparently I found it during one of my episodes."

The room's flooded with light, revealing one wall full of newspaper clippings and another with a large map of Mercy City. Pins have been used to mark certain locations, red ribbon tied between.

Gabby turns to the others as they try to absorb it all. "All of this information relates to the serial murders." She lets out a breath. "And I know who committed them."

Stunned silence is her only response.

"Who was it?" demands her father. "Which demons?"

Colt crosses his arms, staying a couple of feet behind everyone else even as he watches with keen interest. He hasn't said much but it's clear he's taking in everything.

"Actually, it's a bit of a story, so make yourself at home," says Gabby. Sierra rolls her eyes at that and Gabby grins at her. "The spiders certainly have."

"You're lucky I love you," says Sierra with a mock frown.

Gabby blows her a kiss then falls serious again. She moves to the map, pointing at one of the pins. "Mr. Hahn was the first murder," Gabby starts. "A single bachelor living in a studio apartment in Silver Deeps, a south-western suburb of Mercy City. He was found dead, the skin of his chest removed."

"Just like all the others," says Blaise. "Which the police didn't make public."

Gabby nods. "This was six weeks before my first day here. It's around that time I started investigating all this. I could sense the dark powers."

"But you said you only had episodes since last week?" her aunt asks, concerned.

"Apparently not. It seems this has been going on for longer than that, I just never did anything that impacted me like here at the academy. It all came back to me today, thanks to my father," she says, indicating toward him.

"What?" gasps Sierra.

Sierra spins toward Mr. Bishop, except the old security supervisor is no longer standing there. Gabriel, tall and proud, nods regally at her. "I am Gabby's father, Archangel Gabriel."

Sierra's hands bunch into fists. "You have a lot of nerve," she growls, looking away in disgust. "Prick."

Gabriel doesn't acknowledge her fiercely said words, looking as impenetrable as a statue. Gabby's both glad her aunt hasn't let him escape the consequences of his action and that it doesn't seem to have affected her father. She glances away, noting the way Colt's lips twitch and she once more wonders at how much he knows. And how.

She looks back at the map, focusing on what she needs to tell them. "I've been doing all this research at night, not that I realized it at the time. I visited Mr. Hahn's apartment, and sensed dark energies there. Interestingly, I wasn't even tired the following day. The angel part of me was no longer willing to sit around quietly. She did all this."

"And this room?" asks Sierra.

"I set this up not long after arriving at the academy. To have somewhere to collate all the information," explains Gabby. She points to the next pin. "A week after the first, another murder happened. This time, a couple. Mr and Mrs. Geller. An old couple living in a western area called Fraser Town. Same thing. The skin of their chests had been cut away and taken. Again, the same dark energies."

Gabby then moves on the next one. "Mr. And Mrs. Humphrey died next, again the same modus operandi and the energies. They died in Golden Heights. Their son studies here at the Academy, and he was quite rude to me on my first day. I didn't understand it until I remembered that I spoke with him about his parents' death. He was terrified, having witnessed everything himself. He's the one who gave me the description of the killers. There were seven of them, which can't have been a coincidence. Seven killers. Seven days between the murders. And he described wings. That made me reach the obvious conclusion of demons."

Her father nods grimly. "As I suspected," he says, flashing a glance at Colt.

He acknowledges Gabriel's words. "Demons are certainly capable of committing these kind of murders."

"And yet, it never occured to me that—" she shakes her head. "I'm getting ahead of myself. The next murders happened a couple of weeks before I came here, in Mercy City Park. Both, a couple who appeared not have no connection to the first two murders. That is until I dug a little deeper." Gabby points to a stack of folders on a desk. "My research showed that none of them had family in the area. What's more, one person in each couple had the same midwife at their birth. I tracked her down my first night here."

"I didn't see you leave," her father says, frowning.

"I was careful," she says with a shrug. "But when I found her, I discovered she was being hunted."

"Hunted?" says Blaise. "By whom?"

"Demons. Although they didn't hang around. The woman didn't want to speak at first..."

"You convinced her?" asks Gabby's father.

Gabby ducks her head, unsure how she feels about this particular memory. "I told her I'd let the demons take her if she didn't."

Sierra shakes her head. "Gabby!"

"I didn't mean it!" At least, she's pretty sure she didn't.

"Angels will do what needs to be done," grunts her father.

And he certainly would've followed through with the threat. When Gabby came out of her trance, he seemed to instantly realize she was still in control. He'd looked impressed and disappointed.

Doing something that hasn't really been done before means no can be sure what this will look like moving forward. What she'll look like.

"Anyway," she continues, "I found the woman was descended from an ancient bloodline. A direct descendant of the French revolutionary Joan of Arc. This witch told me that they've been tasked with being the protectors of the seven families and always transferred parchments of some kind—which she wouldn't tell me anything about—from generation to generation in those families. These parchments were hidden beneath the skin."

"That's what the killers wanted," says Sierra.

Gabby nods. "That's why the skin of the victims was taken. I returned to the academy and erected the barrier to keep myself from harm. I knew demons were on the loose in numbers."

Her gaze flickers to Colt then quickly away. That was the night she turned up outside his room.

"And then the nightclub massacre happened," she says. "It brought the total to six murders. And I knew somehow there would be more... But getting to the nightclub was impossible, seeing as I'd erected the barrier. Even I couldn't pass through it." She falls silent and looks at the board, focusing on the pin indicating the sixth location of the serial murders.

"You went there, didn't you?" asks Colt.

"I don't know how, but I figured out a way to be in two places at once. During Mrs. Keelin's class, I was not only writing down stuff in my book but I was also checking out the nightclub."

Her father's eyebrows shoot up. "You discovered bi-projection? All on your own?"

"If that's what it's called, then yes."

"If your powers are progressing at this rate, we need to help you harness them," her father says somberly.

"When there's time. While I was at the nightclub, I discovered who we're dealing with. I found myself face-to-face with one heck of a demon. He called himself Belphegor."

Her father's fists clench. "That foul demon is here," he snarls. "He's the one who's murdering these people, ain't he?"

Gabby shakes her head. "I thought so at first, but then I sensed a different aura on him and the leftover energy. Also, I'd already met you then. And the familiarity of that leftover energy matched yours." She draws in a steadying breath. "The murders aren't demonic. They are angelic."

The revelation rockets through the room. Sierra and Blaise look stunned. Colt looks thoughtful. Gabby's father looks furious.

"No angel would hurt humans like this," he scoffs. "You're wrong."

"No, I'm not," she says, noting his surprise at her denial. She supposes if her angel side had won, she'd defer to him more easily. "I looked into it further with the help of the archdemon you seem to hate so much. He knew someone's murdering humans and pinning it on demons, adding fuel to a war already brewing between them and angels. And it's worked. Angels and demons have been concentrating on each other instead of focusing on the dark essence left behind at the murder sites. Including you," she says to her father. "And yet the enemy is very much angelic."

"Who do you believe has done this?" her father demands.

"The Grigori," says Gabby simply.

The next wave of shock has Sierra and Blaise going pale. Even Colt looks a little washed out. Her father's skin takes on a greenish tint.

"The Grigori," says Sierra in a low voice. "They're the stuff of legends and myths. They were tasked with guarding the Garden of Eden, but they failed and were punished. Nobody has heard of them since."

"How could they have returned?" asks Blaise.

Gabby shrugs. "I've no idea, but they're most definitely behind these murders. The demons are sure of it. Even Belphegor remembers their wicked scent."

"And you're taking that foul demon's word for it?" her father fumes, his silver wings unfurling.

"He wants this solved as much as we do," she says with a shrug, noting the way her father's frown deepens. "And with every kill, the Grigori have become stronger. That's what the pyres were about. Amassing power. That doesn't bode well for the final family they intend to kill."

"The seventh murder?" breathes Blaise.

Gabby's gut churns as she points to the six pins. "They form a shape. One that's not complete."

"A heptagon," says Colt, his lips thinning.

"Which means we need to find the seventh family. And we only have a few hours before the Grigori attack. Based on my research I've narrowed it down to three families who live in the south-east of the city."

Sierra straightens. "You can't go after them, Gabby."

"Of course I am. We're going to need to split up. We can't tell the cops, they'll be in as much danger as the victims. And I don't know what's on those parchments, but we can't let the Grigori get their hands on the final one."

Sierra opens her mouth, but Gabby speaks again. "I'm doing this, Sierra. I need to."

Blaise steps forward. "Then Colt goes with you."

Everyone startles at that, including Gabby and Colt. Gabby's father draws in a breath to speak, but Colt quickly jumps in. "I'll go with her."

Gabby's gaze falls on him. For some reason, she likes the idea of them being a team. And she knows he can fight. She lifts her chin. "Let's end this."

24

COLT

C olt climbs out of his car as he stares at the large, sprawling house across the road. Sierra and Blaise went to the address on Foxglove Street, while Gabriel went to Wordsworth Avenue, probably recruiting a few more angels along the way. Colt and Gabby have the Daniels' house on Burlington Road.

Gabby exits, too, and comes to stand beside him, her gaze just as focused on the house. "I think my dorm room would fit in their pantry."

Colt grunts in agreement. The dark green hedge surrounding the large block is as well-kept as the rest of the manicured gardens. The three-story house is just as immaculate and opulent. The Daniels come from money, courtesy of a large portfolio in oil and natural gas.

It's one of the reasons Colt suggested they take it. The place has guards at the front gates, and no doubt top of the range security. After a quick bit of his own research, he figured even if the Daniels were the target, the Grigori won't be getting into here easily.

"The Sins are in Hell, and still, people live like this," he mutters.

Gabby glances at him. "You think they're greedy?"

"Most rich people are."

She angles her head, her curls slipping over her shoulder. "You talk about the Sins as if they're an entity rather than a quality."

Colt slides a glance her way. She's more perceptive than he'd like. "I would say both. Haven't you ever heard of the Seven Sins?"

"In Biblical terms? Yes. But I thought of them more as something we feel or do."

"Some people believe they're demons who inhabit a particular domain in Hell." He stops, realizing he's saying too much. "At least, that's what I hear."

"From where?" she asks, looking even more interested.

The curious way she's looking at him tells him she hasn't learned he's a demon yet. No angel would gaze at him like that, interested and intrigued. It's a good thing. It's an indicator of how well he's masked his aura. If an angel cannot find him, no demon can either.

Perhaps if he ran away now, Belphegor might not be able to follow. Colt could disappear again.

Yet, he doesn't move. Running would mean leaving Gabby behind. He tells himself it's because Gabby obviously means something to Blaise, and therefore, by extension, he'll protect Gabby just like the witch, but he knows he's lying.

He agreed to come here before Gabriel could object. Or offer to go himself.

Colt feels protective of this girl, angel halfling or not. He will not leave her to face this alone.

He clears his throat, realizing too much time has passed since Gabby asked her questions. "Ah, most of my information comes from books, particularly Dante's Inferno," he answers. "It was an interesting take on Sins, that's all."

Gabby twitches her lips. "A martial arts teacher who also teaches music, and you read some weird ass books. Why are you here, Colt? With me."

She asked the very same question he just did himself. But there's no way he's saying out loud what he can't put to words himself. Demons aren't usually protective. They tend to look out for themselves and themselves only.

"That's not a quick answer," he says gruffly. "And we need to focus. What's the plan?"

Gabby turns back to the house, seeming to agree with him. "Protect them."

"That's not a plan," he points out. "That's more of an aspiration."

She throws him a disgruntled glance. "Give me a sec, okay?"

Colt pushes away from the car, every fiber going into high alert. "I can't. They're here."

Gabby's startled eyes follow his line of sight, registering the seven lights descending from the sky.

Straight onto the house.

Without warning, Gabby breaks into a run. Colt sprints after her, quickly catching up. "We should call the others. Even your father."

He can't believe he suggested that, but they're about to face the Grigori. Colt hasn't heard much about them, but what he has tells him they're a formidable foe. And there's seven of them.

"No time," pants Gabby, running straight up the front entrance. "We need to get in," she tells the two guards who just leaped to attention, their hands on their guns.

The two men glance at each other. "Nick off," says the taller one.

"You don't understand," she says urgently. "The Daniels' lives are in danger."

"What? Some sikh wants their oil?" says the other, nudging his friend. "They don't actually store the oil here."

The two men chuckle and Gabby's hands tighten into fists.

"Gabby," Colt starts, conscious of the frustration building within her. "They're just doing their jobs. Maybe we should—"

She takes a step closer to the men, making them tense. "You have no idea what you're up against."

The taller one narrows his eyes. "You threatening us, girl?"

Gabby bristles and Colt quickly steps behind her. He needs to do something before this gets out of hand. He catches the men's gazes and silently mouths a spell. The men blink.

The second one steps back. "Apologies, we realize this must be important. Please, go on through."

The taller guard walks over to the gate and presses a button and they open.

Thankfully, Gabby doesn't have time to ask about their sudden change of behavior. The seven lights have disappeared into the mansion.

Colt and Gabby break into a run just as two screams echo from within. One male. One female. And both terrified.

There's a large stained glass window beside the front door and without breaking stride, Colt powers through it. Colored shards of glass explode but he's unscathed, thanks to a quickly muttered spell.

Colt finds himself in a large foyer, a shimmering humanoid figure before him.

A Grigori.

He opens his hand and one of the shards flies into it. With a quick flick of his wrist, the glass impales the angel. It screeches and runs at him, white fingernails extended, when Gabby crashes through the door with such force, that timber hits the wall on the other side.

Instantly, they're beside each other, fists raised.

The Grigori shrieks again, and six others join it. Seven shimmering beings line up, white fire blazing from their eye sockets.

"Colt," breathes Gabby.

He sees it, too. The one on the end is holding a brown parchment, blood staining the edges.

They're too late.

With a cry, Gabby runs at them, executing a flying kick at the nearest Grigori. It stumbles back but quickly rights itself, leaping back at her, wings now extended. With a move almost too fast to be visible, it swipes a backhand across Gabby's face, snapping her head to the side.

Colt curses. It seems they're fighting seven ancient angels.

With a leap, he spears at the Grigori who just struck Gabby, punching him as hard as he can in the chest. The body he hits is as solid and as cold as marble, and this time, just as unmoving. But the angel's focus is now on Colt, which is what he wanted. He blocks the next strike, ducks the one after that.

There's a soft oomph beside him and he sees that two other Grigori have closed in on Gabby. She's fast as she deflects and punches, but they're faster. And a third is moving to join them.

One lands a punch on Gabby's cheek with enough force to break the skin and draw blood. Fury detonates through Colt and he has to work to contain his wings. He launches a kick that's powerful enough to shove the Grigori back, but as soon as there's an opening, another of the vile beings takes its place.

And this one is crackling with rage.

It spins, contracts, then explodes with energy as two hands propel into Gabby's chest. The force throws her backward, straight through a window on the other side of the room.

"Gabby!" roars Colt.

Torn between going after her and punishing these creatures for hurting her, he lashes out with a ball of fire. It's immediately extinguished by seven counter fireballs, eliciting a cackle from one of the Grigori. The one holding the parchment.

"Too little, too late, demon."

In quick succession, the Grigori vanish, taking the seventh parchment with them.

Gabby comes running back through the shattered window, only to stop when she sees they no longer have any opponent. "Where did they go?" she cries.

Colt lets out a long breath, relieved to see she's okay. "Funnily enough, they escaped with the parchment."

Gabby plants her hands on her hips. "You're going to say we should've called my father, aren't you?"

"It appears I don't need to."

He expects another snarky comment, but Gabby's shoulders droop. "I just wanted to..."

Before Colt can answer, her eyes widen and she rushes into the adjoining living room. He joins her, already knowing what they'll find.

Two bodies lie on the floor, blood soaking into the cream carpet. The skin of both their chests is missing. A heptagon crafted from more blood surrounds them.

Gabby clutches her stomach. "We were too late."

Colt doesn't say anything as he kneels beside the dead bodies, confirming they died like all the others. Painfully, but swiftly.

He sighs. Gabby's obviously hurting at the loss of life. She doesn't need to be reminded they should've had a more concrete plan. She hasn't grown up in this world. The one he's spent hundreds of years in. A world where death waits around every corner.

She wouldn't have considered that if the Grigori weren't so

focused on protecting the final piece of the parchment, then she and Colt would now be in the same state as Douglas and Meredith Daniels.

He did. Which is why they should have at least called Gabriel.

"What now?" she asks, subdued.

"We go back to the academy and plan our next move. The Grigori have all seven parchments now. They'll use them to find whatever it is they lead to."

And Colt can already sense it will be far more dangerous and deadly than any of them can fathom.

She nods mutely as he pushes to his feet.

They've both turned to leave when they freeze.

The wail of police sirens pierces the blood-stained air.

"Skata," mutters Colt.

Law enforcement is the last complication they need right now.

25

GABBY

"**S**hitsticks," says Gabby. "We can't get caught by the police!" Not with two dead bodies beside them.

Right now, very little stands between the Grigori and whatever they're planning. And they're it.

"No, we cannot," agrees Colt.

She glances at him. He curses in other languages and speaks like he's a hundred and five. What is with this guy?

As always, there's no time to unravel the mystery. Gabby looks around frantically. Their closest exit is the window she was thrown through. She noted that the entirety of the rear of the house is surrounded by an eight-foot concrete wall, but maybe they can find somewhere to hide.

There's the soft crunching of glass under boot from the foyer. The cops are entering the house.

Gabby and Colt have seconds before they're caught in the company of a dead Mr. and Mrs. Daniels. And become key suspects.

"We need to run," she hisses.

He shakes his head. "They'll hear us." He grabs her hand

and pulls her over to an alcove with a large vase on a marble stand, tucking themselves behind it.

He's joking right? Colt was obviously crap at hide and seek as a child.

She turns to him but he plants his hand on her mouth, making her eyes pop open. "Shh," he mouths. With his other hand, he waves his fingers over them.

There's no time to object, because two police officers enter the room, guns drawn.

Gabby's eyes widen so much they hurt. She holds still, Colt's hand still across her mouth, pressed against him behind the vase.

One is a young man in a uniform, the other a woman in her forties wearing a navy blue suit, both wearing bullet proof vests. Gabby instantly recognizes the woman from her research on the murders. Detective Riley Espinosa has led the investigation into the serial killings. She's a hard, practical looking woman, her dark hair permanently pulled in a tight bun.

She would totally shoot first, ask questions later.

Detective Espinosa and her offsider enter, guns sweeping the room as they scan it. To Gabby's surprise, they don't see her and Colt tucked behind the overgrown vase, standing as still as statues.

They notice the two dead bodies and walk over cautiously. The male office keeps scanning as the detective squats down. "Same M.O.," she growls. "The bastards have struck again."

"For fuck's sake," says the other cop. "They're turning us into laughing stocks. The media are going to shred us."

Detective Espinosa pushes to her feet, eyes still narrowed. "We're closing in. I can feel it."

Impossibly, Gabby goes even more still. She calcifies every shred of her body. Espinosa is a smart cookie. It's only a matter of time before they're found. Hiding. It couldn't look much worse.

The detective's sharp gaze slowly sweeps the room. Gabby stops breathing, but her heart is like a freight train. Its thundering is surely going to give them away. Somehow, Colt is impossibly calm beside her.

Espinosa's eyes travel straight over the vase, even pause for a second before continuing on.

She didn't see them!

"Let's secure the crime scene," she mutters to the other cop. "Call in forensics."

The two stalk out of the room, leaving Gabby shocked. She turns to Colt, yanking his hand away. "What just happened?" she hisses.

He lifts his other hand, an amethyst ring on it she's never noticed before. "I cast an illusion spell over us. I was gifted this by a powerful witch. It allows me to wield some basic magic."

"Oh." One more what-the-frick piece of information about this guy. "Well, ah, thanks."

He nods, something shifting in his dark gaze.

That's all it takes for her to become aware of how close they're standing. That their bodies are pressed against each other. That their faces are only inches apart.

Sweet ghosts.

The dream she had where she straddled him flares in her mind. Her body temperature spikes.

Colt's chest is all hard planes and intriguing angles. The biceps she's gripping feel like they've been molded from hot steel. And his lips... They part on a barely perceptible inhale.

The motion feels like it's drawing her in. One she has no intention of resisting.

There's something not quite right about him.

Gabby startles at the voice in her head, quickly realizing it's her angelic side. Her freaking Grace is talking to her.

It's why you didn't want to let him pass on your first day.

He's dangerous. You sense it, too.

She pulls back a little, not liking that her angelic part just pointed out what she's conveniently forgotten. There are too many pieces of Colt that don't add up.

He may be dangerous, but so am I, she snaps back, conscious the only person she's giving attitude is herself.

"We need to get out of here," says Colt, stiffening a little.

Gabby removes her hands, trying to gain what little distance she can without knocking over the vase and giving them away. "We could try the window," she says, indicating to the one she was propelled through.

"Is there an exit out the back?"

She presses her lips together. Colt is definitely a guy who likes to think things through. "I didn't see it, but I didn't get a good look. I was running back in here to save you."

He snorts. "I suggest we go out the front door while I maintain the illusion spell."

"Just two invisible bodies, crunching over broken glass?"

"Very well," he says with a huff. "We'll go out the window."

They run as quickly and silently as possible to the gaping opening ringed by shards of glass. A slight breeze tickles Gabby's hair as they dart through the gardens, the first hint of freedom. The white wall at the rear of the garden is just in sight when a voice reaches them.

"Stop!"

Crap! They've been seen.

Neither Gabby nor Colt stop, let alone glance over their shoulders. They keep running, even as she knows there's no way she can scale the high wall.

"Stop, or I'll shoot!"

There's the crack of a gunshot, making Gabby duck but nothing breaks her stride. They reach the wall, Gabby stopping herself with her hands on the rough surface. She runs her hands over it as she looks up. There are no footholds. Nothing for her to grab onto.

She can't make it over.

Which only leaves one out.

She spins around, much to Colt's shock, and faces the cop.

"Don't show your face," hisses Colt.

"Do you have any cash on you?"

"I beg your pardon?"

"You heard me. Maybe we can bribe him."

"You think you'll be able to buy our freedom?" he asks incredulously.

The cop rounds a lush tree, his gun pointed at them. "Put your hands up where I can see them."

Gabby and Colt do as they're told. "Do you have a better idea?" she asks him under her breath.

"We could have used our abilities to jump the wall!"

"Our abilities?" asks Gabby, confused.

"I mean, you're an angel. You could have leaped the wall and taken me with you."

Shit. Why didn't she think of that?

"No more talking," shouts the cop, approaching with the gun steadily pointed at them. "Detective Espinosa is going to have some questions for you."

Gabby clenches her jaw. "We didn't kill them."

Colt's hands twitch where they are above his head. "Be quiet," he hisses. "For someone who was raised human, you certainly seem to know little of their ways."

"Sorry," she snaps. "I've never been caught by the cops before, okay?"

"First rule, don't talk," he growls.

"Quiet!" shouts the cop. "You have the right to remain silent."

"We can't just stand here and let him arrest us!" hisses Gabby. They have Grigori to find.

"Anything you say can and will be used against you—" he stops, his eyes widening as they focus somewhere above their heads.

Gabby takes a risk and looks up, her breath disintegrating. Beams of white lights are streaking toward them.

"Angels," she whispers.

"What the fuck is that?" squeaks the cop as he frantically grapples with the radio on his shoulder.

Gabby's about to answer when he turns and runs back to the house. He's only taken a few steps when he bursts into flames. He doesn't even have a chance to scream before he's engulfed. Stumbling, he falls to the grass, disintegrating into ash.

Horrified, she watches as the angels land on the ground, far more than she expected. Their wings contract but don't disappear. One of them steps forward, dark-haired and pale-skinned. "And here we find the two abominations."

"Samandriel's faction," mutters Colt.

"Samandri-who?" asks Gabby, trying to understand what's going on. These angels don't look friendly. And why would they call Colt an abomination?

"Even less trustworthy than most angels. The scum is mentally unstable."

Which doesn't make anything clearer. A little part of Gabby wishes Detective Espinosa would turn up. Except she'd and her men would probably end up like the poor cop who's now little more than fertilizer for an already lush lawn.

"What do you want?" she demands.

"We don't owe you an explanation," spits the angel. "Only know that you're about to die."

Ice prickles through Gabby's veins. There's a hard edge to the angel's eyes that tells her he intends on following through on the threat.

But why would they want her dead? Does her father know about this?

"If you attack, we'll fight," says Gabby, knowing they have no other choice. "This won't end well for your men."

Colt moves a little closer to Gabby. "You'd be surprised what abominations are capable of."

"Shut up," snaps the angel. "Your talk won't save you. You're vastly outnumbered."

He's right. There's at least thirty of them. And only Gabby and Colt.

The angels spread out in a semicircle, trapping them. Their eyes flash silver fire as they close in, faces hard and cold.

Colt grabs Gabby's hand. "You need to trust me."

She throws him a glare. "You're kidding me, right?"

He's asking her to trust him, when he's more of a mystery than Santa Claus?

"We have no other choice."

He wraps his arms around her, and to Gabby's surprise, she lets him. She has no idea who he is or what he plans, but she finds herself moving closer. Maybe she's drawn to his strength. Maybe she's more terrified than she realizes.

Or maybe she trusts him, even though she has no reason to.

Colt flashes a smile, the jolt of pleasure echoing somewhere in her chest.

Without warning, massive black wings explode from his back. With one powerful pump, the ground disappears beneath Gabby's feet.

She holds onto Colt with everything she has as they soar

into the sky. Somewhere below, the angel calls out but she barely hears it.

Wind is rushing past her face. Her heartbeat is thundering against her eardrums.

And she's trying to process what just happened.

She's flying.

And Colt's a goddamned freaking demon!

To say Gabby's pissed is an understatement. A big one.

Colt's been lying to her the whole time.

She knows she shouldn't be surprised. That she shouldn't be hurt.

But she most certainly is.

They don't go far, landing on the roof of a mansion only a block away. He releases her, the red-tipped onyx wings disappearing like they were never there.

Except they undeniably were.

Irrefutable evidence that Colt is a demon. And according to her father, her enemy.

Colt watches her, his chocolate eyes guarded. He's waiting for her to say something. Gabby's glad there's no time.

She has no idea what to say.

She points over his shoulder at the white beams blazing through the sky. "They're coming."

"Quick," he says through tight lips. "We need to go inside." He opens a nearby door, waiting for Gabby to go through.

She's about to blindly do as she's asked, just like she has every other time, but she pauses. "Where exactly are we going?"

He looks like he's about to frown as he glances at the approaching angels, but then returns his gaze to her. "This is Sinclair Mansion. There's a room on the ground floor that I believe can help us."

"You mean, save your ass," she snaps, striding past him and inside, finding herself at the top of a flight of stairs.

There's a thud behind her. "Run!" shouts Colt.

This time, she does exactly as she's asked. She glances over her shoulder, seeing Colt slam the door shut and wave his hand over it. It rattles as the angels try to open it, but remains closed.

He used his magic to lock it from the inside.

His demon magic.

Stay away from him. I told you he's dangerous.

Not now, she hisses to the voice in her mind. At the moment, the focus is not dying.

They find themselves in a room full of furniture covered in sheets. A crash sounds above them. The angels have broken through Colt's spell.

He runs past her to the door. "Quick, this way."

Another flight of stairs takes them to the first floor, down a narrow hallway, then more stairs to the ground floor. Colt leads the way to the other end of the house, where there are two doors at the end of a corridor. Gabby goes right, pretty sure it's a way out, but Colt grabs her hand and pulls her to the other.

"We can't outrun them."

He yanks her through and shuts the heavy door behind them with a thud. Gabby spins around, finding herself in a large circular room, seven large wooden beams spaced along the wall at regular intervals. Shelves line the stone walls, full of books. The floor is also stone, a strange star carved into the center.

"What is this place?" she asks.

"A sort of supernatural safehouse, I believe," says Colt, looking far calmer as he steps away from the door. "It grants protection from those who would seek to harm you. Whatever the spell, it recognizes the threat and wards you against it. The angels can't reach us."

So they're safe. For now.

Except she's now trapped in a room with a lying-assed demon. Gabby plants her hands on her hips. "We can't stay here forever."

Colt glances around. "Although the reading material would probably be fascinating, no, we can't." He raises a brow. "We need to call for backup."

The angel within her contracts with anger, and for once, Gabby agrees with her.

He's a smug lying-assed demon.

And the truly, deeply annoying thing is, he's right. "Fine. Do it."

Colt looks at her for a long moment and she wonders if he's going to say anything, but he turns away and pulls his cell phone out. His call to her father is short and terse. The animosity between them suddenly makes so much more sense. Colt's call to Blaise is more relaxed and full of assurances they're okay.

Which means Blaise knew all along who Colt is. What he is.

Stinging betrayal slices through the anger. Everyone's been lying to her.

Suddenly, a wave of dizziness washes through her and she presses her hand to her forehead. But the feeling only grows. Gabby staggers and falls to her knees, the pain of the stone floor barely registering.

Reality dissolves as a vision overcomes her.

Seven black stones are sitting on a circular slice of rock, creating the seven points of a heptagon. Inky wisps of smoke rise from each one, oozing as if the small pieces of rock are burning. And yet, they're the color of onyx. Of black ice. Of death.

A hand appears above, shimmering and white, as a voice intones words Gabby doesn't recognize. The rough, harsh dialect grates over her nerves. The stone pieces rise, hovering a few feet above the rock, before spearing to the center. They come together, forming a single, black stone.

There's a blast of white light, the energy powering through Gabby. She cries out, her eyes flying open to find Colt kneeling in front of her.

"Gabby," he says, clearly concerned. "Are you okay?"

She's not, but she shoves his hands away and gets to her feet, glad to find them steady. "I'm fine, thank you very much."

"You just saw something, didn't you?"

Dammit. She forgot he doesn't miss much. Probably a demon thing.

Before she can tell him where to shove his unwanted concern, the door bursts open.

Gabby and Colt are instantly ready to fight. It turns out Colt's intel that this place is a supernatural haven was wrong.

But it's only one angel who enters. Her father.

"We took care of the angels," he announces. "The threat is gone."

Gabby straightens, hoping he's not expecting a round of applause. Her father is simply another person who's kept unforgivable secrets from her.

Sierra and Blaise appear behind him, and Gabby almost rushes to them. Almost. Instead, she takes a small step back, noting the way Sierra frowns.

Her father looks around. "Keepers," he mutters.

Sierra stills, looking around.

Gabby also does a quick scan, wondering what he's talking about. Sierra seems to know. "Keepers?"

He shakes his head. "Nothing. I was just...reminded of something."

Gabby stiffens as she glances at her aunt, but Sierra quickly looks away. More half-truths and lies. More burning anger and stinging betrayal.

"What happened?" he asks, seemingly clueless to Gabby's turmoil. "Why were angels trying to attack you?"

Colt glances at Gabby, then quickly provides a summary of everything that's just happened.

Gabriel's gaze sharpens on her. "You should've called me. You may be more powerful than anyone realized, but you're untrained. You can't run into situations like that."

Her father believing he has the right to chastise her is the last straw. Gabby stalks toward him and punches her finger into his chest. "Look, Dad," she sneers. "If you'd been there for one freaking second of my life, I'd be inclined to believe I can depend on you. But you weren't. So back the frig off."

Her father's blond brows shoot up. The rest of the room is silent.

Probably because he's an archangel. And she just cursed in his face.

If Gabby was smart, she'd apologize for the outburst. But she's still too hurt and angry. Plus, he needs to face the consequences of his actions. He's not waltzing into her life and telling her what to do.

"Now, what do you know about seven pieces of black stone?" she asks, stepping back and crossing her arms. "Each one seeming to have a life of its own, being fused together by an angel?"

A new type of surprise washes over his face. A worried type. "Where did you see this?"

Gabby glances at Colt. "I had a vision just before you

entered. I saw the pieces come together. There was one heck of a mushroom cloud after."

Her father steps back, stroking his jaw. "It couldn't be..."

"What is it?" demands Gabby. She's not going to let him evade her answers this time.

"These seven pieces you saw are part of a dark entity known as the obsidian."

"No, it can't be," breathes Blaise, her face pale.

Her father's face is grim as he continues. "Its creation is a long story, much of which is forgotten, but legend has it that when Christ was crucified, the power from his death was used by Lucifer and his demons to throw this single stone into the world, powered by the darkness of Hell. Once it was let loose in the world, it made humans do terrible things. Evil for the sake of evil. Its power only grew with every kill it inspired. The angel Uriel tried to destroy it but couldn't. So, instead, he broke the stone into seven pieces and hid it in different locations. Those locations he provided to seven families."

Gabby's stomach knots. "That's what the Grigori are after."

"The parchments," gasps Colt. "They contain the location of the seven pieces."

Sierra frowns. "That's why they killed those people."

"Which means the Grigori have the locations of the seven pieces of the obsidian," says Gabby's father. "If they find them and bring them together, the entire world is doomed. It will be Hell on Earth."

Silence, heavy and foreboding, hangs in the room, weighing on Gabby's chest. She knew this was serious. Dangerous. But they're now talking about every life on the planet being the victim of death and destruction.

She throws her shoulders back. "Then we stop them."

Blaise smiles, but it's almost a sad smile. "The Grigori will be hunting down the pieces, yet we have no way of finding them. My spells don't work. We tried."

"I didn't say it would be easy," says Gabby dryly. She turns to Colt, an idea striking her. "What if the angels who attacked us were sent by the Grigori? They'd know where they are."

But Colt shakes his head. "They were Samandriel's angels. I recognized one of them from when they had captured me."

Captured him? Another fact he hid from her.

"Samandriel?" her father asks as he steps forward. "Are you sure?"

Colt nods. "He's here on Earth. Most definitely at the academy."

"And what did he want?"

Colt glances at Gabby, looking almost uncomfortable. "He wanted me to stay away from Gabby."

That startles her, although she tries not to show it. An angel warned Colt off Gabby? And yet he's still here. What does that mean?

Her father frowns thoughtfully, not seeming to think any of that's important. "Samandriel is eccentric and cannot be trusted. Even Heaven refuses to deal with him but accommodates him because he's an angel and a brother."

"Could he have forged an alliance with the Grigori?" asks Colt.

Gabriel looks like he's going to deny such a thing, but he must change his mind. "If it serves his interests," he admits grudgingly. "I need to find out."

He clicks his fingers and vanishes, leaving Gabby blinking at his sudden disappearance.

Leaving her with only three of the four people who have betrayed her.

Colt is the first to move. "Gabby—"

"Don't," she says, meeting his gaze and letting him see what this is doing to her. "You lied to me."

He clamps his lips shut, either respecting her wishes or not having anything else to say.

Gabby turns to her aunt and Blaise. "And you knew he was a demon."

The words are a statement, one that makes the two women flinch.

It's all the confirmation Gabby needs.

"I'm going to stay here and wait for my father to return," she says quietly, deciding it may as well be a sanctuary in more ways than one. "Alone."

She doesn't want to talk to any of them. What's the point?

She can't trust them.

Because they never trusted her.

27

COLT

Colt hasn't experienced much guilt over his lifetime, even as long as it is. He's done what he needs to do to survive and he's ensured he's at peace with that.

It means the tight feeling in his chest is as alien as it is unwelcome.

He strides through the halls of the academy, scowling. He doesn't even know why he feels bad about not telling Gabby the truth. Why should he have told her? They're natural enemies. Ancient enemies.

Because even when he discovered she's an angel, he didn't think of her like that.

Even now, he's not going to let her fight this without him. The Grigori are the real enemy.

Colt senses an angelic aura ahead—one of Samandriel's angels, no doubt—and he takes a sharp left. He knew he'd have to evade them if he returned. And they're not who he's here to see.

He opens the doors he's now standing before, not bothering to knock. Not that it matters. He quickly discovers the dean's office is empty.

"Drek," he mutters, choosing to curse in Slovenian this time.

He slips back out, determined to find Belphegor, only to find a girl standing on the other side.

She smiles, exposing a row of metal braces. "Hi, Mr. Grayson. Have you seen Gabby around?"

Klae. That's her name. He made a point of finding out when he saw her with Gabby. "Sorry, I haven't. I heard she's suspended."

She looks at him for longer than is customary. "Were you after the dean?"

As much as he's keen to get away, Colt wonders if this girl may know where he is. "Yes. I had a matter to discuss with him."

Klae beams, once again exposing her braces. "I just saw him."

"Where?"

She smiles even wider. "I'll show you."

Clenching his jaw, Colt follows her, glad to see she's taking the back corridors. He's hoping to avoid making a spectacle of himself by fighting angels before the student body.

"So, Gabby's been keeping busy," says Klae.

Colt gives a noncommittal answer, not wishing to engage in conversation.

"I mean, her photo is all over the news. Yours, too."

Colt stops, shocked. "I beg your pardon?"

"You're a very good actor," observes Klae. "You should be in one of my plays."

"What do you mean, all over the news?"

She rolls her eyes. "As if you don't know. Being wanted for murder isn't something most people miss."

Wanted?

For murder?

Klae squints from behind her glasses. "Maybe you're not acting. Although you can still be in one of my plays."

"Tell me," Colt grinds out, losing patience.

"You've both wanted in relation to the serial murders. In fact, I saw a couple of cop cars around the back of the building. From what I heard, they've interrogated Gabby's mother." She takes a step closer. "I need you to tell me where she is."

Colt's mind works quickly. It's good that Gabby remained at Sinclair Mansion. The police wouldn't know to look for her there and by now Sierra and Blaise would've warned her to stay there. She'll be safe until they figure this out.

"Right now, I need to find the dean," he deflects.

"Which is exactly where I'm taking you. But after you two have your little chat, I'm coming with you."

Colt shakes his head, admiring her loyalty to Gabby, but having no intention of doing that. "I can't. It's far too dangerous."

To his surprise, Klae smiles again. "Yes, the Grigori are quite terrifying, aren't they?" She shrugs. "But that's not going to stop me."

For the second time, Colt stares at this strange girl in shock. How does she know of the Grigori?

With an impish wrinkle of her nose, she turns and continues down the corridor. "Come on, I thought you said you wanted to talk to the dean."

Jolting himself out of his stupor, Colt quickly catches up. There are no more opportunities as Klae weaves her way through the academy, often having to stop or backtrack as they avoid the police. She eventually leads him to the library when he finds the dean sitting at a desk, reading a book.

"I'm going to go and check on Gabby's friends, Kalisha and Maya, and tell them she's okay," says Klae. "I'll be back when you're finished."

With another quick smile, she leaves. Colt surreptitiously alters his features. It's a risk to use magic as the angels may use it to track him, but he can't afford for the police to interrupt this conversation.

The dean looks up and smiles as he approaches. It's a smug smile. One that says Belphegor knew he'd come back.

One that says he's confident in his hold over Colt.

Colt consciously keeps his body relaxed, even though he has no intention of being under the archdemon's thumb ever again.

The dean closes his book and leans back. "Hello, Colt. I hear you've been busy."

He takes a seat across, keeping his stance casual. "I have?"

He wants to see what Belphegor knows. The old demon has spies everywhere. The police may even have spoken to him, although he obviously hadn't told them anything. The police weren't waiting for Colt when he arrived.

"The demon who escaped me for hundreds of years now has his photo sprawled all over television and papers." The dean smirks. "This girl has certainly had an impact on you. It's as if you have a heart."

"My heart has nothing to do with this," growls Colt.

The dean shrugs. "And you failed to save the seventh family from the Grigori."

Colt's shoulders slump. "They're powerful. Too powerful."

"Yes, they are. I've heard whispers that there's only one weapon capable of killing them." He shrugs again. "Then again, others say they're indestructible, and that's why they were cursed into becoming trees for eternity. There was a book, back in Hell's library, on the Grigori, but a mortal decided he'd prove Hell's existence by walking through the Gates."

Colt's lips twist. "Dante."

"Yes, him," spits Belphegor. "He stole it. Now no one knows

where it is, but it's believed he passed it on to an ancient organization and they've secreted it away."

"That will be a quest for another day. There are more important issues at hand."

The dean nods, looking at Colt as he drums his fingers on the book. "You plan to take on the Grigori," he says. "And you want our help."

"Yes." That's exactly why he's here, despite being surrounded by angels and police. "Any demon you can muster."

Belphegor is already shaking his head before Colt's finished. "While I didn't appreciate the Grigori fueling the angel-demon hatred that resulted in the loss of many soldiers, I'd rather sit on the sidelines for this one. Considering their indestructibility and all that. Not to mention, no doubt there would be angels there, and the last thing we want is another battle. If you haven't noticed, our numbers are dwindling here. And even with the Tear open, fewer can pass through it. " He holds his hand up as Colt goes to speak. "Unless you want me to break open the Gates of Hell and let all the demons out, I won't be persuaded into the 'save-the-human' cause." He shrugs, leaning back. "In any case, you have that archangel with you. I'm sure he will put up a glorious fight."

Colt knew Belphegor wouldn't readily agree. He came here ready to convince him. "You can't just ignore the presence of the Grigori and the threat they pose."

"True," he concedes. "The Grigori winning would be bad for the demons, but even so, I have to give all of this a pass. Demons have no strength left in them to fight a battle that involves the most powerful of angels. I wouldn't want those who follow me to fight a losing battle, and definitely not alongside our bitter enemies, even if they're fighting against the Grigori."

"Think this through, Belphegor," says Colt, letting the

importance of the decision weigh his words. "We can't face the Grigori alone. We need numbers. And any demons, even if only a few, would work in our favor."

They cannot win without it. Gabby's life and everyone else's is in danger.

The old demon laughs. "You expect demons to support you, when all you've ever done is run? You ran away from Hell and your kind and hid in the murkiness of humanity." The smile fades as Belphegor's eyes turn icy. "And now it's to save that same humanity you would ask demons to help?"

"That is my cross to bear," admits Colt. Belphegor is the only one who knows why Colt ran, and the one who most wants to punish him for it. But he can't afford for it to get in the way. "Think about it," he urges. "The demons could come out looking good in all of this."

"Leave the image politics out of this, Colt," Belphegor snaps. "You decided to make this your personal quest, and now you need us to help you with it. That's a big ask from a traitor."

Colt hides his flinch. He may be a demon, but he's always tried to be honorable. But Belphegor's right.

He needs the demon's help.

And he's a traitor to his kind.

He holds the archdemon's gaze as he keeps his voice low. "Please. We need your help."

Belphegor almost chokes on the snigger that climbs up his throat. "You're begging me?"

Colt's hands tighten around each other. His gut clenches. But he doesn't break Belphegor's gaze. "Please," he says again, the word feeling like acid on his tongue.

"This is how low you'll sink? For a girl?" Belphegor demands incredulously. When he realizes Colt is serious, his lip curls in disgust. "You have feelings for her. The Colt I knew would never sink this low."

It may be time to face the truth. That's exactly why he's doing this. To help Gabby.

To save her life.

"I'll do anything," he says softly. Firmly. "Anything you ask of me."

That has Belphegor's eyes turning calculating. "You'll owe me? And when I call in the favor, you won't refuse me?"

"I won't," he promises.

If that's what it takes to stop the Grigori, then so be it.

A cold, hard smile curls across the dean's face. "I'll send my demons, but to create a distraction. Nothing more. We shall not face the Grigori. That will be up to you."

Colt nods. "Very well." It's the best he can hope for.

"And as for the agreement, I'm going to keep the favor you owe me. I'll use it sometime in the future." Belphegor shrugs. "I'm not entirely sure when. Or for what."

Colt nods again, knowing he's giving the archdemon a blank check. The thought makes his skin crawl and his muscles contract, but he has no choice. This is the only way Belphegor will agree.

The archdemon's smile grows. He lifts a finger, the nail morphing into a black pointed tip. He pierces his wrist and holds it up. Colt does the same, hardening his resolve.

They press their arms together, their blood sealing the pact.

Belphegor's demons will help with the fight against the Grigori.

Colt is now beholden to him once again.

With a smile, the dean stands, tugging at his suit jacket. "I'll start to trace angelic essences. The Grigori may need the power of the ley lines Mercy City sits on, but once they gather some power, they'll leave."

Making them even harder to find.

Colt also pushes to his feet. "We'll need to track them down fast, then."

The dean acknowledges that with a short nod before walking away, calling out to a teacher as they walk past.

Colt waits for a few moments, then leaves.

Klae is waiting outside the library, just as she said he would. He doesn't bother to argue with her or ask why she's insisting on coming.

In fact, he doesn't say a word.

The deal he just struck is like a yoke around his neck.

28
GABBY

"So, this is it?" asks Gabby, eyeing the abandoned building on the other side of the highway.

Her father nods where he stands beside her. "Yes. According to the angel I questioned."

Gabby's gut clenches. The angel her father caught was loyal to Samandriel. There's no way he would've given up that information without...incentive. And a whole lot of pain.

But it turns out Colt's instinct was right. Samandriel and his angels have aligned with the Grigori.

She quickly shies away from any thoughts of Colt. He hasn't tried to reach out since he left Sinclair Mansion. She has no idea where he is, or what he's doing.

Just like she had no idea who he was.

She focuses her attention on the dilapidated building, which appears to be an old hotel. There are probably dozens of rooms inside the multistory building. "I can sense their magic. But it's...muted somehow."

Her father nods again. "That would be the wards they've established around it. To protect themselves and the location.

We wouldn't have found it if I didn't interrogate Samandriel's angel."

A part of Gabby knows there was no other way.

The other part of her, the very human part, recoils from the thought of what that would have looked like.

Her aunt shifts a little closer on Gabby's other side, but then stills, as if she thinks better of it. "You're not like them."

Gabby turns to Sierra, unsurprised she sensed her discomfort. When Sierra had returned to Sinclair Mansion—admittedly, where Gabby had holed herself up to lick her wounds—she and Blaise had apologized for keeping Colt's true identity a secret. But there hadn't been time to explain.

Because then she'd told Gabby she and Colt are wanted for the serial murders.

"It's true," her father says. "She isn't like us."

Gabby's gaze snaps to him. Now isn't the time to hear she's let him down somehow.

"You've done what no other angel can do," he says, his eyes a mix of pride and perplexed. Or is that perturbed...

"You haven't allowed your angel total control, like the rest of us," he says. "I don't think anyone knew that was possible."

Gabby just blinks at him. She's at one with her Grace, but also separate somehow. She's still calling the shots.

Because she still wanted to have a heart.

It's Blaise who asks the question trapped in her surprised mind. "What does that even mean?"

"Grace possesses a body in a similar manner to the way demons possess humans. There are differences, like we can't change forms like demons do, we're born into our bodies. Hence why angelic essence takes complete control. It becomes the body. Or so we thought."

"Maybe it's because I'm half human," suggests Gabby.

But her father shakes his head. "That should dilute your ability. Humans are no match for angelic power."

Sierra throws him a baleful glare, but he either ignores her or doesn't notice.

"You're special, Gabrielle," he says somberly.

For some reason, the words make her uncomfortable. She wanted to be normal, not special. And definitely not special by angel terms.

"It makes you an unknown. Especially without any training." He glances at the building. "If I hadn't seen how stubborn you are, I would've suggested you not be here."

That's why he wasn't making the announcement as if it was good news. He thinks she's a loose cannon.

Well, he also thought she'd be a calculating, unfeeling angel by now, too.

"You were right. I have every intention of being here," she says, refocusing the conversation. They can talk about her anomalies another time. "This is my fight."

The Grigori have killed far too many people.

And now it's being pinned on her.

Gabby turns back to the building. Although, being wanted for murders she didn't commit pales compared to what's about to go down.

In that scenario, she comes out alive. There are no guarantees in this one.

There's a gust of wind and the flapping of wings and the four turn around to see a group of angels land behind them. They approach Gabriel, nodding in deference.

"These are my men," he explains.

Gabby does a quick head count. About twenty.

"Is it enough?" she asks.

"They are expert fighters," says her father. "The angels won't stand a chance."

One of the men steps up, his brown hair pulled in a tight ponytail. "Even against Samandriel's craziness."

"Gabby, this is my lieutenant, Moroni."

She offers him a small smile, hoping her father's confidence is well placed. It's likely they'll be outnumbered.

"How do we get past the warding?" asks Blaise. "My magic isn't strong enough."

"Our magic combined should be," replies Gabriel.

"Yes!" says Gabby. "Our accumulated power should do the trick."

Her father nods. "It may take some time, but it should work."

"Let's do this." It doesn't feel like time is something they have a lot of.

Her father glances at her. "Your powers will be stronger if you extend your wings."

Her wings...

Gabby's intentionally not thought about them too much. Despite everything that's happened, sprouting wings is like the final proof of what she is.

Seems a teeny tiny bit of denial is still hanging on.

Letting out a breath, she straightens her spine. Arielle was hurt because she didn't accept this. Who knows what the collateral damage is if she doesn't hurry up and get her act together.

Her father lifts his hand. "I can show you how, if you like—"

All it takes is a thought. An acknowledgement. An invite for the truth to be put on display.

There's an explosion of power through her veins. A whoosh. And Gabby sees two monstrous, alabaster wings in her periphery.

It doesn't even hurt. In fact, it feels...amazing.

And just a little terrifying.

She adjusts her shoulder blades and the wings move, the sunlight catching on their pearly sheen.

She's an angel.

Her father nods regally. "Follow my lead."

His angels line up behind him, each one lifting their hands, palms out, in the same way he has. Gabby copies the motion.

"Project everything you have," he tells her. "We will focus on the entrance."

Gabby nods, noting that Sierra steps back a little.

"Now!" her father orders.

White light shoots from his hands. The angels' hands.

But not Gabby's.

Gabby focuses everything she has, pouring her energy into her palms. Still nothing.

Despite her lack of contribution, the beams hit something several feet in front of the building—an invisible shield—and explode. The area turns into a molten pool of white fire. Yellow fractures spear out, cracking the surface of the ward.

It's working!

Her father and the angels stop, breathing a little harder, as if projecting so much energy took its toll.

Ahead, the veins fade away, the ward healing as if it were never damaged.

Shit. It didn't work.

Her father sighs. "It's an impressive ward. This is why they were chosen to guard Eden."

Gabby throws him an unimpressed glance. Now isn't the time to be appreciating their opponent.

He inclines his head. "It's useful to understand what we're up against."

Ancient, powerful freaking angels. That's not exactly news.

Turning back to the building, Gabby narrows her eyes as she sees movement. Several angels are standing in the doorless doorway, smirking and gloating. One even gives her the bird.

Which just pisses her off.

This isn't a joke, or a test of strength. The people's lives they're playing with are her mother's. Arielle's. Kalisha and Maya and Klae.

Even Colt's.

"Try again," she says grimly.

Her father glances at her, possibly not appreciating having to take orders, but faces the building again. He and his men, along with Blaise, focus and shoot out another beam. It hits the shield, creating a burning crater of white.

This time, Gabby lifts her arms wide. She feels her wings expand behind her. She channels the fury rising within her.

When she brings her hands together, she lets out a cry as she channels her rage at this injustice through her palms.

No beam of light projects. No sonic boom of energy.

She may as well be a cranky butterfly.

Her father echoes a shout beside her, then Moroni and his men. Suddenly, the thick beam of light pierces the invisible shield with such force that the ground shakes. Yellow veins explode over the surface of the ward, fracturing it.

Destroying it.

Gabby drops her arms. The most she just did was act as a cheer squad, encouraging the angels and Blaise to up their game. Her father's right. She needs training.

Except there's no time to appreciate exactly how much she's in over her head. There's a cry from the building and dozens of angels pour out, wings expanding as they prepare to fight.

"Moroni," Gabby's father shouts. "Clear us a path!"

"Yes, sir!"

Moroni and the others run to meet Samandriel's followers. The angels clash, cries and grunts filling the air.

Gabby goes to join them but her father places an arm across her. "They will take care of it."

She watches as they do exactly that.

Moroni and his men show no mercy to the men who were once their brethren. They become relentless assassins, killing Samandriel's soldiers, ripping off their wings, even stealing their Grace.

It's brutal. And bloody. But effective.

Within minutes, the dry grass in front of the old hotel is littered with bloodied bodies and butchered wings.

Her father must register the shock on her face. "They are doing what needs to be done. We cannot afford to have a rogue angel faction siding with one of the greatest threats we've ever faced."

Before Gabby can answer, Moroni and his men run into the building. Her father's face sets in grim lines. "We're going in."

He unfurls his wings and breaks into a run, Gabby right behind him.

It's their turn to fight.

They burst through the doorway, finding themselves in an open space littered with pieces of wood and plastic, trash, and more angel bodies. Another wave of angels pours through several doorways, and Moroni and his men rush forward.

More cries and grunts fill the dusty gloom.

Several of the rogue angels leap over Moroni's men, coming straight for Gabby and her father. Her father runs at two angels while Gabby ducks a flying kick aimed for her head from another. She spins, sending a wing out and clipping it across the angel's cheek. He roars with pain, but her fist is already connecting with his jaw. He flies through the air, then slams into the ground. A piece of wood erupts through his chest as he impales himself.

There's no chance for Gabby to process her first kill. Something slams into her gut with such force she's thrown against the wall, smashing it. Pain shatters through her back and disintegrates her breath. A fist comes for her face and she ducks, the plaster behind her cracking some more. Blinking away the pain, Gabby drops into a squat and pushes up. Her fist rams into the angel's gut, making her double over. Gabby grabs her hair and smashes her head into the same dent her own body just created. The angel drops to the ground, her face blood-spattered and crushed.

Another angel barrels toward her, burly and large. His face twists as his eyes flare with silver fire. He powers a fist into her chest. Then her gut. Then her face. Gabby doubles over, hearing his snarl of victory.

She drops to the ground, spins, and flicks a kick to his shin. He grunts, but she's still spinning, already executing the next kick. The first was only a warm up. She kicks high, aiming for his face. The force of her foot snaps the angel's head to the side and he crumples to the floor, dead.

Straightening, Gabby finds her father across the room, doing something she hasn't seen him do a lot of. He's smiling.

He's proud of her.

It makes her sick, and yet, the power thrumming through her veins exalts in his approval. At the fact she's fighting for what's right.

Her father points to a door behind him. The Grigori must be down there.

Except there are still a dozen or so angels between Gabby and where she needs to be. She drops her chin, preparing to fight again. Knowing she'll have to kill again.

There's a whoosh past her ear as a fireball blasts into the room. It hits the angel closest to Gabby and engulfs him in flames. In a blink, he's nothing but ash. Gabby turns around, finding Blaise and Sierra running into the building, Blaise already holding her next fireball.

She flings it and Gabby focuses on it, making it grow. A slight change in trajectory and it takes out three more angels.

Blaise and Sierra reach Gabby and they weave their way through the battling angels. Gabby notices two blades protruding from the chest of one and she barely breaks stride as she squats down and yanks them out. A second later, they're impaled in another angel about to attack one of Moroni's men.

They reach Gabby's father and run through the doorway, finding themselves in a wide corridor. More broken bodies with crumpled wings are littered around, blood streaking the walls and floor.

"Moroni's gone ahead with his strongest fighters," says her father and he leaps over those sprawled across the hall.

Clearing the path, just like he was ordered to.

Gabby keeps her gaze averted as she follows, Blaise and Sierra with her. This is a baptism by blood.

They run up a flight of stairs finding a large set of double doors at the top. And they're open.

Gabby's by her father's side as they run through, seeking to catch up to Moroni.

Determined to find the Grigori.

They both draw themselves up to a sudden stop, forcing Blaise and Sierra to do the same behind them.

What. The.

29
GABBY

G abby blinks. Swallows. Then blinks again, just to make sure she's not staring at some sort of optical illusion.

What looks like the entirety of the second floor has been gutted, creating a cavernous space.

One that is full of rows and rows of angels.

They stand in regimented lines, their bodies stiff and straight, their wings folded tightly against their back. Blank eyes stare straight ahead, no sign that they're aware four others have entered the room registering across their impassive faces.

What. The. Fuckity. Fuck.

"Not even Samandriel is crazy enough to do such a thing," breathes her father.

"He most certainly is," sneers a smug voice.

Two rows of angels open as another, dark-haired one walks toward Gabby and the others. He smiles, running a hand down the sleeve of the nearest angel. Not even a blink acknowledges it's being touched.

"Samandriel," snaps Gabby's father. "What have you done?"

Gabby holds still as she watches the slimy angel slink forward, taking note of the way the tip of his pointed black hair almost reaches his nose.

"I'd say it's pretty obvious," Samandriel says with an eye roll. "But if you want me to spell it out for the audience, then fine. I've made myself a little army."

Gabby can see why Colt didn't like Samandriel. The guy's an ass.

His gaze falls onto her, flicking to Sierra and Blaise but quickly returns to Gabby. "You humans think you've cornered technology," he scoffs. "We're light years ahead of you. I mean, we do have the advantage of being able to mix magic with technology. Surely your father's shown you the Pearl City." He laughs. "Oh that's right. You're a halfling. Only full angels can enter Heaven."

"What have you done with my men?" Gabby's father demands.

But Samandriel ignores him. "All those silly images of Heaven are full of clouds and pretty flowers. The Pearl City is a technological marvel. Silver skyscrapers, flashy lights, that sort of thing."

"You're testing my patience," Gabby's father growls.

Samandriel turns to him, his black eyebrows pitched high. "Is this the part where I remind you you're outnumbered about a hundred to one? And that every one of those angels are at my disposal?"

Gabby's surprised to see her father do little more than clench his hands in frustration. Seems Samandriel isn't just talking smack.

He turns back to her, obviously enjoying an audience. "Angels can't reproduce," he pouts. "Well archangels can, but not the rest. So we need to bolster our numbers, you see. That's where these adorable clones come in."

"Clones?" Gabby gasps, hearing Sierra's and Blaise's own sharp breaths. "What do you mean clones?"

"The term is pretty self explanatory, my dear. They're copies of us. Essentially, they have the powers we do, but not the Grace."

Which no doubt makes them even more heartless. Robots.

"This is an army for an apocalypse," snarls Gabby's father. "One we will stop."

Samandriel laughs. "With your men? Moroni et al?" Samandriel flicks his fingers in dismissal. "I've banished them. They were cramping my style."

"You're demented and deranged, Samandriel."

"It's too late for flattery," he snaps. "You should've started off with it."

He lifts his hands and opens them, exposing two symbols painted on his palms. In blood.

"No—"

Gabby's father's shout is cut off as he's engulfed in white light. Gabby cries out as it contracts into a single point, flickers, then disappears.

"You bastard! Where's my father?"

Samandriel rolls his eyes. "Somewhere," he says, waving his hand airly. "Mumbai. Moscow. He could be in the Mariana Trench at the bottom of the Pacific ocean for all I care."

Gabby opens her mouth but Samandriel raises a finger. "Shh, now. You're starting to annoy me."

Gabby does as he says, deciding not to antagonize the prick who obviously has a screw loose.

Samandriel turns to gaze at the clone army. "They're quite impressive, aren't they?" He strokes his collar, humming softly. "So, so terrifyingly beautiful."

Nausea settles deep in the pit of Gabby's stomach. The rows of robot angels are definitely terrifying. And now her father's gone, and so are his men, leaving her to try and figure out how to deal with this.

When she has no freaking idea.

Samandriel turns to her, a sweet smile on his face. "Now, the Grigori would like a word with you. Shall we?"

Gabby takes a step backward, pushing Sierra and Blaise closer to the doors. "Fuck no."

"So predictable," he sighs. "You're just like your father."

"What do they want with me anyway?"

Samandriel looks at her, aghast. "It is not my place to question them!" His smooth face settles into an impatient glare. "Now, hurry up. You can bring your little friends if you like."

"As far as I can tell, you're crazy, not deaf. I said no."

Samandriel's nostrils flare. "You will come with me, one way or another," he warns. "You can come willingly, or..."

"I'll take option B," snaps Gabby. She'd rather die than bring Sierra and Blaise to the Grigori.

To her surprise, Samandriel smiles, his lips stretching wide across his face. "Wonderful. You've chosen the fun route."

He takes a step back and raises his hand. One flick of his fingers and the clone army jolts awake. Their eyes snap forward, no longer sightless. Their chests rise and fall with breath.

The crack of hundreds of wings expanding at once is like a cannon.

"See you soon," sings Samandriel, waving coquettishly as he disappears among the rows of angels.

"Blaise," says Gabby in a low voice. Every eye in the room is focused on them, glacial and hard. "Now's a good time for a fireball."

A ball of flames shoots past Gabby, colliding with the first couple of rows of clones. They arch their backs as they open their mouths in silent screams. Bursting alight, they turn to ash a second later.

It's the opening Gabby needed. A powerful beat of her wings has her soaring into the air. Another beat and she's powering back down. She slams into the next row of clones, lashing out with her fists and feet. Several of them topple, but more quickly replace them. Gabby fights with gritted teeth and unwavering determination, flying high to meet those who've taken to the air.

Below her, Sierra battles like a kickass fighter Gabby never knew her aunt was. Blaise launches fireball after fireball, incinerating five or six clones at once.

But from her vantage point above, Gabby sees what she's not willing to admit.

For every clone they kill, there are dozens more. Like neverending rows of shark teeth, ready to slash and kill. They crowd in, leap into the air, snarling in their hunger for blood.

Gabby kicks another clone, sending him powering through a row of others like a bowling ball. She'll tire soon. So will Sierra and Blaise. And she has no idea how to use her powers because her father was never around to train her.

They don't stand a chance.

Although that doesn't stop Gabby from fighting. Trying. Working to rid this Earth of one more angel robot. If she can't stop the Grigori, this will have to be enough.

Sierra cries out and Gabby spins around, seeing a clone standing over her crumpled aunt. She spears down, grabs the angel by his wings and hurls him away. Sierra leaps to her feet, her fists already up and prepared to fight once more even as she staggers. Either in exhaustion or pain. Probably both.

Gabby's heart constricts painfully. Seeing those she cares about die with her is going to be the hardest part.

Blaise shoots off another fireball, but it's smaller than the ones before. It only kills three clones. The five who replace them attack before she can muster up another. Blaise electrocutes one with a single touch and freezes another.

It's possible Gabby can do that, too. But she'll never know.

She leaps to help Blaise, but an angel grabs her midair and yanks her down. Gabby lands hard on the dirty floor, grappling the heartless robot trying to kill her. She has to get up. She has to help Sierra and Blaise.

This can't be how it ends.

The clone lifts its fist, its eyes blank and bloodthirsty all at once, ready to bring the killing blow down.

Suddenly, the angel is gone. Gabby blinks at the exposed ceiling above, wondering what just happened.

Then a face appears in her vision. A beautiful, handsome, guardian demon.

"Colt," she breathes.

He grins as he holds out a hand. "You failed to tell me there was an opportunity to kick angel tuckus."

Gabby takes it and he hauls her up. She looks around, seeing black-winged demons everywhere. They're fighting the angels with fresh energy and dark determination.

Gabby huffs. "Actually, I had it under control."

"I noticed," Colt says dryly. A clone runs at him but a single punch and its chest collapses inward. It crumples instantly, far more mortal than any angel he would've seen. "What are these things?"

"Angel clones," answers Gabby, kicking away another as it tries to attack. "The product of magic, technology, and an insatiable hunger for power."

"Three things that should never be mixed," grunts Colt, sending out a bolt of crimson fire and incinerating another two. "Where is that tuckus licker, Samandriel?"

Gabby leaps, hovering in the air as she sees if she can do the same with her own hands, but nothing happens. Through her frustration, several things start to make sense. If Colt's a demon, he's old. Possibly ancient. It explains the way he talks. The accomplished way he fights.

His hold over magic.

Gabby looks around, seeing a curved staircase on the other side of the room. "My guess is Samandriel's up there." She spins, knocking out several clones with her wings. "Along with the Grigori."

Colt's features harden. "Then that's where we need to go."

Uneasiness coils through Gabby. Samandriel told her the Grigori wanted to talk to her. She suspects it's the only reason she's here and not dead or banished like her father.

Being wanted by the seven most dangerous beings known to man doesn't sit well with her. Not when she's exhausted. Nor can she access whatever powers she's supposed to have.

And yet, the Grigori have the parchments.

They can't get their hands on the obsidian.

She grins at Colt. "First, we see who can get to Blaise and Sierra first."

30
COLT

G abby's smile is all Colt needs to know he's done the right thing.

Irrespective of what it will cost him.

Seeing her glad to see him, the chance to fight alongside her, lifts and calms him in ways he never knew were possible. Belphegor was right. Colt's heart is now involved.

And he wasn't even sure he had one.

Time kills many things. Including the desire to feel too much.

Gabby breaks into a run and he follows, blasting a clone who tries to attack her. No one is going to hurt her. He'll make sure of it.

Colt registers that Blaise and Sierra are ahead, the clones progressively closing in around them. He glances at Gabby. "You first." He smiles a little wickedly. "I'm enjoying watching you in action too much."

Her grin blazes. "Ditto. It's quite a turn on, actually."

With a quick leap and spin, Colt dispatches the clone that was coming from behind, the whole time thinking he's met his match. Not only that, Gabby always manages to take things up a notch.

It's invigorating. Intriguing. Insanely sexy.

Their wings brush as they continue forward, side by side, clearing a path to Sierra and Blaise. They fight together seamlessly. As if they've done this before. As if they've been doing this for decades. They cover each other's backs. One ducks, the other strikes. One attacks, the other defends.

They become an unbeatable team.

In all his centuries, Colt has never felt more powerful.

And it's because he's fighting by this angel's side.

There are only a handful of clones between them and Sierra and Blaise when one launches, teeth bared. Colt releases another of his fireballs, but the clone catches it and throws it back. Gabby leaps out, grabs it and deflects it to the backs of three clones fighting some demons. The demons barely blink as the clones disintegrate, quickly finding their next prey.

Colt and Gabby glance at each other. There are real angels dispersed among the clones.

When they turn back to resume fighting, they find the clones are moving away, clearing a path to Blaise and Sierra.

But it's not Gabby's aunt and the witch who are revealed.

"Samandriel," growls Colt.

A delicate shiver rolls through the angel's wings. "I do like it when you say my name like that," he purrs. He looks to Gabby. "It really is quite...stimulating, isn't it?"

"Get out of our way," she snaps.

"Apologies," Samandriel says with mock sincerity. "I should've realized you wanted to use the exit."

He steps aside, revealing nothing more than a cleared space surrounded by battling clones and demons, the doors they entered through beyond.

Sierra and Blaise have disappeared.

"Where are they?" screams Gabby.

"This was getting boring," says Samandriel on a sigh. He pats the peak of his black hair, glancing pointedly at the staircase Gabby showed Colt. "Tick tock, my dear."

"No!" roars Colt, knowing Samandriel is about to disappear.

He breaks into a run, even though he won't be able to get to the coward in time. At least he'll know the level of fury that will be waiting, banked like an infernal fire, for when they meet again.

There's a flicker of black from above and a demon lands in front of Samandriel, blocking Colt's view. He jolts to a halt as he recognizes who just arrived.

"Belphegor," sneers Samandriel.

The archdemon punches Samandriel in the chest, shoving him backward. "I've been looking forward to this," he snarls, flashing a grin at Colt.

He tries to understand what Belphegor's appearance means. He either wants to finish Samandriel himself.

Or he's ensuring Colt is truly beholden to him by taking part in this battle himself.

Gabby places a hand on Colt's arm. "This is our chance."

Colt's hands are hot fists. He wants to pummel Samandriel himself. Finish him, especially if it means one less debt to Belphegor. The need burns through his veins.

But Gabby's right. Sierra and Blaise have been taken. He's sworn to protect Blaise.

And there's the Grigori.

There's no way he'll let Gabby face them alone. It's why he came here in the first place.

Grabbing Gabby's hand, he turns and runs, blasting any clones who are foolish enough to get in their way.

They make their way to the staircase, leaping over bodies of both clones and demons. They're half way up when an angel appears ahead and flies at them. It dodges Colt's fireball, aiming straight for Gabby.

Colt leaps, twists, and lands behind it. He grabs it by the wings and maintaining his momentum, throws it over the bannister. It flies through air, landing amongst the fray.

"Hey, watch it!" shouts Samandriel. "I will not be taken out by one of my own."

Colt ignores the crazed angel. Samandriel's end is coming, even if it's not today. He'll make sure of it.

He and Gabby reach the second floor.

Ahead are large arched doors. And they're open. Waiting for them.

Gabby doesn't pause, rushing headlong toward them. Colt keeps up, even as his muscles coil. There's no time for a plan. No choice but to go through.

And face what's on the other side.

31

GABBY

Gabby's blood ices in her veins the moment they enter what looks like a large dining room. Sierra and Blaise are here, just as the Grigori.

She cries out, wanting to go to her aunt and Blaise, even as she stops.

Sierra and Blaise are pinned against the wall, several feet up, held there by some sort of magical bonds. The white coils across their bodies crackle and sizzle, the two women's faces twisted with agony as if they're being held with livewires.

Gabby turns to the Grigori. The seven shimmering beings are standing around a large table, paying not attention to the torture they're inflicting several feet away. "Release them!" she screams.

One of the Grigori chuckles. It stares at Gabby as one of the bonds across Sierra's chest flares. She arches her back, the chords of her neck standing out as she tries to contain the scream.

The agonized sound is ripped from her lips, echoing through the room.

"Stop!" pleads Gabby.

"At least you're a quick learner," says another of the Grigori. "You are in no position to make demands, angel."

Another floats closer to the table, making Colt tense beside her. "If you want them free, you need to help us first."

Dread fills Gabby's chest, cold and hard. "What do you want?" she whispers.

The Grigori indicates toward the table with a shimmering hand. "Read the parchments. Tell us where the shards of obsidian are and we'll release the two women."

"You don't, and they die," adds the one beside it. "Slowly and painfully."

Gabby's gaze falls to the table, seeing the seven parchments spread out over it. "I can't. I don't have the ability."

Two of the Grigori glance at each other. The one on the left turns back to her, it's eyes nothing but blazing white sockets. "You do not know who you are?"

"Why, you're the child of the prophecy," says the one on the right. "You're perfectly capable of reading these parchments."

Gabby's too shocked to reply. Are these guys even crazier than Samandriel?

"Yes, we were surprised, too," says another derisively. "You are far from a worthy opponent."

"But, you can read them," snaps the first Grigori who spoke.

"Don't do it, Gabby," Colt says under his breath. "There has to be another—"

His words are cut short as he's thrown backward and slammed into the wall. His body slides up as if he's nothing more than a puppet. The same white coils trap him against the wall, twisting and twitching with energy.

Colt fights it, muscles straining and tendons popping. He thrashes, groaning with pain, but not stopping. The scent of burning flesh tickles Gabby's nose.

"Stop!" she shouts. "I'll do it!"

The sizzling stops, but the bonds holding Colt to the wall remain. One of the Grigori pushes a parchment across the table.

Gabby walks forward, her heart a painful, throbbing mess in her chest and picks it up. She looks to Colt, then Sierra and Blaise.

What choice does she have?

Steadying her hands, she looks at the strange scrawlings on the parchment. They're a language she's never seen before.

And yet, she can read every word.

She looks up at the Grigori. "Release them first. Then I'll try to decipher it."

One of the shimmering beings raises it's hand, but the one beside it reaches out to stop. "Don 't forget they are the ones who freed us."

"They what?" gasps Gabby.

The Grigori smiles. "Yes. The fools thought they were uncovering the Holy Grail. But Cain played them. He brought them to the grave of his dead brother, Abel, trying to resurrect him."

The Grigori chuckle as Gabby tries to assimilate this.

Sierra and Blaise freed the Grigori?

Cain and Abel are a part of this? The first humans to ever walk on Earth?

"But...how?"

"A spell is all it took. One powerful enough to not only free us from our prisons, but to cause a Tear between Earth and Hell. That's where all these demons are coming from. Your precious aunt and her friend are responsible for the scourge pouring into your world."

Gabby shakes her head. It can't be true.

"An apocalypse is coming," intones another of the Grigori. "Which is why we need the obsidian. We will not be imprisoned again. Which is where you come in, child of the prophecy, for you are the seventh daughter of an archangel."

Gabby no longer has the headspace to process this. It's too much. And what can she do about any of it?

"Now, read!" roars one of the Grigori.

Gabby scans the lines, noticing they read from right to left. The symbols shouldn't make sense.

But they do.

"They say...ah...that the first piece is..." She moves the thick vellum closer to her face and then back again, making a show of struggling to read them. "Is somewhere to the east of Mercy City."

"Liar!" the Grigori scream simultaneously. "Give us the exact location!"

The crackling bonds holding Colt, Sierra and Blaise flare to life, making their bodies twitch and tremble. Sierra's the first to cry out. Then Blaise.

"Don't...do...it," groans Colt.

Tears stream down Gabby's cheeks. She wanted to stop this, and now she's making it possible. "The first piece of the obsidian is—"

There's a thundering crack. The wall to her left shatters. Impossibly, a boulder barrels through, coming at them with impossible speed.

Gabby leaps back, although it's unnecessary. The moment the boulder's through, it angles toward the Grigori and gains speed. It smashes the table and ploughs straight through them. They crumple like celestial bowling pins.

Sierra and Blaise drop to the ground, panting. Colt lands on his feet, his wings snapping out, ready to fight.

Relief courses through Gabby. She turns back to the ball of stone that somehow, impossibly, just saved them.

She watches in fascination as the boulder contracts and

shrinks, quickly gaining human form. Gabby gasps in shock as she recognizes the person appearing before her. "Klae!"

But, how?

"She's a golem," mutters Colt, and Gabby's not sure if it's a stunned statement or a surprised question.

Gabby has no idea what that is, but Klae's name is suddenly taking on a whole new meaning.

She runs to Gabby's side. "You'll be surprised how far I'll go to make sure my play goes ahead," she says, pushing up her glasses. She comes to stand beside Gabby. "Even if Grigori are messing with it."

Colt joins Gabby and the three of them watch as the Grigori right themselves.

"We need to attack quickly," says Colt.

Gabby agrees. Her muscles coil, ready to fight, when Klae lifts into the air with a garbled choke.

"No!" Gabby tries to grab her, but Klae's body is whisked toward the Grigori.

"This is what happens when you defy us," they hiss.

Klae hovers before them for a fleeting second before her head snaps to side with a sickening crunch.

Her body drops to the ground, limp and unmoving.

"No!" Gabby screams again, this time the word powered by pain. Not Klae!

"We will fight this," Colt says fiercely. "This is not the end."

But Gabby grabs his arm before he can move. "No. Wait." If they attack, she risks his life.

The Grigori want her alive, unlike the Colt and the others. These evil, heartless angels need her to read the parchments, and they'll make that happen by blackmailing her with the deaths of others.

The pain will never end. Neither will the trail of dead bodies.

And when it's all over, the Grigori will have the seven pieces of the obsidian.

It will only be the beginning of the suffering.

She looks at him, at his fiercely handsome face, at the sacrifice he's willing to make. She glances at Sierra and Blaise, who are wavering on their feet, also willing to fight for this.

Emotion builds within Gabby. Anger at the injustice of seven murdered families. Fury at the loss of Klae.

Rage at what they plan for countless other lives.

The Grigori must be stopped.

Fire leaps from her palms, dancing around her hands, golden and impossibly bright. Blazing like the sun. But it doesn't stop there. It shoots up her arms, explodes across her wings, swallows her torso. Engulfs her entire body.

Gabby raises her arms, feeling energy as pure and powerful as light coursing through her. Around her. Awaiting her command.

She has no idea what she's capable of, but she's about to find out. A ball appears in her hand, golden and fiery. She can't wait to see what it can do.

The Grigori take a simultaneous step back, the white light in their eye sockets dimming.

Then, they disappear.

Vanish.

Flee like the freaking cowards they are.

There's no time to figure out if that's a victory or not. Gabby rushes forward, the fire around her dying, and finds all that's left of Klae is a puddle of mud. She falls to her knees, feeling like her chest is fracturing. "I'm so sorry, Klae."

Gabby hangs her head and closes her eyes as fresh tears track down her cheeks. The sweet girl should never have paid the ultimate price. This is most definitely not a victory.

"It's actually totally fine."

Gabby's eyes fly open to find Klae crouched before her, smiling. "What? How?"

"I'm a golem, remember?"

Gabby nods, then quickly shakes her head. That means nothing to her. She's going to have to do some serious research.

"I'm essentially made of mud," explains Klae. "Pretty hard to get rid of."

Gabby throws her arms around her. "I'm so glad you're okay."

They get to their feet and Gabby blinks. Klae's alive. They all are.

She finds Sierra and Blaise not far away, already holding the seven parchments.

"I'm so proud of you," says Sierra, her eyes shining. "You saved us all."

"We all did." She glances at Colt, her heart tripping. He came back for her. "I couldn't have done this without all of you."

A smile hovers over his lips, but it quickly dies when he turns his attention to Blaise. "You opened the Tear?"

Blaise winces. "We had no other choice. Cain tricked us, and then that spell was the only way we could stop him."

Sierra nods, her mouth downturned. "We didn't know that the Grigori would be released or a Tear would open up, letting demons loose." She turns to Gabby. "We've tried to close it countless times, but have always failed. It's as if there's some spell that holds the Tear open and refuses to allow it to shut."

"We have to shut it," says Gabby, determined. "If you don't find a way, I will."

The world doesn't need more demons. There's enough shit going down as it is.

Sierra smiles. "And you'll do it, too."

Blaise holds up the parchments. "We need to go. Before anyone else gets their hands on these."

Gabby realizes the sounds of battle have stopped. But it doesn't matter whether the angel clones or the demons have won. Neither of them can get hold of the parchments. She nods. "Take them somewhere safe. We'll need to decipher them before anyone else."

With quick hugs, Sierra and Blaise disappear through the massive hole boulder-Klae created.

Klae pushes up her glasses with an apologetic smile. "I'm not sticking around, either."

"What?"

She ducks her head. "I prefer to stay behind the scenes." Her shoulders droop. "And you probably haven't heard. The last family the Grigori murdered—the Daniel's—they were Maya's aunty and uncle."

"Oh." Poor Maya. Another victim of the Grigori's evil. "Of course. I'll be there as soon as I can."

Klae leaves, too, leaving Gabby alone. With Colt.

Who's hovering by the door.

Gabby plants her hands on her hips. "You're going too?"

He stills. "Just saving you having to tell me to. I've lied to you like so many others have."

Gabby walks toward him, noting the way his eyes follow her every move. "And yet, you came back."

One of the many wonders that happened here today.

"You're the one who asked me to leave in the first place," he points out.

She stops in front of him. Colt is as still as a statue, his wings gone, his eyes wary. "Well, I did just find out you're a demon."

He lets out a breath. "Yes, I am. I'm sorry it was...necessary to hide it from you."

"Why?"

"Well, I didn't know you're an angel at first. And then—"

"No," Gabby says quietly. "Why did you come back? Especially when you knew I'm an angel."

Their kind are sworn enemies. They've been at war since time began.

Colt doesn't answer straight away, acknowledging the gravity of the question.

Not only did he come back, he brought a small army of demons with him. It was their strength that tipped the balance.

"At first, I couldn't stay away because I was fascinated by you." His lips twitch. "Then, because I was frustrated by you." His face softens in a way that has Gabby's pulse accelerating. "And now...I can't stay away because I can't bear the thought of something happening to you."

Gabby's breath exhales in a rush. Joy sings through her veins. Rainbows explode in her heart. Somewhere, unicorns are being born.

She steps closer, pressing her hand over his heart and finding it's beating just as fast as hers.

"I really like you, too."

Colt's lips part although he doesn't make a sound. She's not even sure he's breathing. Actually, Gabby's not sure she's breathing.

Every cell in her body has found a new focus. A mantra that echoes through her entire being.

Kiss Colt.

They move simultaneously, the chemistry that always sparks between them flaring. Bodies collide, hands grasp. Lips crash.

Passion detonates.

Gabby pulls Colt closer, wanting to taste, touch, take it all. His mouth is so hot. So soft. So deliciously, blazingly exquisite. The closest this little half-angel will ever be to Heaven.

Their lips meld as their tongues tangle. Gabby spears her fingers into his hair and hangs on for dear life. She moans, her desire only climbing when there's a corresponding groan from Colt. He sounds as lost as she's feeling.

The type of lost where you don't want to be found.

Where you want to disappear into the paradise you just created.

Colt pulls back. "Gabby," he breathes. "We…"

Although he doesn't finish the sentence, she knows he's right. They can't lose themselves to this right now.

And yet, she can't seem to let him go. She smiles when Colt doesn't either.

They rest their foreheads against each other, both panting a little. Gabby reaches out to brush Colt's lips with her fingertips, amazed at the magic they just forged. "This isn't supposed to happen," he murmurs, his breath soft on her skin.

"But it is," she says. Fiercely. Simply.

Whatever this is between them, it's special. Amazing.

And she wants it.

Colt smiles. "It certainly is." Gabby's about to kiss him again, determined to seal their promise, when he stills, his head angling up. "Your father's here."

She huffs in frustration. "Of course he is."

Colt steps away. "The demons will be gone seeing an archangel is here. If there is any fighting left, it's over."

It's finished. The Grigori are gone. They have the parchments. The fighting has ended.

For now.

She sighs, the sound as full of regret as she is. That delicious moment was over far too quickly. "You should go."

"I'm not sure that's—"

"Seriously. It'll be easier if you're not here."

Colt looks like he's debating whether to argue or not, but then he sighs and steps back. "Very well." He frowns. "But don't tell him about...us."

Gabby's barely nodded when he vanishes. A second later, her father strides into the room. "What happened?" he demands. "There are dead clones everywhere."

She holds up her hand. "I'll give you a quick recap. The demons beat the clone army."

Her father's brows shoot up.

"I self combusted and scared away the Grigori."

They climb another inch.

"But we still have the parchments."

Her father relaxes. "That's good—"

"And I intend on seeing Colt," she says, saving the best for last. "I have feelings for him."

Her father's brows slam down so far they almost touch the bridge of his nose. His face turns red. He looks like he, too, is about to self combust.

But Gabby doesn't care. It doesn't matter that she's the daughter of an archangel. That Colt's a demon.

They need to decipher the parchments.

Find the obsidian.

And end the Grigori.

And she's going to do it with Colt by her side, no matter the obstacles.

EPILOGUE

Colt steps up to the counter of the cafe, smiling. He only left Gabby a little while ago, but his lips are still burning. His heart is still trying to find an even rhythm. "One coffee, black, thanks."

The server behind the counter writes down the order. "Sure, thing." He rips off the note and passes it to the barista.

"And one of your delicious butterscotch muffins, please."

"Sorry, man, we're all sold out."

Which Colt had already deduced by perusing the menu scrawled on the blackboard, then the glass-domed platter on the counter. He feigns disappointment. "That's too bad. I was in here earlier with my girlfriend and she had one. She hasn't stopped raving about it."

The guy looks at Colt a little more closely, obviously trying to place him. "Yeah, they sure are popular."

Colt chuckles, holding the young man's gaze. Very subtly, very carefully, he plants the image of Colt and Gabby sitting at a nearby table, drinking coffee and eating said muffin. They're laughing, hands brushing, Colt even feeds her a piece.

Like any normal, human couple.

Except Gabby's mouth closes around his finger, her eyes holding his. The memory of their kiss would have him stilling. Desire would be sparking at that one, moist point then detonating through every cell.

Their kiss confirmed something for Colt. Whatever it is that's kindled between them, it's special.

He spent a long time in Hell, and he's never had his soul scorched like that.

The guy clears his throat, snapping Colt out of the memory he just took too far.

"Oh yeah," says the guy, his cheeks flushed. "I remember now."

"Oh well, I'll have to come back nice and early tomorrow," says Colt good naturedly.

"Sure thing." The young man smiles, now unable to meet his eye. "The red devil cupcakes sell out even faster."

Colt grins. He hadn't meant for his imagination to get away from him, but at least the images now planted in the young man's mind will be memorable.

"One black coffee," calls the barista. Colt pays and takes it, smiling at both of them. "Much appreciated."

He exits the cafe, breathing in deeply. Now that he's created an alibi for the time of the Daniels' murders, he can go talk to Detective Espinosa. Just by turning up, he'll show they have nothing to hide. Add that to the fact they were on a date in a cafe not far from the Daniels house—because Gabby's father doesn't approve of their match so they needed to be away from the academy—and there's no way the police can view them as suspects.

Protecting Gabby feels good.

He feels good.

Good in a way Colt didn't know he could.

He throws the cup in a nearby trash can. There are many

human inventions that should never have been conceived, and coffee is one of them. He's about to turn and walk away, already anticipating telling Gabby the good news, when he registers there was no sound as the cup hit the bottom.

He turns back slowly, century old instincts on high alert.

Dean Roberts—Belphegor—is standing beside the trash can, the coffee cup in his hand. "Hell is a world without coffee," he says. "I could never figure out why you were so keen to leave it."

Colt straightens. "Dean," he says curtly. He's not sure why Belphegor's sought him out so soon, but he doubts it's to talk about the merits of the bitter tasting brew.

"I wanted to congratulate you on taking care of the Grigori."

"They're not dead," says Colt. "But they'll lay low for a while."

"They certainly will, after the girl scared them away with celestial fire."

"I had a feeling that's what it was." He's never seen golden fire like that. It was beautiful and terrifying all at once.

Belphegor nods. "It was certainly powerful. And unique. Angels have long forgotten how to conjure it."

Cold nods, already knowing this. It was something he'd decided not to think too deeply about. He tenses as he realizes something. "So, you saw everything."

"I felt it. It was so unique and potent, it distracted me." His mouth twists. "I was just about to finish Samandriel."

So the crazed angel is still alive. "Gives me a chance to finish him myself," he mutters.

"Angels and demons are mortal enemies, that's the way it should be." Belphegor watches Colt closely, a smile spreading across his face. "Although, that's not why I'm here."

Colt's muscles tense. Foreboding coils through their fibres.

"The celestial fire drew me to the room. It means I heard

everything. I heard Gabby promise she would fix the Tear. She wants to stop the flow of demons to Earth."

Colt doesn't move. He barely breathes. Dread is blooming in his lungs like cancer.

"Now, many have tried to close the Tear and have been unsuccessful. But this angel, she's different. You know it, too. And I don't want the Tear closed. Angels are everywhere, and now the bastards are creating clones. Armies of them. If I'm going to hold them off, I need a constant influx of demons."

Colt knows what words are coming next.

"You need to do whatever it takes to stop Gabby from closing the Tear."

"No." Colt snaps the word out with ferocity. He will not sabotage Gabby.

Belphegor shakes his head, looking almost amused. "I'm calling in my favor, Colt. We lost demons fighting those clones. I was there myself."

Yes, he was. Colt doubts Gabby could've won without them.

"I've upheld my part of the bargain," growls Belphegor, his eyes flashing crimson. "You have no choice. If you don't, do you really think you'll be able to run from me again? That I won't remember how you betrayed me?"

Colt could run, taking the risk that he won't be found. But if he is... Belphegor will drag Colt back to Hell to mete out his punishment. And in both situations, Colt will have nothing.

He'll be nothing more than a traitor.

But worse, he'll have no honor.

And he won't be able to protect Gabby anymore.

"Very well," he grinds out. "I will do as you ask."

"Excellent," breathes the archdemon, satisfaction settling across his features. "And isn't it fortuitous that you're in such a prime position to do it?"

Colt looks away, not answering. His throat is too scorched with bile.

Belphegor ambles away, sipping the coffee, leaving Colt outside the cafe. Disgust at what he must do churns in his gut. How could he have been so naive to think he and Gabby were possible?

He wanted to help her. Protect her.

Now he's honor bound to betray her.

Ready for the next installment in the Keepers of the Light series? Check out CHOSEN ANGEL!

CHOSEN ANGEL

Seven vengeful angels. Seven shards of evil.

One impossible choice.

Gabby may have accepted she's an angel, but she's only just discovering what she's capable of. What's expected of her. And what will happen if she fails. Of course, just to complicate things, she had to go and fall for a demon...

Colt has a past that is centuries old. And a long list of enemies who either want to use him or kill him. A demon far more powerful has called in a favor that requires Colt to do the one thing he never wanted to—betray Gabby.

The seven pieces of the obsidian must be found. The Grigori must be stopped. The war between angels and demons can no longer be contained within the walls of Mercy Academy. Gabby and Colt need each other to succeed, and yet, how can they trust their mortal enemy?

An edgy, epic new adult romance for fans of the Fallen Saga and the Hush, Hush series. Lose yourself in the paranormal heaven that is Chosen Angel today!

GRAB YOUR COPY HERE
mybook.to/ChosenAngel

HAVE YOU READ THE KEEPER CHRONICLES PREQUEL?

As an exclusive for my subscribers,
you can download it for free!!

When Sierra sneaks out, determined to escape her over-protective family, she stumbles across a young man covered in blood. His last words are a plea. *Find the Grail Keepers. Warn them.*

Ryder is the young cop who was last seen with the murdered victim. Sierra doesn't trust him, no matter how drawn she is to him. Except it turns out they're both looking for the same thing—the Holy Grail.

They're quickly drawn into a dangerous hunt involving cryptic clues, a mysterious stone, and a Grail that hasn't been seen for centuries. One that leads to more questions than answers. Can Sierra trust her impulsive emotions? Should she believe Ryder's words or the truth she sees in his eyes? And ultimately, should she follow her heart?

Especially when every decision will decide the fate of countless lives.

CLICK HERE TO DOWNLOAD FOR FREE!

https://BookHip.com/TTBMTTV

ALSO BY TAMAR SLOAN

PRIME PROPHECY SERIES

He failed to shift like every one of his ancestors.

Until he met her.

KEEPERS OF THE GRAIL

The legendary Holy Grail is real.

Yet everything known about it is a lie.

KEEPERS OF THE CHALICE

A vampire. A huntress.

A cure that will change everything.

KEEPERS OF THE LIGHT

Angels and demons have battled for millennia.

Their inevitable war has begun.

KEEPERS OF EXCALIBUR

A fated love. A cursed wolf.

A supernatural war only they can stop.

DESTINED DEMIGODS

Love that defies the gods.

Powers that define destiny.

ELEMENTAL GAMES

Elemental powers. Deadly Games.

No escape.

THE SOVEREIGN CODE

Humans saved bees from extinction...and created the deadliest threat we've seen yet.

THE THAW CHRONICLES

Only the chosen shall breed.

ZODIAC GUARDIANS

Twelve teens. One task.

Save the Universe.

ABOUT THE AUTHOR

Tamar hasn't decided whether she's primarily a psychologist who loves writing, or a writer with a lifelong drive to make a difference. She must have been someone pretty awesome in a previous life (past life regression indicates a Care Bear), because she gets to do both. She divides her time between helping families and writing emotion driven YA stories set in amazing imaginary worlds that surprise even her.

The driving force for all of Tamar's writing is sharing and connecting. In truth, connecting with others is why she writes. She loves to hear from readers. Find her on all the usual social media channels or her website, www.tamarsloan.com where can download one of her books for free.

(Seriously, I LOVE hearing from you guys!)